Jet Fuel Can't
Melt Steel Beams

Jet Fuel Can't Melt Steel Beams

JAMES VACHOWSKI

Copyright © 2025 James Vachowski.

All rights reserved. No part of this publication may be reproduced, distributed, or transmitted in any form or by any means, including photocopying, recording, or other electronic or mechanical methods, without the prior written permission of the publisher, except in the case of brief quotations embodied in critical reviews and certain other noncommercial uses permitted by copyright law. For permission requests, write to the publisher, addressed "Attention: Permissions Coordinator," at the address below.

ISBN: 979-8-88786-055-9 (Paperback)
ISBN: 979-8-88785-056-6 (Hardcover)

Library of Congress Control Number: 2025946951

Any references to historical events, real people, or real places are used fictitiously. Names, characters, and places are products of the author's imagination.

Book design by Allison Chernutan.
Edited by Patterson Hood.

Printed in the United States of America.

First printing edition 2025.

emily@fracturedmirrorpublishing.com
Fractured Mirror Publishing
Knoxville, Tennessee

www.fracturedmirrorpublishing.com

for C and B.

TUESDAY, SEPTEMBER 11, 2001

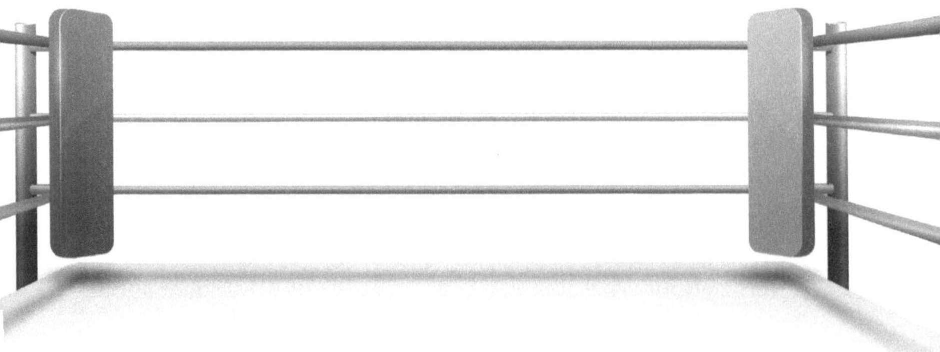

Excerpt from the "Good Morning Show" *live broadcast*
Transcription by Jessie Carpenter

Michael Phillips: "Are we ready? Now, we're going to go live, right now, from Hoboken, where I understand…do we have it? We do. We've got a breaking story for you now, happening right here in New York, and there it is. That's our camera looking north across the Hudson, where a large volume of black smoke seems to be pouring out of one of the World Trade Center buildings."

Cindy Radditz: "That's right. As Michael said, this news story is still developing, but I'm being told that some kind of airplane has apparently crashed into the World Trade Center, just moments ago. We're still gathering information, and very little is confirmed at this time, but on the phone with us is Martha Falcone, who actually witnessed the event from down on the street. Martha, can you hear me?"

Martha Falcone: "Hello?"

C.R.: "Hi, Martha?"

M.F.: "Hi, Cindy."

C.R.: "Hi. You're on the air. Can you please tell our audience more about what you just saw, and give us an update about what's going on there?"

M.F.: "Yes, but I have to tell you, it's absolutely frightening. I think I'm in shock! I just came out of the subway a few minutes ago, heading to work, and as I climbed the stairs, I heard this, this, tremendous boom coming from the south, and then I looked up, and there was this great big ball of fire in the sky! I'm outside Battery Park now, and, listen to this, can you hear all these fire engines and ambulances passing by? This is absolutely unbelievable…hello? Can you hear me?"

C.R.: "Yes, Martha. We can hear you. Please, go on."

M.F.: "…up in the air, and you know, I've never seen anything like it before. It was a ball of fire, literally, up in the air, and then pieces of the building just started falling! And I can't tell, exactly…it looks like the fire might be burning up near the top of the tower, or maybe thirty or forty floors off the ground, at least, but I just…I can't even begin to describe it. This is so horrible; I can't even tell you how bad this is."

C.R.: "Were you able to tell what kind of plane it was?"

M.F.: "What?"

C.R.: "Did you see…do you have any idea what kind of plane it was? The one that hit the World Trade Center?"

M.F.: "Wait, was that what happened? You're saying that an airplane crashed into the building?"

C.R.: "Yes. Did you see what kind of plane it was? More reports are coming in; people are saying that it looked like some kind of an airplane must have hit the tower."

M.F.: "Oh, I…I don't know. I didn't see that. Really, all I saw was, when I looked up after hearing that big boom, was this massive fire. Absolutely massive. Here on the street, we were all saying that it seemed way too high up for a bomb to have gone off. You know? That, like, *couldn't* happen. So yeah, maybe…maybe it *could've* been a plane. But I didn't see it, and I'm not sure anybody else here did. Cindy, I have to tell you, things are flying through the air right now, falling down to the street. This is horrifying! It's unbelievable!"

M.P.: "Martha, we're going to have to let you go, as Cindy and I hand the broadcast off to our mobile reporting team. Please stay safe, and for all of our viewers, don't go anywhere—we'll be right back!"

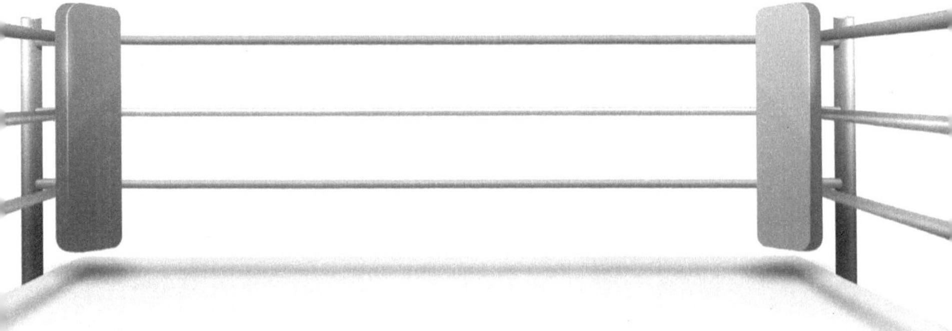

I SLEPT THROUGH THE WORLD TRADE CENTER ATTACKS.

Seriously.

I mean 9/11, the whole thing. All of it.

It's not like I missed anything, though, with all the cable news channels keeping those same video clips on replay for a whole week. I mean, if you were to keep rewatching the same horror film from Blockbuster over and over again, eventually you'd start getting numb to the shock. For me, all that raw emotion just settled down over time, and all those terrifying pictures became just another part of this horrible, new normal.

But I did watch all of the footage.

Every last clip.

Saw them so many times that I even started to see some of them in my sleep. The worst of those scenes actually felt like they could've been permanently seared into the backs of my eyelids.

It took weeks—months, even—before those of us tuning in at home were finally able to process everything that'd happened. Time has a way of blurring as it passes by, so I did my best to track the sequence of events. I took notes, going back again and again to make revisions when new information came to the surface.

It was never my style to focus on the details—not like that, especially not for such a long and involved project.

But what can I say?

I guess some of Burton's ways must've rubbed off on me.

That's why even today, whenever I think back on the events of September 11, my thoughts and memories always form themselves up into this neat and structured timeline. All of those sharp and painful emotions, just mixing in freely with the official narrative.

0846: American Airlines Flight 11, en route to Los Angeles from Boston, crashes into the North Tower of the World Trade Center. Point of impact, floors 93 through 99. The hijackers, flight crew, and passengers are all killed instantly, along with hundreds of people working inside the building.

0903: United Airlines Flight 175, another Boeing 767 on the Boston-to-L.A. route, flies directly into the World Trade Center's South Tower. It strikes floors 75 to 85 on the opposite side of the complex; once again, the fatalities are immediate.

0931: President George W. Bush, speaking from Florida, addresses the nation. He pledges to use the full resources of the federal government to aid the victims and their families, and vows to hunt down the terrorists responsible for the attacks.

0937: American Airlines Flight 77, a narrow-body Boeing 757, takes off from Dulles International Airport before suddenly turning back and crashing into the westernmost wall of the Pentagon. All 59 people aboard are killed, as are 125 military personnel stationed there.

0959: In a matter of seconds, the World Trade Center's South Tower collapses in a cascade of smoldering debris. A billowing cloud of dust erupts and streams through the streets, enveloping lower Manhattan in a shroud of darkness.

1003: Passengers aboard United Flight 93, a second Boeing 757 en route from Newark to San Francisco, discern that their plane is being hijacked. After making contact with family members and hearing about the other coordinated attacks, a small group mounts an assault to retake the plane. Unable to remain in control, the hijackers deliberately crash the plane in a field outside of Somerset County, Pennsylvania. All 44 people aboard are killed.

1028: Exactly 102 minutes after it was struck by United Flight 11, the World Trade Center's North Tower also collapses. The building loses all structural integrity, disintegrating into a massive heap of debris and leaving the New York City skyline altered forever.

1030: My clock radio alarm sounds. The station was Rock 101, of course, but instead of hearing Staind, or even Smashing Pumpkins, it was some announcer talking way too fast, rambling on about shattered windows and broken glass on the streets.

I probably should've caught on that something was up, but for some reason, it just didn't register.

And after a minute or so, I fell back asleep.

1100: The mayor of New York City, Rudy Giuliani, makes the unprecedented decision to evacuate Lower Manhattan. Over a million residents, workers, and tourists are displaced as police officers and firefighters comb through the debris, searching for any survivors.

1300: President Bush speaks to the nation once again, this time from Barksdale Air Force Base in Louisiana. He says that America's armed forces are now on high alert worldwide, and repeats his promise to punish the people responsible for the attacks.

1440: I finally get out of bed. Even though I'd remembered to switch off the ringer on my cordless phone and dial down the volume on the answering machine, it was the whirring of that damned microcassette tape that eventually caught my attention. Tuesdays were my rest day back then—I'd built my schedule so I had the entire day off from classes, except for a lab session that didn't start until 4:00.

1445: I make a break for the kitchen to pour myself a bowl of Count Chocula, more thankful than ever that I'd managed to score one of Dartmouth's prized single rooms. The studio apartment was tiny by anyone's standards, barely ten by ten, but I had the standing shower and mini-fridge all to myself. That semester was the first time I'd ever lived entirely on my own, and the experience was still new enough to feel like a luxury. I started the day with my usual Coke Classic, that cold, twelve-ounce can fitting into my hand just right. Its sweet, syrupy taste hit my tongue sharp but went down smooth.

It was the last moment of peace I'd feel all day.

And for a long time afterwards.

1451: The Navy dispatches a number of aircraft carriers and guided missile destroyers up the East Coast, sending a fleet of ships steaming towards Washington D.C. and New York City. If anybody out there was still harboring doubts, there could be no uncertainty about it now. America was a nation at war.

1455: When I sat down and went through all my messages, my Dad, Uncle Hector, and a mess of friends had already laid it out for me. Daddy had left four messages alone, so I made a point to call him back first. As I turned on the TV set and started catching up on everything I'd missed, I struggled to convince him that the state of New Hampshire hadn't been suddenly overrun by gangs of Muslim terrorists.

At least, not as far as I could tell.

But by that point, everything was right up there on the screen for all of us to see, in full, living color. My dorm room television was just a 13-incher, the smallest set I'd ever owned, an older model where the tube stuck out the back in this awkward, cube-shaped kind of squat. The major networks flashed an endless loop of the same five or six clips, and those gruesome scenes locked themselves into my memory.

The one with United 175 flying low, streaking towards the South Tower, and that hot ball of flame that erupted on impact.

Or that sidewalk video that showed the streets snarled with traffic, a line of screaming firetrucks streaking past.

And one more from later on, when huge black clouds of smoke and ash began billowing down the wide avenues, as terrified people scrambled into the buildings for cover.

1720: Despite not being struck by a plane, the complex at Seven World Trade Center collapses after several hours of uncontrolled fires. The 47-story building has already been evacuated, but the fresh disaster forces rescue workers to pause their operations and flee the area.

2030: Back at the White House, President Bush addresses the nation for a third and final time that day. He calls the attacks "evil" and "despicable" and promises that America and its allies will stand together to win the war on terrorism.

2045: After a countless number of lost hours, I finally manage to break my gaze away from the screen. With the set muted, I just sat there in this mesmerized kind of silence. The second-shift news anchors had managed to regain some composure by then, even though their coverage was still just a highlight reel of those same few home videos. There wasn't any new information to pass along, but that didn't stop those reporters from analyzing the President's every word. Each and every one of those broadcasts, they all seemed to have reached the same conclusion. Those reporters were so resolute in claiming that the crashes were acts of terrorism, almost as if the FBI and the CIA had already wrapped up the investigations they'd launched only a few hours before.

Right after that, though, is where my timeline always seems to go blurry.

I honestly couldn't tell you just how long I sat there at my tiny desk, numb and silent.

But once I finally did manage to get up and get moving, the only thing I could think to do was reach down underneath the bed and pull out my old memory box. That plastic Rubbermaid tub had been collecting dust through my time at college, yet I'd never been able to make myself leave it behind at home.

Inside was a dozen birthday cards wrapped up in a bundle, all of them signed by Mom: one for each of the years she was with us. The very last one had a picture of Inspector Gadget holding a cake with twelve candles in his go-go-gadget arms.

Then there was my old field hockey shirt from senior year, the varsity one. The uniform that Coach Raeke had made it a point to issue out himself, once I finally got good enough to come off the sidelines in the last few minutes of the games.

The entire box was full of junk like that. The stuff I still hung on to for some reason or other, even if I couldn't fully explain why. Old pieces of the past, things that had stuck with me even as I'd grown older.

And then, at the bottom of the box, there was that old yearbook.

John F. Kennedy Junior High School. Home of the Hawks. Class of 1993.

The light from the television flickered against the cinderblock walls. They were completely bare, the same way I'd found them on the day I'd moved in. I hadn't even bothered to hang any posters, since graduate students were supposed to be way past all that kid stuff.

Right?

But even with the television muted, the baseless speculation still echoed in my ears. Could all four of those planes possibly have been hijacked at the same time, in an amazingly complex and coordinated act of terrorism?

Could the United States of America really be at war, even when it still wasn't clear who'd attacked us?

And since it seemed pretty obvious that there wouldn't be any new information coming that night, every other American must've been thinking the same thing as me:

What in the world was going to happen tomorrow?

But see, the difference between me and everybody else on the planet was, I already knew.

As if all those broadcast images weren't shocking enough, I knew that our world had already begun changing, and that we were watching it happen, live.

While everybody else could only imagine the horrors yet to come, I was having visions of heavily-armed soldiers loading up onto dozens of transport planes, headed for the far side of the world.

Just like Burton had said.

The moment I heard that a plane had struck the North Tower, I knew my stepbrother had been telling the truth.

A surge of electricity shot through my fingers as I ran them across the yearbook cover, resting them over the embossed, blue letters. It struck me as funny, almost—the fact that a dumpy little middle school like JFK would even go to the trouble of putting out a yearbook.

I mean, does anyone actually *want* to remember that time in their life? Has there ever been a single kid, in the long and vaunted history of public education, who actually grew up and still kept in touch with their ninth-grade classmates?

Let's face it, in junior high, there's no such thing as friends. Only allies.

The goal isn't education; it's survival.

I pulled my legs up onto the chair, crossing them over into a tight yoga position while I flipped through the glossy pages. And right then—if only for the briefest of moments—I swear, I could actually feel time's strong pull, drawing me back to that era.

The grip was fleeting, sure. But it was there.

Undeniable.

Time travel was possible, just like Burton had said.

Which meant that my stepbrother had been real, too. The older one, I mean.

And if that was true, it meant that the spring of 1993—all of it—had actually happened.

MONDAY, JANUARY 4, 1993

I SLAMMED THE FRONT DOOR BEHIND ME, DOING MY BEST TO KEEP THE cold air shut outside. My legs shivered beneath those thin Bugle Boy jeans, a single layer of denim not nearly enough when the temperatures dropped down into the teens. I'll admit, it was stupid not to have layered up with a pair of sweatpants when I left the house that morning, but it was just as well—going to school at all turned out to be a huge mistake. Big surprise, John F. Kennedy was just as much of a shithole in January as it'd been the year before. If anything, the three weeks off for Christmas had just made it harder to go back.

I'd walked home in a mental fog, the same way I'd passed the entire morning. The only time I really focused at all was after I caught creepy old Lesane giving me the hairy eyeball during American History. But I wasn't worried. Not really. That buzzard was off in his own world half the time. He had this way of pacing around the classroom when he lectured, always with one or two shirt buttons undone. It was almost like the guy was more preoccupied with the War of 1812 than with dressing himself properly.

I doubt he would've been able to smell the liquor on my breath—not through that thick walrus mustache of his, anyway. But still, my Dad would've killed me if he found out I'd copped another suspension, so the moment Sleazy Leazy came striding towards my desk, I jumped up, snatched the hall pass, and made for the girls' room, cutting back at the fire doors to make my escape. That fifth of Malibu I'd slammed during homeroom had kicked in by the time I made it out onto the blacktop, but somehow, I managed to stumble to the sidewalk without being spotted.

Hell, even if anybody *had* seen me, I was probably way too blitzed to hear them calling me back.

"Jessie? 'Issat you, girl?"

Crap.

"Uh…yeah. It's just me!" I started down the hallway, kicking myself for not thinking that anyone else might be home. I must've been damn near wasted if I'd managed to climb up our steep driveway without noticing the huge Ford Bronco parked outside. That thing was impossible to miss: it was lime green, with dark limousine window tint and a massive chrome brush guard, all of it jacked up over a set of 33-inch mud tires.

Esmerelda stuck her head out of the kitchen, the cordless telephone pressed up against her ear like always. I swear, that lady wore a phone like it was a fashion accessory, the white plastic handset complementing her powder blue Adidas tracksuit. "Hey, 'joo home early, huh, babe? 'Joo not sick again or something? No?"

My face flushed with embarrassment. "No, we just… it was a half day. Early release. Must've been one of those teacher workdays, I think."

"Izzat right? I sorry baby, I did'na see that one on the calendar your Daddy left!" She turned back towards the kitchen. "Now how in the worl' I miss that? Lemme go back, ha' another look…"

My mind shuddered into gear, fighting through the haze. It was a struggle for me to think at all, let alone come up with a good lie, so I settled on telling the truth.

Kind of.

"And yeah, the thing is, I just didn't feel so hot. So I decided to come on home and rest for a while."

Aunt Emmy had already popped back out of sight, but it sounded like she'd bought it. Either that, or she just didn't care all that much. "Aw, baby! Okay, why don't joo jus' go lie down, then? Take a load off. Joo'll feel better in a coupla hours. Huh?"

"Thanks, Aunt Emmy. I'll be in my room." I couldn't be certain she'd heard me, but she'd already switched back to speaking Spanish. Esmerelda was my Uncle Hector's wife, and neither one of them were true family. Hector and my Dad had worked together for years, so they'd gotten really close, like brothers almost. And not having any kids herself, Emmy always drove up to stay at our place whenever my Dad and Samantha were both out on the road at the same time.

When I reached the foot of the stairs, I saw my stepbrother Burton pop his tiny head out of the kitchen. He was clad in his everyday attire: a skintight pair of boxer briefs. Black, of course, with a matching set of hot flames striped down the sides. The kid always went shirtless indoors, and on that day, he bore a striking resemblance to some babyface rookie wrestler.

Burton stared at me with that silent gaze of his, not speaking a word.

Like always.

It was almost like he was looking straight through me, as he chewed away at that Granny Smith apple, probably his third or fourth of the day so far. Burton still hadn't started talking yet, but in my opinion, that was just as well. I mean, who really cared what a three-year old had to say, anyway? Me, I'd stopped trying to interact with the kid altogether. Burton seemed to prefer screaming and kicking over actual communication. His tantrums could get downright nasty, especially when somebody made the mistake of trying to run a comb through that tangle of dirty blond hair.

"Burton!" Emmy shrieked. "'Joo get back here right now, boy! I mean it! Tha's your fourth apple today. Ain't I already say 'joo ain' s'pose to have no more? You think I wanna spend all day cleaning up the toilet when 'joo get the shits again, huh? 'Joo still hungry, get back in here, eat some of this peanut butter sandwich!"

Burton flinched. His tiny body tightened into a knot of muscle and bone, fists wound into compact balls of flesh. The moment I spotted his jaw clench down, I knew what would be coming next. I ducked off into the living room, unlatched the liquor cabinet, and snatched up a handful of mini-bottles without even stopping to see what they were. The kid's high-pitched shriek echoed down the hallway, but at least it drowned out the sound of the cabinet door as it clicked shut. Those tiny glass bottles clinked softly in my palm as I sprinted upstairs.

"Burton, baby! Can't 'joo see I'm on the phone? It's long distance! Ow! Hey!"

The wail broke off for a split second as Burton gasped for air, but the kid filled up the silence by lashing out at Aunt Emmy's legs. The whipping sound of his tiny fists pounding away lasted for a few seconds, before a single dull thump pounded against the drywall. I'd witnessed enough of these fits to know that Burton must've just chucked the apple in frustration, but as bad as all this sounded, I knew the kid was just getting started. Yeah, for a toddler who couldn't speak, my stepbrother still had his own unique ways of expressing himself.

"Burton, 'joo knock dat off! Jessie, baby, 'joo still down here girl? Come on now, give me a hand with your brother, hey?"

"He's not my real brother," I muttered, careful to keep my voice low. I slammed the bedroom door harder than I needed to, hoping Aunt Emmy might take it as a sign that I hadn't heard her. Those old, thin walls never did much to keep noise out, and Burton's wailing permeated our entire house. His high-pitched screams were punctuated by rapid hammering as the kid threw himself on the floor, pounding his fists in a rage.

As for me, I walked over to my desk and clicked on the television, then surfed up through the channels until I reached MTV. There was another thick manila envelope waiting there next to the set, which had to have come in the morning mail. It could only have been the latest VHS tape from my Dad, but I left it there, unopened. As talented as the man was, I just wasn't in the mood to watch him perform again. As I sat there waiting for the picture to come into focus, I cranked up the volume, hoping to drown out Burton, yet not make so much noise that I'd risk Aunt Emmy barging in. By that hour of the day, there was at least a fair chance of catching a Rage Against the Machine video in between all the crappy dance music.

I pulled open my mini-fridge next, grabbing an open two-liter of Sprite and pouring in all the liquor, one bottle after another. The streams of Malibu rum, Jose Cuervo tequila, and Bombay Sapphire gin sank to the bottom, sloshing back up in an angry fizz when I capped the bottle and gave it a shake.

Downstairs, Burton's screams were still going strong, and it took all of my concentration to block them out. I knew from experience that the best thing to do was just leave the kid alone, let him run out of steam on his own, and hope that none of our nosy neighbors felt the need to call the cops.

But the shrieks were piercing, almost unbearable, and I wondered if my normal afternoon buzz would be enough to drown them out.

So after a moment's consideration, I dashed down the hall to our bathroom and snagged a bottle of Robitussin out of the medicine cabinet.

"Jessie! Girl, where you at? Sure could use a li'l help down here, huh?"

I tiptoed back to my room and closed the door just as quietly as I could manage, then clicked in the button lock for good measure. With any luck, Aunt Emmy might assume I'd put on my Walkman headphones and laid down for a nap. Back at my desk, I uncapped the Sprite once more and poured in the cough syrup. The clear liquid morphed into a purple mist, all those different drinks swirling together in this oddly hypnotic fashion.

"Jessie! Girl, 'joo better get down here!"

I braced myself for the taste—needlessly. The stuff wasn't half bad. Sweet like soda, of course, but the cough syrup gave it a thicker consistency and toned down the bite from the tequila. It was kind of like drinking a watery milkshake, but with one hell of a kick. I could almost feel my buzz spike after that first swallow, but I managed to keep my shit together long enough to ditch the evidence. The Sprite bottle went back in the fridge, half-empty now. The mini bottles got bundled up in tampon wrappers, buried down deep at the bottom of my wastebasket. That done, I flopped down on my quilted comforter, that deep haze washing over my body just as "November Rain" came up on the screen.

It was so relaxing, just lying there and letting the alcohol rinse my frustrations clean. The stress and drama of my life, all of it, seemed to wash away, carried off on a soundtrack of Guns N' Roses.

All of my cares—every last one of them—faded into nothing, melting away just like that video's picture-perfect wedding.

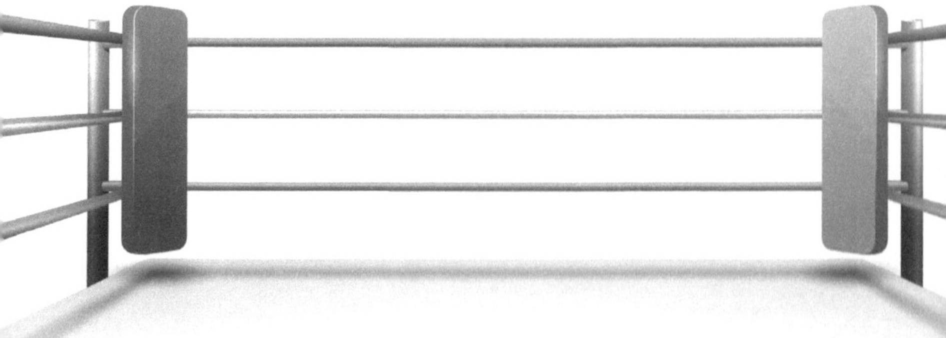

WHEN MY EYES FINALLY OPENED, THE ONLY THING I COULD MANAGE TO do was just lay there wondering how much time had passed. It was dark outside, so it could've been anywhere between four PM and six AM. Night came early during those cold New England winters.

After listening carefully for a few minutes, I was relieved to hear only silence. Burton must've already gone to bed, and Aunt Emmy, too, if she hadn't gone down to the Blessed Sacrament for bingo, I mean. My television set was still on, still tuned to MTV, although I didn't recognize this video. A couple black guys, gangsters decked out in hooded sweatshirts and hockey jerseys, were cruising around the Los Angeles freeways in some kind of tricked-out Cadillac convertible.

I hated rap music—couldn't stand it. For some reason, though, I just couldn't bring myself to reach up and change the channel. My body felt numb all over. Tingling. I couldn't move at all, like I'd been paralyzed from the neck down somehow. When I tried to raise an arm to reach for the remote, nothing happened. Like, my brain knew exactly what I wanted to do and all, but I just couldn't couldn't trigger my muscles into action.

I tried to wiggle my fingers next, just the tiniest movement.

Still no luck.

And now in hindsight, I know that should've been a sign that something was seriously wrong with my body—but at the time, I was too whacked out to comprehend it. In fact, the whole situation just didn't register, at least not fully.

Not until the volume meter suddenly popped up across the bottom of the screen, and those small green bars clicked steadily to the right. My bedroom filled with the synthesized bass beats of "Nuthin But A G Thang," a song which had been simply unavoidable that month.

And then, after several more seconds of having to watch those two thugs parade around at a cookout, I heard this soft little cough from the corner of the room. The noise took me by surprise, since I was positive that I'd locked the door. But all I could do was tilt my head to the left, and only ever so slightly.

There in my beanbag chair—the old blue vinyl one that had a way of leaking tiny bits of polystyrene foam stuffing all over the carpet—sat a full-grown man. And the weird thing was, the old guy was just sitting there, doing nothing. Nothing at all, except watching television.

Or to be more precise, he was watching *my* television, and the rap videos playing on it.

I guess the whole crazy scene probably should've surprised me a whole lot more than it did, but at the time, all I remember thinking was that the situation just seemed a bit…odd.

And so I ended up lying there.

Taking it all in.

Like, what else could I do?

Fighting through the mental haze, I did my best to study the guy closely, committing the details to memory.

The stranger was an old, white dude. Somewhere between forty and fifty, maybe. And skinny. His hair was a wild forest of uncombed fibers, mostly brown, with a couple gray strands mixed in there at random. His face was lean, yet still somehow roundish, as if the guy still had one last stubborn layer of baby fat tucked in around his cheeks. But the thing that really struck me was his clothes! The dude was middle-aged, but he was dressed the same as any of my classmates at JFK—or like the rich kids did, anyway. Those privileged few, whose parents could afford to shell out for a brand-new wardrobe every season. His down jacket was a puffy Triple F.A.T. Goose, warm and comfortable. A twinge of envy struck me, and I silently wished that I'd had the foresight to crawl beneath the covers before I'd passed out. A bright red hooded sweatshirt was peeking out from underneath the coat, this well-worn zip-up Champion, hanging loose over a pair of stonewashed carpenter overalls and a set of Timberland work boots. Brand-new, tan, with no scuffs. Thin wire headphones rested against the back of his neck, with the yellow wire cord streaming down to a Sony Discman Sport that was clipped on his belt.

Finally, the horrible video faded away and *Yo! MTV Raps* cut to a commercial break. I watched as the intruder reached for the remote, pressing a button that made the word "MUTE" appear in the screen's upper-right hand corner.

I looked at the guy.

He stared impassively back.

The expression on his face—or rather, the complete lack of an expression—probably should've frightened me a whole lot more than it did. But even from the far side of the room, that long, silent gaze just struck me as kind of…familiar. You know? Almost as if I'd seen it somewhere before.

The guy? Definitely not.

But his face? Absolutely.

And then, after a long, awkward silence, the dude twitched his nose with a sniff of disdain. "You know," he said, "if you were trying to kill yourself tonight, it didn't work. Believe it or not, you're still alive."

There was absolutely nothing I could say to that. Honestly, I wasn't even sure I still had the ability to string a sentence together.

"I'm not saying you *should* kill yourself, now. That's never going to be the right choice. But if you *are* going to do something—anything—then you owe it yourself not to half-ass the job. So if offing yourself is what you really want to do—what you were *trying* to do just now, whether you realize it or not—I'd recommend you check out our parents' bedroom first. Mom's been taking sleeping pills for the past couple months, did you know about that? Helps her to rest in between all the road shows."

As I lay there, I swear, I could actually feel each individual bead of sweat as they streamed down my forehead. I hadn't known about Samantha's pills, or else I probably would've been swiping them already. But man, I was so far gone that I didn't even have the strength to argue that while Samantha might've legally become my stepmother some months ago, I'd be damned if I ever called her Mom.

As it happened, though, all I could manage to do was listen.

"You just go on ahead—mix up that same drink you did this afternoon, but drop in five or six of those pills, too. If you do that, everything will take care of itself before long. You'll just drift off to sleep, same as you did today, and you won't have to worry about waking up anymore. Not ever. Can you even imagine that? Never again having to deal with this absolute mess that you call a life."

When the Clearasil zit cream commercial ended and the next video came on, the guy pressed the mute button once again. I recognized the singer, a big dude who called himself Heavy D. The nickname seemed appropriate, but I had to admit, it *was* kind of impressive, how he moved that big frame nimbly back and forth between a squad of backup dancers. The music, though, that was absolutely terrible. I couldn't stand those urban rhythms, and I wanted to beg the guy to change the channel, but I didn't even have the strength to ask. My eyes just rolled back in my head as my gaze drifted up towards the ceiling.

The dude's attention was back on the television by that point, and I'm pretty sure he might've said something else. But that was right when the blur faded in, and I drifted off into a deep, dreamless sleep once again.

MONDAY, JANUARY 11, 1993

AND THEN ONE AFTERNOON IN THE SCHOOL LIBRARY, AFTER I'D GOTTEN back up on my feet, that was when I first took notice of John Nguyen. I mean, *really* noticed the kid. He and I'd been going to the same schools for years, as long as I can remember, so I imagine he must've always been there in the background. Probably since kindergarten, even though I'd never actually spoken to him.

Never had a need to.

And to be honest, I don't know if I'd ever even taken a real good look at the kid, either.

Not before that day, anyway.

John Nguyen was just one of the dozen or so retards they let attend JFK. But not one of those Down Syndrome kids, the really disabled ones, who were so hard up that they went to their own special Life Skills classes, studying things like how to tie their shoelaces, then getting a fake high school diploma after twelve years of babysitting. No, for some reason or other, he'd ended up in most of the mainstream classes—whenever he bothered to show up, that is. Our teachers generally tolerated the kid, or ignored him at least. Yeah, for the most part, John Nguyen was pretty much invisible, except for those times when he opened his mouth to say something dumb.

School was a different world back in the ninth grade. John F. Kennedy Junior High was basically just this place where I went because it was expected of me. Whenever Dad and Samantha were back in town for more than a weekend and I was forced to keep up appearances, or whenever I just wasn't up to forging Aunt Emmy's signature on my sick notes, I'd head off to school as a way to pass the time. The place was a hassle, but at least it was warm in the winter.

It was an open study period, I remember that. Those were regularly scheduled at least once a week, or irregularly whenever one of our teachers needed to duck off to their lounge for a quick drink. I was passing the time the same way I did in all my classes, with my head tucked down low over my books. The phony show of concentration was usually all it took for me to get away with dozing off. My teachers had already learned that if they left me alone, I was much less likely to disturb their lessons, and at JFK, silence was enough to pass for good behavior.

Naturally, I didn't make eye contact when John walked in and chose a seat at the far end of my table. I swear, when that kid said "Hey" in that whiny, high-pitched voice of his, the greeting only made him seem even more annoying than usual.

Like, if that was even possible.

I only spared him a glance when he pulled a glossy wrestling magazine from his backpack. He slapped it down on the table, licked his fat thumb and began flipping through the pages. It was the latest issue of *Turnbuckle*, one I still hadn't gotten around to reading. For some reason or other, I found myself wondering if there might've been any pictures of my Dad inside, even though I knew damn well there wouldn't be.

My eyes must've lingered a second too long, and the kid finally sensed my gaze. When John Nguyen looked up again, I was struck by his resemblance to a caveman. That thick, sloping forehead of his jutted way out over a pair of thick black eyebrows, both of them joining together so that they were damn near perfectly centered above his plump brown nose. I couldn't hold back a shudder, and I had to turn my attention back to the textbook before he had a chance to say anything. American History wasn't my favorite subject, but it would have to do. Any distraction was better than staring at the yellow layer of fuzz coating John's crooked teeth.

But even as I tried my damnedest to ignore him—while at the same time ignoring our classmates, the rest of the school, and the whole damned world—I couldn't quite manage to block out Nelson Madeiros and Manny Ramirez when they wandered over. Those two goons, they were nothing but trouble. Like me, they only came to school when they didn't have some place better to be, and I could tell what they were thinking the second they chose their seats. Nelson and Manny pulled up chairs on the other side of my table, sandwiching John Nguyen in between.

"Whatcha reading, John?" Nelson asked, snatching the magazine away. "Wrestling! Huh." He shot a glance my way, so I did my best to look like the Battle of New Orleans was more interesting than the skirmish taking place in front of me. "You trying to get in good with your girl Jessie? Huh? Maybe strike up a conversation with her?"

He lifted his elbow and used it to bump John Nguyen in the shoulder.

Hard.

"You got a crush on that little honey, don't you? Yeah, I knew it! Can't say I blame you, that fine little body and all. Girl'd actually be kind of cute, if she ever got that acne cleared up. But you better be careful of her daddy. You heard? The Daydreamer's liable to come after you, you don't treat her right!" Nelson sneered in my direction again. "Although, I ain't sure that washed-up old man would still be able to *do* anything. Whenever he steps in the ring, he spends most of the match on his back!"

I felt my pulse quicken, but did my best to keep cool. My shaking hands flipped the page, and I played it off like I hadn't heard anything. Yeah, my dad was a jobber. That was no secret. Dad never won many matches, but that was only because his real talent was making all the up-and-coming wrestlers look good in the spotlight. Helping them get over with the fans. That was the job, and Tommy Carpenter did it better than anyone.

Manny shook his head with an air of scorn, then turned his attention back to John Nguyen. He licked his lips and blew a few loud air kisses, reaching over to rest a hand on the kid's thigh. With his other arm, Manny reached around John's shoulder and pulled him into a close embrace. "John, it's okay," he lisped. "Really! Everybody knows you're a faggot, so hey, it's cool! There's nothing wrong with looking at photos of half-naked dudes…I mean, it's not what *I'm* into, but if that's your thing, then man, there's no need to *apologize*." Manny took the magazine away from Nelson and flipped it open to a spread of Johnny Forbes, then pressed the pages into his victim's face. "Here, this guy's pretty cute. Give him a kiss!"

John Nguyen laughed. It came out as this nervous little whinny, as he shook his thick head from side to side with embarrassment. "Come off it, guys! I'm trying to read."

Nelson leaned in from the other side, giving John a quick shove. "Dude! You fucking stink! I mean, really, bro. Do you have any idea just how ripe you are right now? When's the last time you took a shower, anyway?"

I sighed, wrinkling my nose as I flipped the page. It was true, John Nguyen usually *did* carry around a unique funk. The odor was a peculiar mix of body sweat and halitosis, combined with the fumes from old clothing worn for days on end. I'm positive that the kid would've *had* to have taken a bath every so often, but I was also certain it couldn't have been an everyday thing.

Manny leaned in close, pressing his cheek against the wispy layers of peach fuzz that covered John's face. He pulled the magazine away, holding it about an inch from the kid's nose, riffling the pages to make him flinch. John's head eased back much slower than I would've expected, more of a delayed reaction than an actual reflex.

"Let me tell you something, Johnny Boy," he hissed. "You want to make it with any of these hunks, you're going to have to scrub up a little. Do something about that stench, maybe splash on a little cologne every so often. Here, let me help!"

And before John Nguyen had a chance to respond, Manny dipped a hand into his jacket, coming back up with a small spray bottle. The flat black color was unmistakable: Drakkar Noir, the preferred fragrance of every hormonal teenaged boy in greater Lowell.

"Here, bro," he said. "You can borrow some of mine." Manny thumbed the cap and worked the spray nozzle loose, holding the entire container upside down above John Nguyen's head. Nelson leaned in and pinned John's arms behind his back, so he couldn't stop that clear liquid from spilling all over his thick mess of black hair. It ran down his face in wide streams, pouring along the sides of his fat neck, too. Those two jerks cackled with laughter as the cologne slowed to a trickle. Across the room, I saw our worthless librarian, old Mrs. Kushner, shoot our table a fierce glare of disapproval over her windowpane-thick bifocals. The old bag sure didn't trouble herself to do anything more than that, though.

As the fragrant liquid dripped to a halt, Manny gave the spray bottle one last shake, then dropped it into John's lap. "There, see?" he asked, as the powerful stench wafted out across the room. "Now, isn't that better?"

And the whole time, John Nguyen just sat there and took it. Those big hands of his stayed planted beneath his hammy thighs, and I shook my head in disgust. Not just at the shameless bullying, but at John's complete refusal to defend himself. I mean, that kid was nearly as big as Nelson and Manny put together! If he only knew how to use his size, and his reach, I'll bet he could've taken on both those twats at the same time. But no, John Nguyen just sat there with this stupid smile plastered across his fat face, almost as if he believed he could've gotten himself out of that mess just by laughing along with them.

Who knows why?

Maybe he figured that if he acted like he was in on the joke, those idiots might get bored eventually, and maybe leave him alone. Like he was hoping for some kind of escape to just magically appear all of a sudden.

But I knew better.

This wasn't professional wrestling.

This was real life, and there was no such thing as an easy way out.

I covered my nose as that strong, citrusy fragrance overpowered the space. "Fucking morons," I muttered, careful to keep my head down, even though the struggles of a growing nation seemed even less relevant than usual.

"What was that?"

I didn't bother to respond. Just flipped on to the next page, never mind that I hadn't finished reading the last one.

"Hey, skeezer! I'm talking to you." Nelson flung a chewed-up number two pencil my way, sending it clattering across the tabletop. "I know you didn't just say something! Did you, bitch?"

Thankfully, *I* didn't flinch.

I took a deep breath, then raised an open palm, flipping my left hand around to shoot that dick the bird. Out of the corner of my eye, I saw Mrs. Kushner had chosen that exact moment to abandon her desk and go work the card catalogues. It was just as well, really. I could deal with any heat from those two heels, Manny and Nelson, but the last thing I needed was to cop another detention.

"Holy shit! It lives!" Manny chuckled, then pushed back his chair. The kid took his sweet time about it, too, reaching down to adjust his crotch as he stood, then strutting a wide path around the table. "What's the matter, Jessie the Junkie? Did I offend you? Look, I'm sorry, okay? I didn't realize the two of you were an item! You're just sticking up for your boyfriend, am I right?"

With a heavy sigh, I flipped my textbook shut. Honestly, it was just as well. There was no chance in hell I'd be able to catch up on all the reading I'd missed, at least not with those two assholes hanging around. I could almost feel my next suspension looming, but figured that I might be able to cover it up by faking sick again. And really, what choice did I have? If there's one thing my Dad taught me, it's that sometimes you've got to stand firm. You can't afford to wait and do nothing, hoping someone else will come along and stick up for you. No, you've got to fight your own battles. And the sooner you draw that line in the sand, the better.

Rising, I stuffed my notes into that beat-up old Jansport bag and stepped off in the other direction, careful to keep a chair in between us. I held the History textbook loose in my right hand, knowing full well that Nelson would be lunging in to block my path. I swear, those two clowns made one of the weakest tag teams I'd ever seen, stumbling about like a pair of gooseshit green punks straight off the indie circuit. Their movements were stiff. Jerky. Telegraphing their intentions, clear as day. That routine of theirs was so bad, even the most gullible mark up in the nosebleeds would've been able to call the next shot.

"Where you think you're going, freak?" Sure enough, Nelson puffed out his thin little chest as he jumped in, standing way too close now. There wasn't enough space left for that dumbass to throw a punch, not without having to step back for the windup. From that position, the only move he had left was a shove.

On the left, I spotted Manny hustling over to cut around behind me, and I knew he'd probably be dropping down on all fours. I made my decision without thinking about it, and before Nelson had a chance to buck up, I shrugged, letting my backpack fall loose. When it thumped against the floor, I whipped my arm forward in a tight arc. The move was quick, strong and violent, and the book's spine struck hard against the bridge of Nelson's nose.

"What in the hell!"

He stumbled backwards, creating the gap I needed to repeat the move twice more. A bright red burst of blood began spraying from his nostrils, my cue to lunge forward and plant a shoulder in his solar plexus. I felt that warm blood spatter all over my new mock turtleneck, but by that point, I just didn't give a shit.

Nelson's legs buckled. He tripped over a chair leg, going down hard on the cold linoleum. I heard a loud shriek from somewhere across the room, but I was way too focused to bother turning around to see who was watching. With Nelson out of commission, I whirled on my heel, snapping my arm forward to chuck the book down at Manny. That douchebag had already dropped into a low squat, all ready to trip me up, but the sudden attack had caught him by surprise. The book caught Manny right in the temple, crumpling him into a ball right then and there.

The job was done, but I stood there in place for a few more seconds, just staring at John Nguyen and his look of confusion. That same, stupid expression which seemed to be permanently pinned to his wet, sticky face.

And right then, in that awkward, uncomfortable moment, I heard the moron let out this low, little whine.

For a second, I almost thought the kid was about to start crying.

But he didn't.

Softly, speaking so quietly that only he and I could hear it, John Nguyen whispered, "I'll show those guys. Some day. They'll never be able to bother me again."

I broke off my gaze, rotating my head around the library to make eye contact with all of my classmates who were bold enough to stare back at me. That room was as still as death, filled with the overpowering scent of Drakkar Noir. Even Mrs. Kushner, who under normal circumstances would've seized any opportunity to curse me out, had been stunned into silence. But I knew the moment would pass quickly, so I bent over to grab my bag while both Nelson and Manny were down for the count. I left the textbook lying there, its pages stuck together with blood.

As I hoofed it out into the hallway, I could practically feel all those sets of eyes watching me. The back of my neck was warm, as if countless pairs of laser beams were boring holes into my skin.

"She's such a freak," someone hissed.

I kept my head down. My legs churned, propelling me away from the scene of the crime.

"Totally," another voice said. "Like, complete and total washout."

EVEN BEFORE I'D MADE IT HOME THAT DAY, THE SUSPENSION NOTICE was waiting on the answering machine. The charge was fighting—second offense—which carried a one-week minimum sentence. There was no appeal process, and of course the whole incident would be marked on my permanent record. At least I'd managed to escape any consequences at home, since Aunt Emmy had been out somewhere running errands. I played the tape through, then hustled down to the Li'l Peach to dial our number from the pay phone there. Of course I'd left my parka behind, so I damn near froze to death waiting on the beep. With my bare hand covering the receiver, the recording only picked up a long, silent stretch of heavy breathing, which could've come from any old creep in town.

That done, I jogged back up the hill, raced in the door, and re-played the tape so Aunt Emmy wouldn't spot the blinking red light. And later that night, I concocted another cover story about not feeling well, probably because of a pesky bug making the rounds at JFK. Even though I'm sure she must've suspected something was up, it *was* cold and flu season, so I got a pass.

But after just a couple days of hiding out in my room, I was starting to get bored with the routine: sleeping late, ducking Aunt Emmy until she took Burton to daycare, and then heading off to McDonald's for hotcakes and sausage, bumming around the restaurant until the lowlifes who worked there tossed me out. Believe it or not, all that nothingness was finally beginning to wear on me. After three or four straight days of this, as I trudged back home on a cold and windy morning, I even found myself wondering what might've been happening at school! Yeah, even the luxury of being able to watch MTV all day was feeling more and more like a grind. I guess I'd just never noticed how often they played the same videos on that channel, and I mean, like, over and over again. I swear, I must've seen that "Tears in Heaven" song a hundred times, if not more.

Eventually—more out of boredom than from any real desire to get high—I dipped back into the fridge to finish off the rest of my Sprite and Robitussin cocktail. The drink went down quick and easy. I ditched the empty bottle in the trash, then settled in to savor the buzz. In a matter of minutes, my body felt lighter and lighter, almost like I could've been floating over the bedsheets instead of laying between them. I wiggled my toes back and forth inside those wool raglan socks, marveling at the way they seemed to drift up and down under their own power.

And the very last thing I remember was glancing sideways. Towards the bedroom door.

There in the corner sat the same creepy old guy, kicked back in my beanbag chair once again. His skinny legs were splayed out straight, shamelessly sporting a slick new set of black Reebok Pumps. Sitting there all casual, like he was trying to pretend that new color hadn't been sold out in the stores since Thanksgiving.

After a moment, the guy turned away from the television. He glanced my way, shaking his head in this sudden bobble, which caused the hood of his dingy red sweatshirt to slide back.

I lifted my neck, getting a clear view of his face for the very first time. The dude's cheeks were covered in a thin layer of stubble. The light gray shade marked him as middle-aged, though somehow he still could've passed for a student at UMASS. Okay, maybe a graduate student, but my point is, the guy was clearly old, yet he still had this youngish kind of look to him. It was almost eerie, the way he managed to look like he was two different ages at once.

He glanced my way and sniffed his nose. "Hey. Did you ever get around to stealing Mom's sleeping pills?" He craned his pencil-thin neck and cast a gaze around the room, letting his eyes linger on the Nirvana poster I'd hung beside the window. "No, I guess you didn't. Never mind, then. I was going to say, if you couldn't find them or something, you might try drinking bleach instead. Though, you'd probably need an entire bottle to do the job. And trust me, you don't want to go that route. It tastes horrible, bleach does. And you might just vomit it all back up, accomplishing nothing. You'd be right back where you started: still alone, still miserable, and on top of all your other problems, you'd have severe intestinal damage to deal with."

A cold chill ran up my spine. I had, in fact, conducted a thorough search of the master bedroom. In the drawer of Samantha's nightstand, I'd found a dark brown pill bottle, about half full of Ambien tablets.

Just like this creep had said.

I'd been careful to leave everything exactly as I'd found it, though. Knowing that witch Samantha and the way she always watched me like a hawk when I passed by the liquor cabinet, I figured that my stepmother probably kept a close count of her pills.

Finally, after an infuriatingly long struggle, my lips formed up properly and produced a few coherent sounds. "Who?" I asked. The question had been weighing on my mind for the past week, which is probably the only reason I managed to choke it out. "Who *are* you?"

He sniffed again, making a scornful appraisal of my haggard appearance before turning back to the television. "Burton" he said. His voice was soft and low, so I barely caught the words that came next. "Your brother."

But by that point, my mind was already fading off into a dark, drunken oblivion. There was absolutely no way I could've processed that wild claim, but I kept it together just long enough to toss out a single, weak jab in reply.

"Burton's not my real brother," I whispered, as I slipped off into the void. "He's Samantha's kid…"

TUESDAY, JANUARY 19, 1993

OUTSIDE, THE COLD WIND HOWLED ITS WAY DOWN OUR STREET IN A series of sharp, whistling gusts. Even bundled up beneath a mound of flannel blankets, that sound alone was enough to make me shudder. I'd always hated that time of year, when winter was at its darkest, and the temperature dropped too low for snow to fall. I guess that's why, when the intruder handed me a steaming cup of hot cocoa, I gratefully accepted it. The first sip was so hot it scalded my tongue, but that warm ceramic mug felt good in my hands.

Calming.

I watched the oversized marshmallow melt into a sticky white goo as I rotated the cup around in my palms, blowing the steam away. And then finally—once it'd become apparent that this guy wouldn't be the one to speak up first—I nodded towards the match playing on my television set. "You know…most grownups couldn't give a damn about professional wrestling."

He nodded, but his eyes stayed fixed on the program. "Their loss. People focus on the cheesy storylines too much, instead of just appreciating the athleticism and the whole performance aspect. I mean, I'm sure you must've heard people say that wrestling isn't a real sport. Not like, I don't know. Baseball, or football maybe."

I shrugged.

"But I always wonder, how much more fun those team sports would be to watch if the announcers focused more on what happens off the field, in between games? Like, the camera could maybe go back into the locker room, or even follow the athletes' daily lives, like some kind of afternoon soap opera. I don't know, it's just an idea. But a little drama might make more people tune in."

I nodded, even as I wondered how the playoffs were shaping up. I grew up in Massachusetts, and the Sunday afternoon Pats games were pretty much required viewing, but there'd just been so much going on in my life that year that I hadn't bothered to watch a single one. Feeling almost embarrassed, I made a mental note to check the standings in the paper before my Daddy called again, so we'd at least have something to talk about.

Besides school, I mean.

The two of us sat there in silence for a good, long while. The announcers' voices filled the room at irregular intervals, interrupted by bursts of tapping as the stranger banged away on this weird-looking computer terminal. It was one of those portable models, about the size of a suitcase. The dude had this odd method of typing on it, almost like a rhythm, where he'd press play on the remote control and let the videotape run for about ten seconds or so, then pause the action as he wrote. Sometimes he'd have to rewind a bit and listen to the dialogue a second time, but not often.

Curiosity finally got the better of me. I pulled myself upright and stared in his direction, even though the sudden movement set my head spinning in giant orbits. "What… what in the fuck are you supposed to be doing?"

He ignored the question. Just went on with his typing, picking up the remote after he'd come to a stop. "Language," he eventually sighed, not even bothering to answer my question. He just pressed the play button again, like I wasn't even there.

I bit my tongue, slowly counting to ten as I waited for the typing to stop. When the guy's fingers ceased moving, I rephrased the question, but minus the four-letter word. "What I meant to say was, what are you doing?"

He tossed a stray glance my way, his hands still planted atop the keyboard. "Writing."

I couldn't be certain whether his single-word answer had been intentionally crafted to piss me off, or whether this dude was just that uninterested in talking to me. And so even though my mind was still clouded with fog, I was determined to press him for a real answer. "So, like. Um. What are you writing?"

"A transcription."

I bit my lip. Clenched my fists. Then slowly, carefully, eased my fingers back out again. "A transcription, huh? Of what?"

"Of the match."

I'll admit, I was damn near completely lost by that point. I honestly couldn't tell if the guy was pulling my leg, the build-up to some kind of horrible prank. Painful as it was, I had to hold my tongue for a couple long minutes.

Saying nothing.

Just watching him closely.

The dude's concentration was amazing. His eyes would fix squarely on my television set, then on that laptop computer of his, and then back again. As far as I could tell, it looked like he really *was* trying to take down the commentators' every word, plus a couple notes on the in-ring action. And even though I tried my damnedest to think of a reason *why* that dude might've been working so diligently at such a pointless task, the whole situation was unexplainably weird.

Like, beyond belief.

I watched him go through one more cycle before I butted in again. "Okay, I give up! I'll bite."

He must've heard the question, but chose to ignore me. Cycling through that same process once again.

Press play.

Watch for ten seconds, give or take.

Press pause.

Type.

And only after that was done did he bother to respond. "What's that?"

I sighed. "Why, exactly, would anybody bother to transcribe a professional wrestling match? Like, I'd be willing to bet that WWW probably has those recordings down in their vaults somewhere already! And besides, this is just a dark match! All those videotapes are. Dad only sends me the clips that don't make the live broadcasts, so why in the hell—I mean, why in the *world* would anybody ever care about them?"

He nodded, holding his skinny arms out straight and then cracking his knuckles, one hand after the other. The sleeves of his red hooded sweatshirt stretched to their limit, with the splotchy, stained fabric around the elbows looking threadbare and worn. "So, you really mean to tell me that you haven't watched any of this month's tapes yet? The ones with Dad's most recent stuff?"

I felt my face flush. Normally I made it a priority to watch every single VHS tape that my Dad mailed home from the road, but lately, things had been…different. Especially over Christmas, when he and Samantha had both been home at the same time, and for an entire week. That whole vacation had just felt so, I don't know. Awkward. With her fawning all over Burton, and making a big fuss over her kid like always, but then all of a sudden trying to act all motherly towards me, too. "I…I've been meaning to," I said. "It's just…I just haven't gotten around to them."

He let out a scornful sniff as he squeezed the pause button. "Yeah. You've been busy."

I tried to focus on the screen, same as he was doing, but those athletes seemed to keep blurring together in a series of colorful swirls. Even the announcers' words—the back-and-forth patter that helped set a tone for the match—all that speech just drifted past my ears in waves of muted sound. I could feel the warm grip of sleep trying to pull me under again, but I struggled against it, and stayed conscious long enough to blurt out one last question.

"But…why? Why are you doing it?"

He sighed, but turned and gave me his full attention for the very first time. I saw his features soften with a look of concern, right at the same moment the darkness enveloped me. "I'm making sure that Dad's matches are documented for posterity. All of them, even the dark ones. This is history in the making, and we're lucky to be witnessing it."

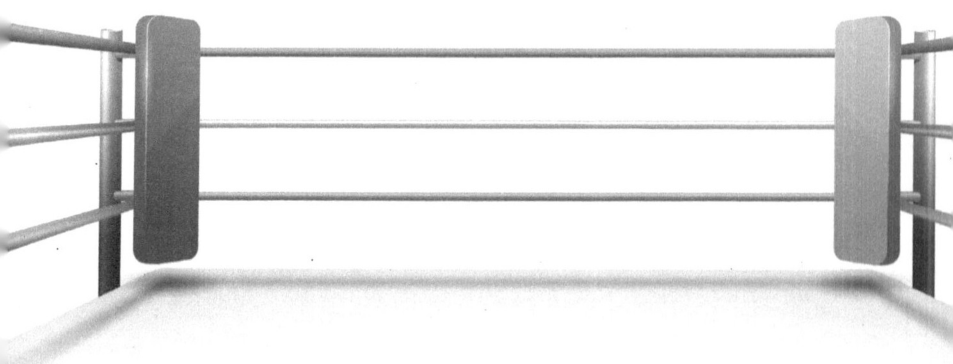

TO: JessieBear1979@AOL.com
FROM: DayDreamer@AOL.com
SUBJECT: Hey, Bear!

Hey, Bear!

Sorry I missed you last night! Esmerelda said you were still under the weather, so I didn't want to bother. I hope you're taking care of yourself, staying out of the cold and all. Did they give the flu shot at JFK this year? Trust me, you don't want any part of that virus. When that bug starts going around, it's absolutely vicious!

Anyway, just checking in to see how you're doing? We haven't talked much lately, and I know you're real busy with school and with helping your Aunt Emmy look after your brother, but I wanted to ask, have you watched those tapes?

It's crazy, right? I still can't believe it myself, how everything's finally starting to come together, but it just goes to show you. Work hard, believe in yourself, and sooner or later, the opportunities have to come knocking!

So yeah, I know how slammed you must be, but I wanted to make sure you'd be tuning in on Monday. Yes, it's a school night, but you won't have to stay up too late! I'm on the undercard—as usual—so it'll probably be the very first match. A curtain jerker, but at least it gets me back on the live broadcast. And I know this is going to sound like I'm cutting a promo right now, but trust me, you will <u>not</u> want to miss this match!

I'll try to call again this weekend, if I can. And Samantha and I are hoping to make it home again next month, but I guess now we'll have to wait and see how this next match goes over?

Study hard, Jessie Bear! I love you!

Dad   XOXO

MONDAY, JANUARY 25, 1993

MY HANDS WERE TREMBLING BEYOND CONTROL AS I MADE MY WAY downstairs, heading for the telephone in the hall. Aunt Emmy had already headed off to bingo, and with Burton tucked into bed, I'd be able to have a private conversation for once. Looking back, I don't really know *why* I'd waited so long to ask my Dad for his advice, especially seeing as how that weird stranger had come and gone *twice* already. I mean, who knows? I guess I could've dismissed that first visit as a hallucination, maybe. Nothing more than a bad reaction to the booze and the cough syrup. But the second time? Well, the longer I'd stayed sober, the harder it became to deny the whole situation. And after a couple days of thinking about it, somehow, I guess I just came to accept both of those visits really *had* happened.

But in this strange sort of way, the extra attention wasn't entirely unwelcome. With my Dad out on the road so much, I mean, and Samantha on my permanent blacklist even when she was home. Aunt Emmy, well, she'd just never been much good for conversation, what with the language barrier and all.

And Burton?

Hell, the only thing that kid was good for was screaming.

Honestly, once I'd managed to convince myself that the creepy old dude wasn't planning to rob our house, or rape me at knifepoint or something, I actually found myself kind of curious about when he might show up again. I didn't believe anything he'd said, mind you…at least, not at first. But I guess you could say that after a while, I started not *disbelieving* him either.

I know, right?

Like, the whole situation just sounded so incredible. But on the other hand, there was always the possibility— however small—that there just *might* be some shred of truth behind everything.

And if there was? Well, that would be nothing short of *impossible.*

But of course, I'd already forgotten which city my Daddy was scheduled to appear in that night. I had to dial his Motorola pager, wait for the beep, and key in our home phone number.

And after a split second, I punched in the numbers "911."

Not two minutes passed before the handset buzzed. I answered on the first ring and heard the unmistakable chaos of a crowded locker room. Yells and shouts of laughter— nervous energy from the wrestlers as those massive athletes pumped themselves up to perform for a capacity crowd. I'd been backstage a ton, of course. Whenever Dad got booked to do the job at the Worcester Palladium, and even once at the old Boston Garden. It was kind of a trade secret, a pesky little fact that World Wide Wrestling would never cop to, how all of their wrestlers always ended up sharing the same dressing room. The babyfaces suited up right alongside the heels, never mind who was supposed to have heat with who. I did my best to keep the illusion intact, blocking out those voices I recognized, even though my Uncle Hector was impossible to ignore, shouting my name and blowing loud air kisses in the background.

"Hey, Bear!" My father shouted. "What's wrong? You know I don't like to make calls from the set! Those limp dicks up in Creative are going to think I'm leaking dirt to the sheets!"

I honestly couldn't remember the last time we'd talked, and I silently hoped it hadn't been as long as Christmas, back when we'd shared a quick hug outside the limo, right before it carried him and Samantha off to Logan Airport. I tried my best to push the guilt from my mind, thinking about how expensive all those long-distance calls might've been. Even though we were pretty well-off back then—especially by Lowell standards—we still weren't *rich* rich. At least, not yet. Whenever the monthly AT&T bill came in the mail, Daddy *still* took the time to read it over, and I mean line by line, with a highlighter marker ready. I guess when you've come up from the bottom the way he did, you can never really shake that habit of watching every last dime.

"Yeah, Daddy," I finally answered. "Everything's…fine."

"Good to hear. Hey! I'm real sorry we haven't talked much lately, but, well? You know how this business can be. Listen, I need to get out to the ring here in just a minute! They've got me facing off against the Tennessee Mule. You're watching, right?"

"Of course!" I hustled into the living room and clicked on the big screen. As that massive 65-inch television set warmed up, I clicked the remote to dial down the volume on the commercials. "It's just…I wanted to…no, Daddy. It's *me* who should be sorry. I just needed to call and ask you about…well, about something important."

I took a deep breath and swallowed.

Bracing myself to ask a question that was inevitably going to come out sounding stupid.

"What would you say if somebody tried to convince you of something that you *knew* just couldn't be true? Something so far out, it would literally be, like…impossible?"

There was a pause.

A long one.

I knew my Daddy had to have been subconsciously calculating the cost of the call, which was growing larger by the second.

When he finally answered, his tone had dropped lower. The conversation sounded almost confidential now, and I was touched by the concern I heard in his voice. "We're not talking about guys here, are we? Because, you know, Bear, you're entirely too young to have a boyfriend."

"Dad!"

"I mean it! You know what? If any of those mill town peckerwoods ever tells you he loves you, you need to know in advance, *that* shit's impossible. Flat out, you hear? Kid's just trying to work his way into your pants."

"Daddy! Please! This is serious."

"Okay, okay. Just as you're long as you're not pregnant or anything, huh? Little Bear, let me tell you. The Daydreamer might be getting older with each and every passing day, but I'm still not ready to be a granddaddy to some bastard."

I fumed. The only way I had to vent my frustration was to hold up the staticky line with another long silence. Biting my tongue, until the expense grew so big that it prompted him to apologize.

"Go ahead, kid," he snapped. He was speaking quickly now, impatient. "I'm listening. But cut me a break, okay? I'm just trying to make sure there ain't no pimple-faced loverboys sniffing around the house while I'm out on the road. Take my word for it, Bear, boys are good for nothing. Not a damn thing! They'll just lead you on and make a whole lot of bullshit promises, none of which they're able to keep."

I smiled in spite of myself. That was my father for you: even if he was just a jobber, he'd always been just as tight on the microphone as he was in the ring. But because of that, I could never be sure whether he was a hundred percent serious, or just rehearsing for the next promo. "It's nothing like that, Daddy. I guess...I guess I just really needed to hear from you. You know? Get your thoughts on this situation."

A pause. "Well, baby girl, you got me. You always got me. And I hope you know that."

"I do, Daddy. I do. But I need to ask you something important. Have you ever tried to get your head around something that's just…impossible? I mean, something so far out there, you couldn't believe it was true?"

Another long moment of silence passed, which is how I knew he was taking my question seriously. "Oh, I have, Bear," he finally answered. "And you know what? I still do. Every God-damned day of my life, I do."

"Well, how?" I blurted. "How did you ever convince yourself to believe some crazy shit like that? How can a person get to the point where they can accept the impossible?"

I heard my Dad take a deep breath, a sign that he deemed the question worthy of an honest answer.

"You know what I say to that?"

His voice had turned soft, almost gentle now, which concerned me. In all the years I'd known my father, there'd never been one thing gentle about the man.

"What, Dad?"

"I say, if anybody ever wants to see real, tangible proof of the impossible—something that's pretty damned close to being beyond belief—all they'd have to do is take one look at my career."

There was nothing I could say to that. Absolutely nothing. I'd heard my Daddy tell his origin story any number of times, so I just leaned against the wall and listened. With the cordless phone pressed close to my ear, the rise and fall of his voice carried me right along with it.

"Seriously, Bear! I only wish you could've seen what my life looked like, fifteen years ago now. Back then, I was just one more no-account piece of white trash from Lowell, Massachusetts. Didn't have no damn job back in the day, and I sure didn't have no diploma. You hear me?"

I heard him.

"Ever wonder why I ride you so hard to keep your grades up? Huh? Why I nag you to do your homework each and every night and to get your hustle on in the classroom? Well, maybe that's 'cause the only thing that really scares me is the thought of you slipping up and heading down the same road I walked. You ever think about that?

I couldn't bring myself to answer.

"Huh?" he prompted. "You ever think about how it'd feel to sleep on a cold closet floor 'cause you can't afford no place of your own? Ever think about how it might feel to choke down your pride every day, when you're slumming it in some shitty triplex apartment over in The Acre? Baby girl, I've lived that life! You think I want the same for you?"

I shook my head, staring mindlessly out at a soda commercial which was flashing across the big screen. The colorful label of that Pepsi Clear bottle was a stark contrast from my father's hard luck story. "No, Daddy. No, I know you don't."

He rolled right along, not missing a beat, his speech steadily growing in intensity. "You're damn right I don't!

Shit! If you go by the statistics, I probably ought to be dead already, or maybe just another burnout junkie, locked up in Walpole or some other prison. Some loser who's gone and pissed away all his chances. You really think back then—back when I had to scratch and claw to come up with a couple sheets of toilet paper every single time I needed to wipe my ass—that I could have *ever* imagined living the life we have now? No way, Bear! You want to know the type of jackass kid I was? Huh? Back when I was eighteen years old and thought I knew everything? Let me tell you, I was a washout! A nothing! Just a punk who couldn't see past his own nose, and couldn't think any further ahead than the next Friday night! I probably would've gone on like that forever, living for absolutely nothing and nobody, if I hadn't made the decision to hitchhike into Boston that one night. If I hadn't blown the last five dollars I had to my name on a ticket to see Bubba 'The Haystack' Samson perform live and in person."

I must've heard the story of that fateful night a hundred times. More, probably.

It was one of my favorites.

"It was cold, Bear. Damn cold. Wind blowing steady, temperature dropped close to zero. Thought I might've gone and froze myself to death on the ride home, rolling up I-93 in the bed of some random dude's pickup truck like some bummy-ass hitchhiker, my ears gone numb to the point where I thought I might lose 'em. Now, you really think that if I could talk to the kid I was back then, show him just a *glimpse* of everything we've got going for ourselves now, that there'd be any chance in hell he might *possibly* fucking believe me? Huh? Or do you really think, back before the day I walked into Sully's gym that first time, that I could've *ever* imagined breaking onto the indie circuit, even? And shit, that gig only paid fifteen bucks a show! Yeah, kid, there was no way in hell. Not a chance! Because let me tell you something, I just didn't have time to daydream about building a career in World Wide Wrestling—grinding out a living in the squared circle—not back when I always had to worry about where my next meal was going to come from."

I shifted my weight on my feet, staring over towards the muted television. Its bright glow filled the room, lighting the space in a way that was oddly comforting. I could already feel those first thick tears starting to build, welling up in my throat, but I did my best to choke them back. My father had gone and got himself all fired up, so it would've been a shame to interrupt him by crying.

"Listen here, baby girl. Hunger's a bitch. You want to know something about hard times? Well, you better pull up a chair and get comfortable, 'cause this might take a while. God knows I ain't no smart man, but damn it, I got me a graduate degree from the School of Hard Knocks! And I can tell you 'cause I know, it's damn near impossible to listen to your heart when you can't hear it 'cause your stomach is rumbling so loud from hunger! But hear me out, now. Once I finally *did* reach a point where I could lay out plans more than a day in advance—once I started working out, and once I found the focus I needed to consider my own self-worth every now and again—that's when I got this completely new perspective on life. And when *you* finally reach that point—when *you* find yourself lifting your chin up ever so slightly, casting that first glance beyond the horizon—let me tell you, that's some powerful shit. And that right there's when maybe, just maybe, you'll start to realize how much untapped potential you really have, tucked down deep inside and just waiting to come out."

I bit my lip as my Dad came up for air. My face felt hot. A single warm tear rolled down my cheek.

When he spoke up again, his voice was softer. Calmer, even.

"But hey, Bear? You still got the TV on, don't you?"

I glanced around the living room, noticing for the first time that I wasn't alone. Burton had gotten out of bed somehow and crept his way downstairs. My stepbrother looked uncharacteristically calm, sitting up there on the reclining sofa and grasping his silk blanket in one hand, the other one jammed down inside a sack of Ruffles potato chips. I watched as a shower of green-speckled crumbs sprayed from his lips, fluttering down and powdering the front of his Batman footie pajamas with a fine mist of sour cream and onion.

And I guess I probably should've been more shocked than I was to see that strange man again.

Sitting right there next to Burton, dressed in a stonewashed pair of Guess jeans and that same ratty, red Champion hoodie.

But at that particular moment, the whole scene just didn't seem nearly as weird as it did before.

In a way, it almost felt natural.

I mean, kind of.

Burton, for his part, seemed completely at ease with the guy's company, happy to share that big bag of chips. The kid looked relaxed, even, in a way I'd never seen before.

"Bear? You still there, honey?"

I could barely find my voice to answer. "Yeah, Daddy. I'm still here."

"Good. Now listen close, because in about sixty seconds or so, I'm going to have to haul ass and get out there. It's going to be the match of my life, so I want you to watch every second. The Mule's getting old, but he's no slouch. The man's three hundred pounds of pure Tennessee muscle—hell, you know! Stubborn bastard nearly got the better of Kilimanjaro at last year's Fall Brawl, remember? Had that monster dead to rights, at least until that cheating son of a bitch blinded him with a sack of chalk powder."

Of course I'd seen that match, with its hokey, screwjob ending.

"But hey, kid? Tonight, all I want you to do is sit there. Just sit there, and watch the show. And you don't need to say anything right now, not a damn thing. You just wait, and you'll see what I'm about to do to that man. Because you already know, when I climb in the ring, I ain't focused on nothing else but the fight at hand. I got me a job to do, so I do it, and I do it well, that's for damn sure. But tonight?

Yeah, tonight might be a little different, if you catch my drift. So as soon as the ref hits that three count—once he slams his arm down on the mat for the last time—win or lose, I'm going to stand up and point straight at the camera. And right then, at that very moment, I'm not going to be thinking about anything or anybody else besides you, kid."

I swallowed hard, biting back the lump in my throat.

"So, when you see me do that, I want you to think about something. When that moment comes, I want you to stop and ask yourself if your old man really could've risen from nothing—and I mean—*absolutely—fucking—nothing*—and broken into the field of professional sports entertainment—not to mention, raised two beautiful, brilliant kids and landed another smoking-hot wife—an absolute bombshell, same as your mom—and whether I could have it all—literally every last thing I ever dreamed of—if for just one second, I hadn't dared to believe that me, myself, and I—this no-account scrub from Lowell, Massachusetts—wasn't capable of doing the impossible?"

His words hung over the crackly, long-distance line. Echoing, almost, like they could've been hanging there under their own power. I could still hear the commotion in the background, the athletes' excitement reaching a fever pitch. In front of me, the credits for some lame sitcom were rolling down the screen, and I knew that *Monday Night Titans* was just moments away.

"Damn it, Bear, I've got to run! But listen, you remember what I said. Okay? There's nothing in this world that's impossible. Not a single, God-damned thing. Remember that shit, okay? And remember I love you, kid. I love you."

And with that, he was gone.

The line disconnected.

I held the phone in place for a long moment afterwards, and the dial tone had already begun to beep in my ear before I managed to whisper the words, "I love you, too."

I said them to an empty line.

Those pent-up tears began pouring down my face, rolling freely and unchecked. I reached for the remote control and cranked up the volume, hoping to drown out the sobs that I couldn't choke back any longer. The show's theme music set that oversized subwoofer rumbling, sending waves of powerful sound rolling through our big, old house. The walls vibrated in time to the words of Dr. John Burnham, WWW's legendary announcer, and as those cameras panned the crowded stadium, I stole one more sideways glance across the room.

Burton's eyes were glued to the set. The kid looked fascinated by the show's opening sequence, all those glossy images of powerful athletes with the WWW logo whipping past.

The new arrival, though? That stranger I'd eventually come to know as 'Old Burton?'

Well, all that guy was doing was just staring back at me, saying nothing.

And right then—after one last, long moment of hesitation—I made my decision.

I shook my head from side to side, suspending any last remaining traces of disbelief. That done, I sat down on the couch and joined my stepbrothers—both of them—to watch the show.

What can I say, really?

When it comes to my Daddy, I'll always be a mark.

NOW NORMALLY, ONE OF THE BEST PARTS OF A WRESTLING MATCH IS the commentary. A great play-by-play announcer doesn't just call the shots, he helps the audience interpret what they're seeing. I mean, if you were to just sit back and watch the fight, it'd be easy to think that's all there is to professional wrestling. The pulled punches, the oversold holds and whatnot, plus a few high-flying stunts thrown in every so often for extra drama.

But actually, the performance is so much more than that.

Like always, the color commentator blew right past my Dad's introduction. Jobbers were basically just expected to pace around the ring and look menacing while the favored opponent made a showy entrance. And as always, the cameras flashed a single quick shot of Tommy Carpenter, while he stretched a hamstring out on the bottom rope. But even playing his role as the pre-determined loser, that look of fierce determination showed clear in my Dad's eyes. I watched closely, noticing that he'd dropped a couple pounds since the holidays. And he was definitely moving a step quicker than usual as he shuffled from side to side during his warm-up, even though the on-screen text read the same as always: six foot three, two hundred seventy-five pounds. Everybody knew those measurements were fudged, but nobody ever seemed to mind.

I watched, fascinated, as they made a big show of calling down the Tennessee Mule. His twangy, pop-country theme music boomed across the stadium as that big bubba of a man lumbered down the ramp, clad in his trademark dingy overalls and stained yellow T-shirt. The Mule, he was another career wrestler—not quite a legend, but close. A survivor of the game, already in his forties, and the age was starting to show. But no matter how road-worn that guy might've looked, the hometown favorite still brought the crowd to their feet for a good ninety seconds. That dude strutted his way to the ring, moving in no particular hurry, stopping every couple feet to slap hands with all the local kids seated up along the rails.

"So, who are you supposed to be, then?" I asked the sudden question more as a way to break the ice, rather than because I actually gave a damn about his circumstances. "I heard you say 'our Dad.' Right? And I know you called Samantha 'Mom.' So, what does that make you? A second stepbrother or something, like that little dude sitting next to you?"

He shrugged. "Kind of? Not quite. But yeah, I guess so."

I pondered that response while the Tennessee Mule

made a long, slow lap around the ring apron. "So, uh, how does that work? Don't tell me you're, like, an older version of this kid?"

He just shrugged, so I used the opportunity to study him more closely. He was tallish but thin, and that old hoodie wasn't quite baggy enough to conceal those bony shoulders of his. Without a jacket, I spotted a bold, black-and-white patch safety-pinned over his heart, making that circular "A" symbol the first thing anybody would focus in on. So, even though the fabric was spattered with what looked like ketchup, and even though this dude was *way* past an age where he could've pulled off the punk look, I had to admit, the sweatshirt was pretty cool. I dug it.

I watched as he twisted his thin lips up into a scowl, pondering my question. Setting aside the sheer scientific impossibility of the situation, I had to admit, the two Burtons *did* share an uncanny resemblance.

"I guess you could say that," he finally answered. "Yeah. I'm him, and he's me. Or to be more precise, I *was* him, and eventually, he'll grow up to become me."

I swear, I'd never been more grateful for that big television set of ours. The way that projection screen just sat there against the wall, so huge and imposing, gave us something else to stare at besides each other.

I mean, could our first real conversation have *been* any more awkward?

I avoided making eye contact, silently processing the dude's words. Although, I guess I also ought to mention, the weirdness of the encounter certainly didn't take anything away from the match. It was awesome to see Dad working again, and in a prime-time broadcast? Beyond thrilling! His bright, blond hair was trimmed back some—barely shoulder length now—and he'd doused it with water, combing it to the back all slick-like. But even though he'd already dropped his trademark tie-dyed dressing robe, Tommy "The Daydreamer" Carpenter was still working the crowd, throwing out a two-fingered peace sign to draw heat.

The three of us watched, enthralled, as the Tennessee Mule squeezed his way underneath the bottom rope. And right then, all of a sudden, that's when the realization hit me. When I looked over at Old Burton again and saw him just *sitting* there, kicked back on the couch, relaxing.

Just watching the match, same as me and Burton were doing. Same as any other viewer.

And *not* typing away on his laptop.

"So, wait," I said, raising a hand. "Hold up a minute! Where's your computer, dude? Don't you have to type a transcript for this match, too?"

"No need," he replied. "I've seen it before. Hundreds of times. Out of all Dad's matches, this one's my favorite." The guy's cheeks twitched, rising up to form a tight, little smirk. "And besides, I'd be willing to bet that WWW probably has these recordings down in their vaults somewhere already."

I picked up on the jab but couldn't hold back a smile. "Well, then," I said as they rang the bell at ringside. "If that's the case, it should be easy to prove you're telling the truth.

About everything. If you've already seen this fight—if you really *are* my stepbrother—then tell me something, who's going to win? Our father, or The Tennessee Mule?"

He shot me a sour look, one that carried a clear meaning. Obviously, Old Burton was in on the kayfabe. He knew Dad's job would be to throw the Mule one hell of a challenge and then lose by a hair to give the man one last, thrilling win before heading off into retirement. My Dad had been wrestling professionally for over a decade by that point, and nearly as long as I'd been on the Earth, but in all that time he'd only "won" a handful of matches.

After a long, silent pause, Old Burton nodded towards the big screen. Dad had already gotten himself knocked to the mat, and he was struggling to regain his footing. Most of his matches only lasted a few minutes, so I figured we were in for another quick ending, but over on the couch, this old dude was careful to keep his expression blank, not dropping a single hint. "Just watch," was all he said, as my Dad rolled clear of a vicious boot stomp.

So, that's what I did.

I watched.

And even though I must've seen my Dad do the job a hundred times before—maybe even a thousand, if you counted every time I'd rewound those VHS tapes—it was still mesmerizing to watch two top athletes go at it. Dad had always made a point of staying in peak condition, but that night, he looked absolutely chiseled! The man must've been putting in two-a-day workouts for the past couple months, on top of the usual in-ring drills. The sharp edges of his shredded muscles stood in stark contrast to the Tennessee Mule's body, with all those rolling layers of flab. The Mule was wild and unkempt, fueled by raw hillbilly strength. Of course, my Dad was a big guy, too, but by comparison, the man seemed downright agile. I watched as he snapped upright and ducked down twice in quick succession to dodge a pair of flailing haymakers.

Old Burton angled his head my way. He held the blank stare for an uncomfortable moment before seeming to come to some kind of a decision. "Open-hand slaps," the guy whispered. "Two of them, to the jaw. Right first, then the left."

My jaw fell slack as I watched my Dad execute the blows.

His hands moved like lightning, hammering down two vicious slaps to the Mule's carotid artery, both shots landing loud, like thunder. The vicious hits echoed throughout the packed arena.

I could almost feel the small beads of sweat forming up along my hairline, and it was a struggle to keep my composure. "Come off it! Anybody could've seen those coming. Dad's a brawler, always has been. This proves nothing."

The guy who claimed to be my stepbrother dropped his chin, dipping his head in a slight nod of acknowledgement. All three of us were watching closely as the Tennessee Mule staggered about the center of the ring. "Okay, then," he breathed. "Fine. Those were just a set-up for the Irish whip."

I watched in amazement as my Dad—the man they called The Daydreamer—went on the offensive for once. He charged forward, ducking another wild blow, then snatched the Mule's free arm and used the dude's momentum to swing him around. When that big bruiser hit the ring ropes at full speed, I swear, it looked like they stretched out just as far as they could go, damn close to breaking. And when the Tennessee Mule came thundering back in the opposite direction, his thick legs were chugging away at full tilt.

"Into the clothesline."

Dad's arm shot out at a neat right angle, clipping the Mule right in the neck.

I looked on, stunned.

It was almost like the blow had struck me, too.

The mountain man went down hard, but the sound of the impact was lost among the screams of horror. Man, that crowd! Those Memphis fans just couldn't believe what they were seeing. Thousands of ticket holders rose to their feet in a wave of screen-printed T-shirts, whipped into a rage by such a dramatic reversal of fortune.

And the whole while, there in the center of the ring, stood my Dad. Poised and calm, ignoring the madness, impervious to the fury that was boiling up around him. He dropped to one knee, fighting to lock in a grip.

The roar of the crowd was amplified by the Dolby surround sound speakers, so I could barely hear Old Burton's next call. "Finishing move coming up, so watch close now. He'll make a quick transition to the Boston Crab."

I shot to my feet, my face hot with fury. "Bullshit!"

I snatched the remote control and whipped it at the guy's head, but without aiming. It sailed high and right, striking against the wallpaper with a hollow thud before clattering down to the floor. A pair of double-A batteries rolled free and disappeared underneath the sofa.

Burton, though, he didn't flinch. His gaze stayed focused, eyes locked on the big screen.

Both Burtons, I mean. The new guy, plus my little stepbrother.

"Dad's no grappler!" I screamed. "When in the hell would he have had time to master a submission hold like that? You're a lying bastard, Burton, or whoever you are! You know what? I want you out of my house. This minute! Like, right, fucking—"

And then it happened.

Old Burton raised an arm and pointed silently towards the TV.

And just like that, my rage fizzled away entirely.

Somehow, my Dad had managed to get his powerful biceps wrapped completely around the Mule's hammy thighs. I watched, stunned, as he hoisted the big man with ease, rotating his huge body up and around, before sinking his own hips down to cement the painful lock-up.

Even little Burton, the greenest of wrestling fans, seemed impressed by the maneuver. That kid was frozen in rapt wonder, the bag of potato chips completely forgotten. It was almost as if he could've somehow known that something really special was about to go down.

Something unbelievable.

A shower of paper cups rained down from the upper decks, littering the ring and soaking the mat in a wash of beer, soda, and shaved ice. The live audience was howling in protest, filled with rage at the sight of their hometown hero in peril.

And then, only seconds later, it happened. Or maybe an eternity went by, I don't know. But whenever that shit finally did come to pass, I swear, it really *did* happen.

The Mule tapped.

The God-damned Tennessee Mule tapped!

A twenty-year veteran of World Wide Wrestling and perennial mid-card favorite, just ended the very last match of his career—in his own hometown—with a fucking tap-out.

And it was Tommy Carpenter who'd made him do it!

Those fans roared up a storm, rocking the Mid-South Coliseum and bombarding the ring with a shower of trash. Me, I didn't know what to think, but as soon as that first steel chair came flying in, a pack of security guards appeared from out of nowhere. They scrambled and shoved their way down to the apron, linking arms to hold back the angry mob. While the Mule lay prone on the mat, still writhing in agony from that vicious spinal stretch, the referee grabbed my father's arm, raised it high in the air, and then dove off to safety.

And then—just like he'd promised—my Dad swiveled his head from side to side, searching for the cameraman.

Ignoring all the missiles being lobbed his way, Tommy Carpenter stalked to the corner of the ring, grabbed the turnbuckle, and stepped up onto the bottom rope. The focus camera zoomed in as my Daddy pointed a single, calloused finger out at the television audience.

Out at me.

A cold chill ran down my spine. It was almost as if the two of us were staring right at each other through that live satellite broadcast.

And just then, a deafening burst of hip-hop music exploded from the stadium speakers. Those low, vibrating bass beats set that Deep South crowd into an absolute fury. The camera pulled away from the incensed crowd, panning back down to the announcers' table where Dr. John Burnham ignored the incoming loogies long enough to call the decision. "Ladies and gentlemen! I don't believe what I've just seen here in Memphis, Tennessee! Your winner… and proof that anything really *is* possible…The American Dream, Tommy Carpenter! Don't go anywhere, folks! We've got lots more wrestling action still to come, right here on *Monday Night Titans!*"

And just like that, the program cut away to a Snapple commercial. I tried to process what I'd just seen, but it was just too much to comprehend. My Dad, a perennial jobber, had pulled off a major upset, and he'd done it on a live television broadcast. Now in all the years I'd been watching World Wide Wrestling, I don't think I'd ever heard of the Tennessee Mule tapping out. Not once! That monster had crippled more wrestlers than steroids, but on that night— his *last* night—he'd come up short. The fan favorite, a heel who'd earned so much respect that he'd nearly managed to pull off a full face turn, had just been laid low on the final match of his career.

And for him to have gone out like that? Tapped to do the job in his own hometown?

Well, that was just unprecedented.

Unbelievable, almost.

For whatever reason, it looked as if WWW had decided The Daydreamer was worthy of a little push. It was an absolutely crazy angle, but I guess the Creative team figured my Dad's re-branding was worth a shot, especially since that particular match wouldn't upset any of the ongoing storylines. And judging by the sound of all that heat, the surprise ending would surely bring a spike in the television ratings.

I glanced sideways once again. My little stepbrother had already turned away, his attention span well past its limit. Old Burton, though, that dude was still staring straight ahead, lost in his own thoughts, like always. At some point, he'd pulled his legs up onto the sofa and crossed them over Indian-style.

I managed to catch his eye during the split second in between commercials. My heart was pounding now, and I stuck my hands beneath my legs, hoping it wouldn't be so obvious how badly they were shaking. "Hey, man! Yeah, you. Burton, right?"

The guy lifted his stubbly chin.

"You mind telling me what in the hell that was? Whatever we were watching just now?"

A thin smile flashed across Old Burton's lips. He dipped into the front pouch of that grubby sweatshirt, coming back up with a slick, yellow Sony Discman. He pressed the Play button with his index finger and thumbed at the volume wheel, looping those narrow wire headphones deftly up into place with his free hand. The second I heard that tinny, synthesized rhythm, I recognized it as the new Ice Cube song that had just come out. The one that seemed to playing on MTV about every fifteen minutes or so, even though I tried my damnedest to avoid it.

"That?" he answered, nodding his narrow head to the beat. "That spectacle you and I and me just witnessed? Well, that was history in the making. That match? That single five-minute bout? Well, to put it simply, that was a whole new start for our family."

I shook my head, struggling to clear away the confusion. "But...but what exactly *was* it?"

Old Burton sighed. "Wasn't it obvious? After Dad's given so many years of his life to the business, doing the job without question in a countless number of matches, I guess World Wide Wrestling is finally thinking about putting Tommy Carpenter over."

FRIDAY, FEBRUARY 26, 1993

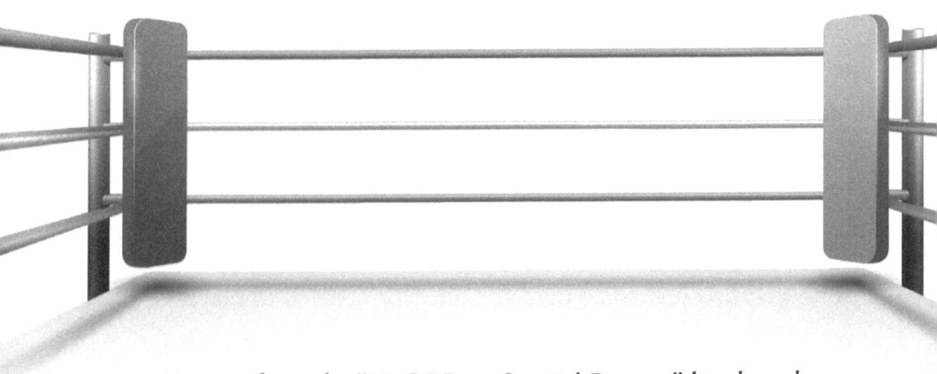

Excerpt from the "ABC News Special Report" *live broadcast*
Transcription by Burton Carpenter

Don Larsen: "We're coming to you live, now, from the World Trade Center here in mid-town Manhattan where it appears that a full evacuation is underway. I'm speaking to Judith Leoni and Molly Frizzell, and, well, as you can see from their appearance—now, that is not dirt on their clothes, that is—I guess, dust, and smoke, and ash I would assume, and… can you tell us exactly what happened inside the building? I understand you both work on the twentieth floor of the North Tower? What did you see, and what did you hear?"

Judith Leoni: "I didn't see anything, really. Like, I was just sitting there at my desk and then I heard this big, I don't know, explosion! It almost felt, like, the whole building had blown up or something. I nearly fell out of my chair! And then the next thing I know, somebody was shouting that we needed to evacuate, and that's when I got up and left."

D.L.: "Molly Frizzell, what about you? What did you see, and what did you hear?"

Molly Frizzell: "I…I actually saw the walls start shaking, so at first I thought it must have been an earthquake, but then I heard that bang! I can't really explain it. It was just… terrifying, really."

D.L: "How much smoke was inside the building? I'm guessing there must have been a lot, because you're—well, you're both *covered* in dust, but how much was there? Were you able to see at all?"

M.F. "We were…I'd been up on the twenty-second floor at the time, and then I met up with Judy in the stairwell, coming down. And it wasn't that bad, really, not until the tenth floor or so. From there all the way to the ground, you just couldn't see anything. Nothing at all. It was so dark, but then all of a sudden, there were people with flashlights, guiding us out of the building."

D.L: "And while all this was going on, was there anybody who—did anybody tell you what actually happened?"

M.F.: "No, not at all! We were just, like, following the crowd. You know? It must've taken us ten, maybe fifteen minutes to make it all the way outside. It was absolutely terrifying, the entire time, I mean. I was just about panicking in the stairwell, and then it wasn't until we made it outside before we saw all the smoke and the fire trucks and everything. And then one of the police officers said that some kind of bomb had gone off…"

TUESDAY, MARCH 2, 1993

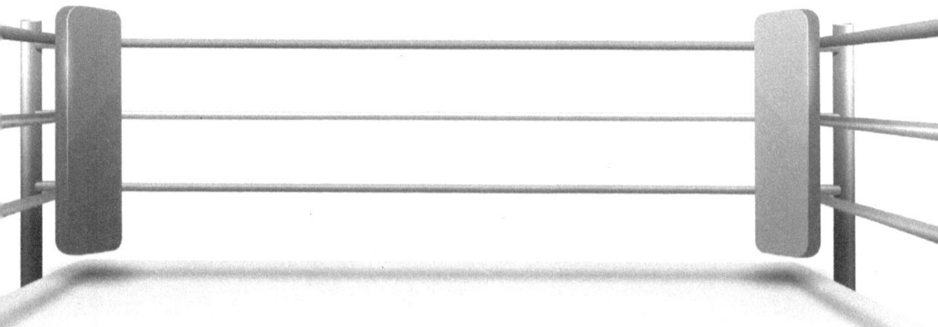

A COUPLE WEEKS HAD PASSED. THREE, FOUR MAYBE. I DON'T KNOW.

The both of us, me and Old Burton, by that point, we'd reached what you might call an understanding. Without actually saying anything, we'd come to decide that Burton could just show up at our house whenever the hell he felt like it, and also that I wouldn't bother to question him about it.

We'd always hang out in the living room if Aunt Emmy was away, mostly watching television. Whenever we'd had enough of replaying the previous week's matches, Burton would usually switch the channel to whatever cartoons happened to be on. I'd hand over the remote without complaint, leaving that old weirdo to flick back and forth between *DuckTales* and *Gummi Bears*. Me, I'd never been real big on those animated shows. Normally, I'd just sit there quietly, marveling at the sight of a fully grown man so fascinated by a children's program. About the only shows we could ever agree on—apart from World Wide Wrestling, I mean—was the Friday night lineup on ABC. I thought that nerdy Steve Urkel was an absolute riot on *Family Matters*;

Burton loved how Patrick Duffy and Suzanne Somers had blended their families on *Step by Step*.

Finally, one cold and rainy afternoon, I guess I must've been feeling a little more comfortable around the guy. Or at least, comfortable enough to ask him the question which had been rattling around inside my brain. "So, Burton. Tell me something, okay? Why are you here?"

Of course, he didn't bother to answer.

The guy did that a lot, though. Just ignored me.

Like at the beginning, when he first started coming around, I thought he might've been hard of hearing or something. And then, later on, I got to wondering if maybe he might've just been choosing not to listen. Like he was working my nerves, or something. Eventually, though, I came to realize that this dude simply had his own unique way of holding a conversation.

For instance, whenever he wasn't quite ready to answer my questions—or if maybe he just didn't feel like it—then he wouldn't, simple as that. Or then sometimes, Burton would answer, but only after he'd taken a good long while to consider his response. I'd had to sit there in awkward silence more than a couple of times, gazing absently at the television for so long that it almost seemed like the man could've drifted off to sleep or something before he finally came back with a reply. And then there were other times, if Burton happened to be particularly engrossed in whatever show was on, that the television set just took priority over verbal communication.

That seemed to be the case on this particular weeknight, when the two of us were just lounging around, killing time with a rerun of *Ren and Stimpy*. I realized my mistake right after the question left my mouth, me being so foolish as to speak up while the program was running, so I had to wait until the next break before trying again. With my eyes locked on his, I spotted that first flicker of disinterest when a Snickers commercial rolled across the screen. "So, bro. You want to tell me why you're here, anyway?"

Burton rolled his thin neck from side to side, as if his muscles had gone stiff after so many hours of channel surfing. His eyes seemed distant and unfocused like always, but I could tell by the way he fiddled with his headphones that my stepbrother was actually thinking about how to answer. No matter how blank his expression seemed—almost ghost-like at times—there were always a few telltale signs which meant he was open to conversation. And, like always, Burton waited until he was good and ready before answering the question.

And then, of course, he didn't.

"Maybe I just like your company," was all he said, punctuating the vague response with an irritating shrug of indifference.

"Knock it off, douchebag! You know what I mean."

The show resumed, and his gaze came back into focus. "Language."

"Fine, then. Would you prefer to be called a dirtbag?"

Burton tilted his head to one side. "No, not really. But at least that's not a curse."

"Dirtbag it is, then. But seriously, if you really *are* my stepbrother, then why are you here with me, instead of off in the future somewhere? Like, it stands to reason that traveling through time must take a whole lot of effort. Am I right? Or at least some kind of special energy, like the way Doc Brown had to steal all that plutonium in the beginning of *Back to the Future*."

Burton opened his mouth, but I charged ahead before he could interrupt. "Why would you go to all that trouble? Coming back in time from—well, from wherever it is that you started from—if all you were planning to do was just hang out here with me? I mean, seriously! We've been playing video games and watching reruns of bad television for weeks now. What's the matter, don't they have VHS tapes in the future?"

Burton shifted his weight on the couch, turning halfway around to meet my stare. "Like I said. Maybe I just enjoy being around you. After all, we're family, right? So, why can't we just spend time together?" He went on, clearly frustrated. "Look. Here we are, the both of us, just relaxing. Does it really have to be any more complicated than that?"

But by that point, I'd had just about enough of the guy's crap. I reached behind my back, grabbed a throw pillow, and launched it towards his head. "Knock it off, dickweed! See, that's how I know you're full of shit. And I still haven't figured out how you managed to call that live match, but don't worry. I will, and soon enough!"

Burton didn't say anything. He only shrugged.

I pressed on ahead. "And let me ask you something. Just one thing, okay? If you really *could* travel through time— like, if you actually *were* one of the first people in the history of the whole damned human race who got that kind of technology to work—then, don't you think you might've been more inclined to accomplish something worthwhile? Like, say, killing Hitler? Or maybe bringing back a cure for AIDS? Or using all those future resources to help wipe out suffering in the world, or at least to make peoples' lives a little more comfortable?"

"What makes you assume that I'm capable of either of those things?" he snapped. "First off, I'm no assassin. And sure, I might have a doctorate in Physics, but that's not the same as being an actual medical doctor. And what's your basis for thinking that a disease like AIDS will ever be cured? Huh? You think that just because one single scientist happened to stumble across the secret to time travel, that all of a sudden, all of the world's problems will just up and disappear?"

I raised an eyebrow in his direction.

"But in any case," he hurried on. "Even if there *was* a cure for AIDS, or cancer, or *whatever*, I probably wouldn't tell you. If some random person ever had advance knowledge of the future, well, it could be dangerous. To themselves, to others. Even to the future itself. There's such a thing as ethics, you know. Even forty years from now, some of us still have principles."

I let out a sigh of frustration. "But see, that's exactly what I'm talking about! You expect me to just—I don't know—*believe* you can travel through time, first of all. And that you keep doing this, over and over again, all so we can sit around watching cartoons, and music videos, and endless replays of Dad taking bumps?" I waved my hand towards the big screen. "Let's be real for a minute. These shows, they all kind of suck."

Burton went mute. Seconds passed, then minutes. And when he finally did speak up again, it was in this soft voice. Almost hollow, as if the force of my words had struck him right in the gut.

"And just how do you know that what we're doing right now—spending quality time together, even if all we're doing is watching these stupid shows—hasn't already made a positive impact on your world?"

I sneered. "Umm…hello? What kind of good could we possibly be doing by watching wrestling and listening to all that God-awful rap music?"

Burton tilted his head back to the other side with this slow, pronounced roll of his neck. "Rap artists are the poet laureates of your generation," he sighed. "You know how they still make kids read Shakespeare in school? Well, I suspect that fifty years from now—or it might even be fifty years from *my* now—but eventually, middle-school English teachers are going to build lesson plans around this stuff. Handing out essay topics like, 'Describe the main social critiques of Public Enemy's seminal 1990 album, *Fear of a Black Planet.* Five pages, single-spaced.'"

I shook my head and flopped back against the couch.

My eyes rolled upwards and came to rest on the ceiling. With nothing left to do but sit there, I let my gaze wander absentmindedly across the popcorn-textured coating.

Finally, Burton reached over, snatched the remote and clicked off the television. When he broke the silence, I could tell by the guy's stern tone that he meant business. "So, what would you say, then, if I just came right out and told you everything I'm doing here? And that all of it—all of *this*—was being done for a very specific reason?" He paused to suck in a quick, sharp breath. "Lounging around with you, right here in 1993, just happens to be part of the plan. The most important part."

I didn't quite know what to say to that.

"And as for all those cartoons, and the music videos? The wrestling?" He scratched at his chin, running an index finger over that thin layer of gray stubble. "Well, I guess I just like all that stuff. So I kind of thought you might, too."

I snorted. "So, you just up and decided to come popping in and out of my life, for what? Four weeks now? Showing up without notice every time, never telling me nothing, not even when I might expect to see you again? Now how is *that* supposed to help anyone?"

Even looking straight up, I could hear him shifting about on the sofa. "Well, how about this? Since I've been coming around, have you swiped any more bottles of Robitussin from the Brooks pharmacy? Even a single one?"

I froze in place. My entire body had gone cold.

"Or, what about here at home?" he pressed. "Nobody's

accused you of raiding the liquor cabinet lately, have they? I mean, it's not like Dad or Mom ever kept close track of how much booze they had on hand, but at the rate you were going, I'm sure they would've noticed eventually."

I sat there, motionless, as small beads of sweat began coasting down my forehead. About the only response I could come up with was, "You do realize, Samantha's not my real mom. Right?"

"No, she's not. But she's mine, and she's a good one." He paused to take a deep breath, then went in for the kill. "And what about me? Huh? The 1993 me. Your little brother."

"Stepbrother," I snapped.

"Family's family. But, well. Have you seen me break into any tantrums lately?"

The answer was obvious. I didn't bother responding.

"Why do you think that is? Even someone as stubborn as you has to admit, I'm a lot calmer whenever my future self is nearby. Being around people who know how to deal with problem behaviors, that makes all the difference."

He had a point. Young Burton wasn't exactly giving off any signs that he was about to start speaking in complete sentences or anything, but that kid really *had* seemed a lot more relaxed lately. Especially on those afternoons when his older self stopped in, as much as I hated to admit it. It was the first time I'd ever seen the little guy trust another person, and the two of them had managed to develop this strange, unique kind of bond.

And I guess that's the reason why—even if I still wasn't completely buying the whole time travel bit, that over-the-top work Burton was selling—his story *did* seem to make sense.

I mean, in a way.

"No, really," he went on. "Just think about it. Has it ever occurred to you that the reason I keep coming back in time, and the reason I wanted to spend so much time with you, was that *you* might be the one who could do something positive? Not me?"

No, I thought to myself. *Of course it hadn't.*

"That it was *you* who had the power to make an impact? After all, this is *your* time, not mine. I'm just a bit player in your life story. All I'm here to do is meet you and spend time with you and maybe—just maybe—give you a little push in the right direction."

I felt this thick, uncomfortable lump begin to rise in my throat. I swallowed hard, trying to force it back down.

It didn't work.

Although, my mind was finally able to see the situation for what is was. Like I was thinking clearly all of a sudden, for the first time in who knows how long.

My heart was thumping hard in my chest. I had to jam my hands beneath my legs to hide the trembling.

"Okay, then. So what do we do next?"

He smiled. "We're doing it."

THURSDAY, MARCH 11, 1993

BURTON'S VISITS GREW LONGER AND MORE FREQUENT. I'M STILL NOT certain whether he'd managed to refine his techniques for time travel, or if it was just that sobriety made me more aware of his presence. Whatever the reason, my older stepbrother had somehow managed to become a permanent fixture of my ninth-grade experience. And over time, I don't know, I guess I just got kind of used to having the guy around.

In the afternoon, he'd be waiting there when I got home from school.

Weekends, he'd stay up late with me watching *Saturday Night Live*. Or, whenever he had the remote, *The Arsenio Hall Show*.

And Old Burton would've always disappeared by the time I woke up the next morning, even though I can't remember ever having seen the dude come or go. Eventually, I guess I just came to accept the peculiar arrangement as the way things were going to be around our house.

And yes, before you ask, I *have* heard that science fiction theory about how time travelers aren't supposed to be able to meet up with their own selves in the past. And I'm here to tell you, that's bull. I watched Burton like a hawk anytime his future self was present, and not once did I ever see either of those two suffer any ill effects.

The universe never splintered up into an infinite number of dimensional vortexes. Or, at least, if it did I never noticed. And neither of the Burtons ever keeled over in shock or vanished into thin air or anything.

Far from it.

If anything, the younger Burton seemed to thrive during those visits. Hell, sometimes, the kid was literally glowing with happiness. There was absolutely no way that bugger could've known he was looking at an older version of himself, but for some reason, I always suspected he did. Burton just seemed so much more comfortable whenever Old Burton was hanging around. The kid was so calm when he was in his own presence.

Peaceful, almost.

Even Aunt Emmy looked forward to Burton's visits. That was only because I'd lied, though, and said the guy was a junior professor at UMass who was tutoring me for some volunteer work hours. It must've seemed like an odd arrangement, having this old dude coming around at all hours, but she never once questioned it since the extra supervision meant she could head out to bingo any time she wanted. And it didn't hurt one bit that my grades really *had* started improving. Or at least, they'd stopped sliding down into oblivion. Turns out, showing up for classes really *did* make a difference.

Whenever we got tired of watching wrestling, Burton would boot up the Sega Genesis, and we'd get down to business. It'd be *Mortal Kombat* if I'd won the two-finger shoot, but if he'd come out on top, then it'd be one of the lame ones: cartridges from the reject pile, games I'd been given as birthday or Christmas presents and quickly forgotten. Titles like *Michael Jackson's Moonwalker,* or maybe *Ecco the Dolphin,* or if Burton couldn't decide between the two, then sometimes he'd compromise with *Sonic the Hedgehog.*

That guy drove me crazy with how he played *Sonic,* starting over from the very beginning each time. It was infuriating, the way he never got any better. Not one bit. Burton would carefully pick his way through the Green Hill Zone, one of the easiest stages in the history of video games. The dude scrolled along just as slowly as he could manage, careful not to miss a single one of those shiny gold rings. His turns could last half an hour or more, huge chunks of my life that I'd never get back. I swear, if I hadn't actually known the guy better, I might've suspected he was playing that way on purpose, just to piss me off.

But I'd chosen odds over evens that day, and won the contest by upturning a middle finger when he flashed two. Grudgingly, Burton popped in *Mortal Kombat* and passed me a controller.

He chose Johnny Cage, like always.

Me, I went with Sub-Zero. Cold and lethal.

The second the fight started, I launched a quick ice burst. He jumped it with ease, so we both hung back, settling into our rhythms. I used the game as an opportunity to grill him some more, since I'd found that our conversations flowed more freely when Burton was distracted by some kind of activity.

"So, listen. As much as I've been asking, you've never come right out and told me. What do you think it is I need to do…brother?"

I'd tossed that word out there on purpose, hoping it might trip him up, but Burton's concentration was unbreakable. His eyes never left the screen.

"So, you're asking me about your purpose in life?" he finally answered. His thin fingers blazed away, strutting Johnny Cage back and forth in this showy little shuffle. "That's pretty deep stuff."

I launched Sub-Zero into an airborne flip, tossing off another pair of ice bursts which sailed harmlessly by. "You know that's not what I meant!"

Johnny Cage charged forward to close the gap. "It might not be what you meant, but it's what you said. Choose your words more carefully next time."

If his criticism had been meant as a distraction, it worked. I hesitated for a split second, just long enough for Sub-Zero to cop a high kick to the chin.

"What I should've said was…"

I struggled to find the words, scrambling to pull my character back to safety.

"…was, well. Why are you here? Shouldn't you be back in your own time instead? Don't you just, like, belong there?"

I feinted, then caught Johnny Cage with a flurry of quick punches, pummeling him backwards across the Warrior Shrine. Burton's skinny fingers flashed above his controller, escaping the assault with a high jump and acrobatic tumble. His character safe for the next few seconds at least, he reached up and wiped his nose with a grungy sleeve.

"Now, that's a fair question." He spun Johnny Cage around in a series of leg sweeps, leaving me no choice but to hang back. "I'm no philosopher...but I guess when you really think about it..."

He darted forward with a shadow kick. It fell just short.

"...if you believe in God, or fate, or whatever, then you might also believe that all of us are here on Earth for *some* reason or other." His fingers were moving at lightning speed, firing off jab after jab. "And in that regard, I'd have to guess that I ended up exactly where I was meant to be."

He mashed his thumb down hard, landing an uppercut that sent Sub-Zero flying.

"Or in my case, it's exactly *when* I'm meant to be, even if neither of us are fully able to explain why."

My train of thought swayed perilously on its tracks, coming dangerously close to derailing. The conversation was way too heavy, and my lapse in attention had left Johnny Cage with an opening. I watched, stunned, as the shirtless movie star lunged in and proceeded to beat Sub-Zero senseless.

But before Burton had a chance to claim the fatality, I squeezed the Start button and paused the game.

"What exactly do you mean by that, man?" I raised a hand to cut him off before he could even begin to offer a response. "No, just listen! Okay? I'm actually willing to accept the possibility that time travel could really be a thing. After all, you're here, or at least I *think* you are. Right? So, like, here it is: as of this moment, I am officially, once and for all, acknowledging your presence."

Burton tilted his chin to one side, lifting his gaze up towards the ceiling. "Well, that's something. Thanks, I guess."

I sighed, tossing down my controller in disgust. "Listen, man! You've been coming around here for like, *weeks*, now! And in all that time, you still haven't told me *why* the year 1993 is so damned important to you."

"Jessie, listen. I've already told you…"

"Yeah, yeah. I know. You *can't* tell me, because it could be harmful or something."

He shrugged, lifting one bony shoulder. "Or maybe it's like I said, and I just enjoy your company. You're a lot of fun to be around, you know that?"

"Knock it off! After all this time, I think you owe me some answers."

He turned sideways, which is how I knew I'd finally caught his attention. "I *did* mean what I said, Jessie. You're my big sister, and I love you. Honestly, that's the only reason I keep coming back here. I just want to spend time with you, and visiting 1993 is the best way for me to do that."

I threw up my hands, then pounded two fists down against the sofa cushions. "Oh, come off it! I get that the two of us are supposed to be siblings—that's fine, whatever. But if we really *are* related, then tell me something. Why don't we just hang out together in *your* time? 2033 or whenever? I mean, there's got to be more interesting stuff we could do there—then—besides just sitting around and playing video games, for Chrissakes! Like, we can't hang out at a bar yet, or go to a club, or anything. I don't even have my license!"

His nose twitched in a quiet little sniff as that same look of impassiveness came back across his face. "No, but that didn't stop you from borrowing Aunt Emmy's truck last year."

My mouth fell open.

"Remember? The day the new *Alice in Chains* album came out, and you just couldn't wait to get the CD from Sam Goody?"

I'd nearly forgotten about that. It was the one and only time I'd committed grand theft auto, and I'd gotten away with it, despite nearly causing half a dozen separate wrecks on the drive up to Nashua.

"Wait…what? That was last year! How in the hell could you possibly know about that?"

Burton shrugged. "I saw you leave. Remember? Uncle Hector flew in and took Aunt Emmy out for lunch, and they asked you to watch me. You handed me an entire box of Oreos and left me here watching Sesame Street, and if I recall, you made it back home just a few minutes before they did."

I bit my lip, struggling to push the repressed memory back down where it belonged. "Well, it was worth it. That album is a classic."

"If you say so."

He'd put me on the defensive, and I struggled to regain momentum. "Dude, I'm being serious! What's stopping the two of us from getting together in the future and…"

A horrible thought flashed through my mind.

"Burton! Wait a minute! You said…you said this whole…thing of yours…was the best way for us to spend time together. Right?"

He nodded.

And even though he knew perfectly well where I was going with my thoughts, that old bastard still made me go there.

I swallowed. "So…is there some reason why the two of us *can't* meet up then? I mean—what I'm trying to say is…"

He looked me straight in the eye this time. "You want to know if you're dead. Is that it?"

The direct question caught me off guard. I mean, I'd long since realized that Burton had a complete and utter disregard for social graces, but every so often, his bluntness still came as a shock.

"Well…yeah," I finally managed to stutter. "I guess that *is* what I mean. In the future, in the time you left, am I already dead? And if I am, what the hell happened?"

I watched as his gaze flickered back to the television screen. Both of our characters stood there, motionless. Frozen in place.

Sub-Zero, dazed, his masked face tilted down.

Johnny Cage, striking a pose as he waited to deliver the fatality, flexing his muscles for an unseen Hollywood audience.

"You know," Burton whispered. "I honestly don't think I should tell you that."

I flopped back against the couch, the video game completely forgotten. My mind was still struggling to process the specter of some dark and foreboding ending, a certain demise that was waiting for me somewhere, out there in the shadows of an uncertain future.

And even though I'd never given a whole lot of thought to my own death before, the idea now seemed more pressing than anything else I could imagine.

Burton must've picked up on my discomfort, and he made a weak attempt to soften the blow. "Look here, Jessie. You've got to believe me when I say it, the only reason I came back in time *was* to be with you. Okay? That's it. But maybe, just maybe, by doing this, we'll be able to create a better future. Not just for the two of us, but for a lot of other people, I think."

I cast a wide, empty gaze out the window, contemplating all the possibilities which lay beyond the present day.

Would I have a chance to graduate from college?

Or even high school?

The possibilities seemed infinite, far too many to comprehend. But out of all the hypothetical scenarios I'd considered, I just couldn't imagine a world without me.

"Tell me something, Burton. How *exactly* are you proposing we do that?"

He leaned forward, bringing his body directly across my line of vision. "Look, sis. I already told you. Nobody else can change your future for you. You've got to do it on your own. You said it yourself: 1993 is your time, not mine."

I opened my mouth to reply, but the dude cut me off.

"Just stop, and try to listen to yourself for a minute! Okay? If you did, it all might start making sense. You talk about this future you've never seen like it has to be some kind of utopia, but have you ever thought that we might have our own problems to deal with? Serious ones! Things you couldn't imagine, not in your worst nightmares. And yet here you are, only concerned with yourself and with your own life. You know what that is? It's selfish, plain and simple."

I clenched my fists but managed to bite my lip and avoid showing any emotion. "You're an asshole."

Burton cocked an eyebrow at the weak comeback. "Takes one to know one?" He inhaled, allowing himself a deep, calming breath, before spreading both arms wide. "Listen to me, Jessie. Hear me out. What if I told you there was nobody in the world more important to me than you? No one at all. Would you believe me?"

"I guess so?"

I mean at that point, what choice did I have?

"Then would you trust me enough to do something? Just this one little thing which has the potential to put a whole chain of events into motion. Which could maybe, possibly, help change your future for the better?"

My teeth dug down hard into my lower lip.

But by that point, my mind was too far blown for me to even try holding back the tears.

"So?" I finally choked, as a warm stream of water rolled down my cheek. "Let's talk. What is it you need me to do?"

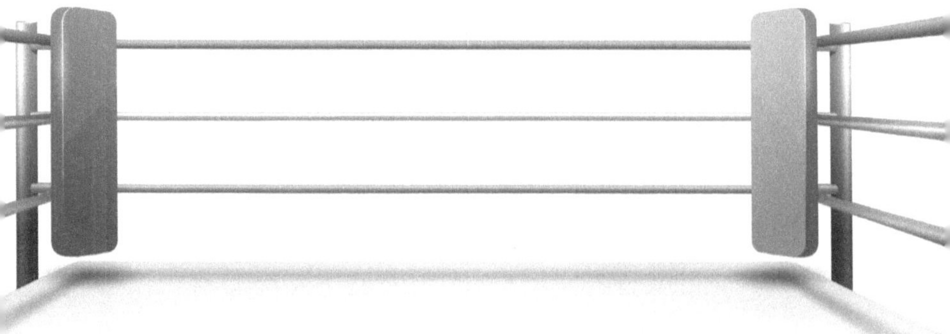

AND THEN THERE HE WAS AGAIN. BACK IN THE SAME EXACT SPOT AS always, legs still crossed up on the couch, Indian-style, almost as if he'd never left.

But hell, who knows? Maybe he hadn't.

Maybe it was that same damned afternoon, and I'd just messed up on the dates.

But I doubt it.

It'd been a good long while since I'd gone off on a serious bender, even if I did still find my way into the liquor cabinet every so often.

But it was one bottle at a time now. No mixing.

So, yeah. Even though the conversation felt like it blended right into our last one, it could've easily taken place later that evening, or anytime that next week.

The important thing was, I knew for sure that it happened.

It did.

"No," I finally said, breaking the silence.

I waited a long moment before going on, nearly as long

as I'd spent considering his request. And then I said the word again, just to avoid any confusion.

"No."

But even saying the word aloud, I couldn't hear any conviction in my voice. It sounded almost like I'd repeated myself more as a form of consolation, than to actually reject his proposition.

And what's worse, I could tell that Burton knew it. That guy could sense he'd already won the argument.

"Don't be like that," he said, once a respectable amount of time had passed. "You need to keep an open mind about this or else there's no way it'll work. None of it. Now, I know how you feel about John Nguyen…"

I opened my mouth to interrupt, but he raised an open palm.

"…I know. But you've got to trust me. I've got an idea."

I reached down and grabbed my legs, pulling them up into a cruel mimicry of that dude's cheesy yoga pose. "So, you mean to tell me," I snapped, more forcefully than I meant to, "that the whole reason you traveled several God-damned decades back in time, using some kind of advanced metaphysical future technology or whatever the fuck it is—"

"Language."

I sighed in frustration. "Fine. Whatever. So, you're saying that everything you've been doing, however the *heck* you've managed to do it, was all because you want me to be *nice* to someone?"

His head tilted back and to the left in that same quirky way of his, that facial tic that pissed me off so much just a short month ago, back before I realized that was just how Burton looked when he was deep in thought. "It's more like 'need,' not 'want,'" he eventually replied. "And not just somebody. It *has* to be John Nguyen. I need you to try to and become friends with him, and the sooner the better."

"Now, wait just a minute! That's about the stupidest thing I've ever heard, and believe me, I've heard some shit. I mean, I guess it wouldn't *kill* me to be nice to some other kid. Fine, whatever. But you seriously expect me to go and buddy up to that retard? The biggest burnout in our class, *John Fucking Nguyen?* No way in hell, Burton. You can get bent!"

I braced for the guy to flag my foul language again, but the reprimand never came.

His gaze was still hanging off in the air somewhere, but even though it looked like he wasn't listening, I knew he'd heard me.

When he finally did speak up, Burton's voice was quieter, little more than a whisper. "He's not retarded, you know."

"The hell he isn't! That kid's a disgrace. There's not a single damned person at JFK who can stand to be anywhere near him, and I mean, not even the teachers!" I exhaled, my fingers counting off all the ways in which John Nguyen had offended me. "For one thing, he fucking stinks. I swear, I've seen him go an entire week without changing his clothes, and I bet he didn't shower that whole time. And the way he acts? Shuffling around, head down, with that creepy smile plastered across his fat face, mumbling under his rotten breath all the time? Ugh!"

Burton shrugged. "I don't know about that. I've never met the kid."

I let out a sigh. Even as I unclenched my fists, I could still feel the beating of my heart as it thudded away in my chest.

Burton sniffed, then scratched his nose absentmindedly. "But let me ask you something, sis. Have you ever taken a minute to consider *why* John Nguyen acts the way he does? Why he can't seem to make eye contact? Why he talks so slowly, or why sometimes it even seems like he *thinks* slowly, too?"

I folded my arms up in a show of defiance. "Nope. Never spared a second thought for that loser, and I'm not about to start now."

Burton tilted his chin again, that tic of his just slightly more irritating than usual. "Well, maybe it's time you reconsidered."

"What in the hell is *that* supposed to mean?"

He nodded towards my little stepbrother, who'd just plodded into the room. As usual, Burton was wearing nothing more than his favorite pair of black boxer briefs.

The moment was almost surreal. Both of us just sitting back, silent, watching Burton—the three-year-old Burton—who for his part, didn't appear to take notice of us at all. The kid gazed vacantly around the room and then laid down flat across the carpet, basking in the light of a sunbeam like a cat might've done. I guess the warmth probably felt good on his bare skin or something.

Old Burton was the first to speak up. "John Nguyen's not retarded, you know. He's autistic. Like I am. And kind of like…"

He raised an arm towards his toddler equivalent before dropping it just as quickly.

"Like *you* are?" I offered.

"Thank you." Burton twisted his lips, searching for the right words, struggling to describe his condition. "See, John Nguyen and I are a lot alike. Especially in terms of our behavior. He's obviously much farther along on the spectrum than I am, but I'm also willing to bet that he didn't get nearly as much childhood support as I did, or I mean, as I will." He sniffed again. "Probably none at all."

"What do you mean?"

"Well, Jessie. It's like this. Even though John Nguyen and I could've been born with the exact same mental capacity, the two of us were raised in completely different environments. Take *him*, for example. I mean, *me*."

Burton tossed a hand idly towards his younger self. I watched closely as my stepbrother ran his palms back and forth across the shag carpet for no other reason than the sensation of it. Of course I'd noticed that same kind of repetitive behavior before, but I guess I just hadn't paid it any mind.

Never had a reason to.

"When a kid's got any kind of developmental issue—like in my case, when I'm going on four years old, but still not speaking—eventually the parents will catch on that something's wrong. And once they link up with the school counselors or get an outside specialist involved, it's usually just a matter of time before the kid starts improving." He turned his head sideways to make eye contact. "That's how it went with Dad and Mom, at least. But just wait, you'll see what I mean before long."

I snapped at him more as a reflex than because I was actually upset. "You mean *your* Mom! Samantha caught my Dad on the rebound. That woman might stay here when she's not out on the road, but she damn sure isn't *my* mother."

"That may be true, but at least she's trying to make the relationship work. Even if you aren't."

I felt my face go hot.

Burton pressed on with his line of reasoning. "But, as I was saying. Once our parents finally *do* catch on that I'm a little different, things will start happening fast. All my nonverbal behavior, the grunts and screams? The tantrums that spring up from nowhere, anytime there's a slight change in my normal routine? Turns out, those reactions are pretty standard for kids on the autism spectrum. When I was a child, they'd manifest anytime my senses got overloaded, whenever my developing brain was unable to process everything going on around me."

I didn't know what to say but still nodded along, pretending that I understood.

"I didn't remember 1993 very clearly, since I'm still so young right now. But I know it won't be much longer until Mom and Dad really start getting involved in my education, spinning up all kinds of treatment routines. I'm talking regular appointments with a psychologist, plus occupational therapy and a speech counselor. The whole deal. I even had a personal aide there for a little while, helping me settle in when I started kindergarten. There was a whole support staff on my side, helping me grow up. People who dealt with autism every day, and who knew how to manage the condition."

I grimaced, imagining the price tag that must've come with such an intensive regime. "Sounds like an awful lot to go through."

"Yup," Burton said. "Expensive, too."

I shrugged, trying to shake off the creepy sensation I always felt when it seemed like that guy was peering into my private thoughts.

He went on. "Thankfully, we're pretty well off right now. And I don't want to spoil the show for you, but our parents' careers still have a lot more room to grow. They'll be able to pay for all those treatments, no problem."

"Well, that's good news, at least."

"But do you think that John Nguyen's family is anywhere near as fortunate as we are? Do you even know the first thing about that kid's home life?"

I sighed. "Nope, but let me guess. You do?"

"I've done some research. John's parents? Well, his mom and dad are still together, but just barely. And that's only because neither one of them's ever stayed sober long enough to file for divorce. Most weekends, the two of them end up getting wasted and beating on each other."

I blushed with embarrassment. My body moved on its own, doing its best to squirm down into the cushions and disappear. "Sounds rough."

"They live in that trailer park down by the Acre. You know it? It's a tough neighborhood. And besides being an alcoholic, John's dad's been in and out of prison his entire adult life. The guy hangs drywall for a living…can you imagine? Hauling around those big heavy sheetrock panels all day long, coming home covered in sweat and gypsum dust every night? Nothing to look forward to in your life besides whatever's on television?"

I grimaced. Evenings in the Nguyen household sounded an awful lot like Burton's visits, but of course I knew better than to say so.

"John Nguyen's spent his whole childhood living that way, day after day, for years on end. And let me tell you, it doesn't help one bit that his dad's still carrying around a host of issues after two tours in Vietnam. He can't hold a job for more than a month before going off on a bender, waking up a few days later over in Lowell County Corrections. Judging from his criminal record, it looks like the man's done time for at least six separate counts of driving under the influence."

I bit my lip.

"But even when his Dad's on lockdown, John's home life isn't any better. His mom normally heads to Lawrence and shacks up with this Dominican guy who doesn't have any papers and keeps a Camaro registered in her name. So yeah, I guess you could say that John Nguyen's folks aren't around all that much." He tossed a glance my way. "Sound familiar?"

I couldn't think of anything to say, so I didn't.

It was probably better that way.

"But the difference between him and me is, whenever his parents *do* happen to be home, they're simply not paying the kid much attention, if any at all. John's an only child, and I'm willing to bet he was an accident. He's an afterthought, so most days he's left to his own devices, probably glued to the television watching wrestling, or cartoons, or whatever's on, until he gets bored enough to head out to the woods and start setting fires. Nobody around him cares enough to show any interest, and by now, his parents have probably just dismissed him as retarded, same as you have. I doubt they've *ever* considered looking into how to support his disability."

He reached up and tapped the side of his head.

"See, if you think of the human brain like an automobile engine, John Nguyen's is just running on a different set of gears. His mind probably works a lot like mine—moving at a different speed and in a different direction, so who knows? Maybe that kid might've had a real chance in life, given a different set of circumstances. But when it comes to autism, it's the extra effort that makes such a difference."

I shuddered again. The deep conversation was making me uncomfortable all of a sudden. I couldn't tell whether that was because I'd started feeling the slightest bit sympathetic towards John Nguyen's circumstances, or if I was just embarrassed by my own self-centered attitude.

"Okay, then," I finally answered. "Let's suppose all that information really is true. I'm not saying I understand it—at least, not everything—but let's say for the sake of argument that you're right. Maybe John Nguyen's not a full-blown retard. Fine. So, he's just an autistic, who hasn't gotten the support he needs."

Burton nodded.

"But if that's the case, then what in the hell do you expect *me* to do about it?"

He leaned back against the sofa, shifting his body to face his younger self once again. "The way I see it, all you *should* have to do is just be nice to the kid. Or at least, try to. Now, does that really sound so hard? Would it *kill* you to try, for once in your life, being kind to John Nguyen?"

AT LEAST A WEEK HAD PASSED AFTER THAT LAST VISIT.

Longer, probably.

Enough time went by that I started to wonder if I'd ever see Old Burton again, and as much as I didn't want to admit it, I actually began to miss the guy's company.

As the days passed, I got back in the habit of arriving at school before the late bell. It was still such a strange experience, coming through those doors clear-eyed and sober.

First thing in the morning, those hallways always seemed so clean. The linoleum floor shined so bright, it was almost intimidating.

But as uncomfortable as I might've felt, none of my classmates spared me a second glance. I suppose it was possible that all those kids were ignoring me on purpose, but it was much more likely that nobody at John F. Kennedy really cared all that much about my comings and goings. And most days, that arrangement was fine with me, although I still took care to duck low every time I passed by the Administration Office's big plate glass window.

Force of habit, I guess.

I rounded the corner as quickly as I could. No sense in risking another confrontation, after all.

And then when I saw the kid, I froze up.

Yeah, I know. Even though I'd agreed to take a shot at talking to John Nguyen, I guess I'd secretly been hoping for a little more time. Mid-morning would've been better, maybe after we'd both gotten past a couple classes. But even though the circumstances weren't ideal, I knew I had to act fast. John Nguyen might have been autistic, sure, but he was also just as big a slacker as me. I couldn't risk stalling, since there was no guarantee he'd still be at school by the time the dismissal bell rang.

Or me, for that matter.

I caught up to John Nguyen as he stopped to hunch over the water bubbler. The kid looked a mess like always, wearing an old T-shirt that was at least half a size too small for his thick frame. The hem stopped about an inch short of his belt loops, and a soft roll of belly fat peeked out from underneath.

The kid's dark black hair was done up in its usual tangle, uncombed, and dusted with a layer of dandruff which floated down onto his shoulders in a fine, powdery mist.

And as far as his body odor? Well, I caught my first whiff from across the hall. That pungent, lingering smell of two overripe armpits which had probably never seen the business end of a deodorant stick. The kid's fragrance was what I imagined it'd be like if you'd misplaced an apple core somewhere, and after a couple days, it'd started to rot, but you just couldn't find it to throw it away.

I took a deep breath, partly to steady my nerves, and partly to suck in one last gulp of fresh air before entering the contamination zone. That done, I took a single, bold step forward.

And then I stood there waiting, for nearly a full minute.

Now, I know for certain that kid must've seen me, but for some reason, he seemed determined to ignore my presence completely. Even after swallowing enough water to drain the Atlantic Ocean, he kept his back to me as he eased upright and ran a chubby hand through the fountain's arc of cool water. John Nguyen looked fascinated by the way it flowed through his fingers, almost exactly like how Burton always loved to splash around in the kitchen sink at home. The bubbler seemed to have captured John Nguyen's imagination, or at least, he found it more interesting than anything I had to say.

Eventually, I got tired of waiting, and opened the conversation with a simple, "Hi, John." I spoke slow and clear, so he couldn't pretend not to hear me. "How's it going, man?"

The first bell had already rung, so there wasn't anyone else around. Him and me, that's it. I watched, intrigued, as John raised his massive head ever so slightly, then bent back down to take another slow sip.

The kid was stalling, most likely hoping I'd give up and go away.

But I'd probably been bullied, beaten up, and pushed around just as much as he had. I recognized the tactic, and it didn't work against me.

I slid my Reeboks across the slick floor, inching my way closer. Thin streaks of water were still visible on the linoleum, a sure sign that Mr. Vorela had just come by with a wet mop. Honestly, I had no idea why that old guy never waited until school let out to clean up. Who knows? Maybe some kid had come in sick and laid down a trail of early-morning vomit or something. I know showing up at JFK always made *me* feel like puking.

I took another tentative half-step forward. "Having a good day, man?"

Up close, I had a clear view of the kid's big, brown eyes. They shifted up and to the left, almost like he needed a moment to think before answering such a simple question.

I couldn't have guessed how long John Nguyen might've stood there in silence, but thankfully, the late bell rang at the exact same moment my patience ran out.

"Well, I've got to get to class," I grunted. I bit down hard on my lip, fighting back that feeling of annoyance. There was absolutely no reason for me to be concerned with punctuality, not by that point in the semester, but the bell made for a handy excuse to disappear. Even though I didn't have a single damn thing better to do, I was pretty sure I could find something. "I'll see you around, John Nguyen." The kid's first and last names rolled together naturally, almost like he was a reverse version of one of those single-name celebrities, like Madonna. Or Prince.

Like he was famous for some reason or other. Or more likely, notorious.

As I turned to hustle off down the hallway, I saw the kid's eyes go wide with confusion, bulging out from beneath a set of flabby round lids.

But honestly, I'm still not sure what I'd been expecting might happen after that first meeting.

Like, maybe the two of us could've had some kind of miraculous interpersonal breakthrough, right then and there.

You know. A conversational exchange of historical magnitude, or some shit.

But honestly, I was just happy that the short chat hadn't driven John Nguyen into a meltdown. The way I saw it, the fact that the kid hadn't broken down into a sobbing mess *had* to count for something.

Didn't it?

WEDNESDAY, MARCH 31, 1993

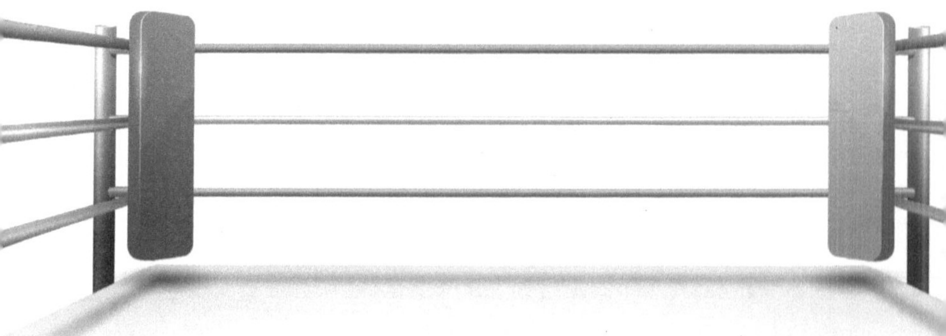

I SAT THERE IN SILENCE. NEARLY MOTIONLESS TOO, BUT FOR ROTATING my head from side to side every minute or so, looking back and forth to make a careful examination of both of them.

There was the three-year old Burton: the kid I'd always known, yet never understood.

And then there was the middle-aged Burton: the one I'd only recently met, but who already seemed so familiar.

I watched closely, scrutinizing their physical appearances. The similarities were undeniable. They both had the same eyes, for sure. Between their round shape and that deep shade of sky blue, it wouldn't have been nearly enough to just say that there was a strong resemblance. And even a stranger would've been able to recognize those facial structures, with a sharp, sloping curve falling down along both sets of narrow cheekbones. Both of the Burtons sported wide patches of freckles, stretching from cheek to cheek, and their messy blond hair looked like it could've been styled by the exact same windstorm.

And, just as amazingly, the two of them even carried themselves the same way.

And I mean like, identical.

From that constant slouching posture, to a preference for loose and relaxed clothing.

Come to think of it, I'd never seen either one of those guys with their shirts tucked in. And whenever they were near each other, it was almost comical. Both sets of shoulders rolled forward, chins tucked down, nearly to their chests. Sometimes, if I hadn't been paying particularly close attention, it would still come as a shock to glance across the couch and spot the two of them sitting there, side by side.

Mirror images, they were, but like something out of a carnival funhouse. Except for their different ages and sizes, the two might've been able to pass for blurry reflections of one another.

But even after I'd come to terms with the idea that those two humans were the same person, over time, I managed to pick up on a few subtle differences. Take my stepbrother, the one who actually belonged in 1993. That kid never made eye contact unless he absolutely couldn't avoid it, like if he needed to get my attention for some reason or other. But Old Burton? Well, even though that dude had a lot of the same behaviors, it was obvious he'd spent some time practicing how to hold a conversation. The very way he spoke—waiting until after he'd finished a sentence before looking my way—showed that even after decades of training, making eye contact still came as something of an afterthought.

"So, that's the reason why he—why *you*—still aren't talking yet?" I paused for a moment, stumbling over the pronouns. "Because you're autistic?"

He nodded, closing his eyes as he collected his thoughts. The two of us turned our attention towards the kid lying there on the carpet, watching him stretch his body back and forth in the warmth of a long, clear sunbeam. Burton wasn't paying us any mind, his thoughts occupied by some other pressing matter, one known only to him. He was going through some kind of repetitive process with his lips, blowing saliva into an endless series of small bubbles. At moments like these, it almost seemed like Burton lived within his own little world.

"Yeah. See, when you talk about autism, you've got to understand, it's not just a single, fixed condition. More like a range of different traits and behaviors, all of them falling somewhere along a really wide bandwidth. And autism's not particularly well understood right now—at least, not in 1993. Most people aren't aware of the full spectrum, so a lot of these kids slip past, unnoticed. Sure, Mom and Dad must've realized that I'm a bit off, but with both of them out on the road so much, it's hard for them to see the full scope of the issue. It'll be another couple months before they really catch on and drive me down to Boston to meet with a child psychologist. After that initial diagnosis, things will start improving pretty quickly." He paused to inhale a short, sharp breath with this annoying little sniff of his nose. "See, it's simply not possible to address a problem when you don't realize you have one. Understand?"

I sat there, still and quiet, listening to Aunt Emmy bang a bunch of pots and pans around in the kitchen. There wasn't a single person who'd ever accused that lady of knowing how to cook, but that fact hadn't stopped her from trying.

"So, like, will anybody ever find out what causes it? And will there ever be a cure for the disease?"

Burton's eyes flickered. "First of all, autism's not a disease. Not the same way the flu is, or AIDS, or whatever. The autism spectrum is more like a span of disorders. *Conditions*, really, that a person just happens to be born with. When you say somebody's autistic, it's almost like you're describing another aspect of their personality. You know? Just a single characteristic that happens to affect someone's personality and behavior."

I nodded. "Okay, I think I've got it. So, autism is more like a handicap, then?"

The guy let out a sigh, but at least it didn't sound like he was upset.

"Kind of? Right now at least, yes, most people might still see autism as some kind of disability, but only because nobody really understands it yet. Wait a decade or two, give the doctors and psychiatrists some time to do their research, and all of these conditions will get re-labeled without nearly as much stigma attached." He leaned back against the cushions, reaching up towards the ceiling and stretching both arms overhead. "Lots of things are getting misunderstood these days," he said, folding his hands back behind his head. "Autism's just one of them."

I grimaced. "Yeah, I guess I can see that." Watching Burton, I took note of the way he fanned his fingers along the back of his neck, spreading them out wide and then bringing them right back in again. The guy repeated the motion over and over again, almost as if he wasn't even aware he was fidgeting.

"So, that's why Burton acts the way he does? I mean, why *you* acted the way you do…did…back in the day? Now?" I gave my head a quick shake, trying to clear the frustration that always came on whenever I tried to work through the gnarled branches of our family tree. "The tantrums that come out of nowhere, the picky eating and stuff? All that comes from being disabled?"

He lowered his chin with a single, slow nod. "Well, I prefer to think of myself as *differently* abled. I mean, I hold down a regular job, same as most other autistic adults. I'm capable of maintaining healthy relationships with other people—a few close friends, at least. But yeah, without getting too deep into all the neuroscience, you're basically correct."

When Burton finally turned his head my way, I fixed him with a careful, considering gaze before speaking. "But you're not that way anymore. Are you? Like, you're still autistic, obviously, but look at you! You grew up and became a normal adult. Or, at least, you seem to be."

A sad smile crept across his freckled face. "Thanks. I think?"

I felt my face go hot, but Burton unclasped his hands and raised one in my direction.

"No worries, sis. I mean, I guess I should take that as a compliment. But yeah, there's a ton of different treatments and therapies out there, and as peoples' awareness of autism rises, these will only become more prevalent. Right now, yes, it might seem like my childhood self is living in his own world, but that'll change. Man! I wish you could see what I'm like by the time I leave for college."

I felt a slow smile growing across my face as I tried to imagine what my little stepbrother might look like in another fifteen years or so. And where *would* that kid end up going to college? You know, if it turned out there really was some kind of misunderstood genius hidden deep down underneath that outer layer of silence. Was I, right now, looking at a potential Harvard graduate? Or, maybe a brainy kid like that might end up enrolling at the Massachusetts Institute of Technology. No doubt, he'd definitely be bound for one of those Ivy League genius schools.

Burton drew his slim headphones up from his neck and fitted them carefully over his ears. He looked tired all of a sudden, almost as if the brief conversation had worn him out.

"Remember, sis." His eyes were fixed straight ahead, gazing out on his younger, contented self. "You can't ever allow people to hang a label on you. We're all dealing with issues of some kind. Every single one of us. But whenever you really set your mind to something—and I mean, really put yourself out there, with a goal and a solid plan to make it happen—you should know, there's not a thing in this world you can't do. If you believe in yourself, there's no such thing as a disability."

I didn't quite understand, but I nodded to let him know that I'd heard. And as I turned my attention back towards the big screen, I kept quiet, letting Burton's words roll their way through my mind.

That last line in particular.

It sounded just like something our Dad might've said if he was cutting a promo.

I'm not sure how much time passed, but when I finally glanced back across the couch, Burton had disappeared. Gone back to his own time, I guess.

He'd slipped out in that quiet, unobtrusive way of his, and I was left to watch Burton fall asleep on the shag carpet. As I listened to that kid's snores, soft but steady, I passed the time by thinking about his future, as his older self had just described it. All the uncertainty made it seem so fascinating…and the only thing that really worried me now was the fact that I wouldn't be around to see it.

WE WERE HANGING OUT IN THE LIVING ROOM AGAIN.

Like always.

This time, though, Burton's serious tone had caused the familiar space to take on a completely different feel. He'd gotten up from the couch and switched off the television set, for the first time in I don't know how long.

No distractions.

For once, my mind was crystal clear, and I finally felt ready to listen to whatever he had to say. Anything.

For his part, it seemed like Burton could tell I was serious now. At long last, the dude was ready to lift the curtain and reveal how he made it all work.

The two of us were sitting on the floor. His legs were crossed up Indian-style, and I was doing my best to mirror the position. We held our arms still, folded open and hanging to the sides, elbows resting on top of our thighs.

And then eventually, Burton spoke up. His voice came out soft, barely a whisper. "Okay, nice work. Not bad for a first effort. How are you feeling?"

I'd promised him I'd be honest, so I was.

"How am I feeling? I'm feeling like an absolute tool, that's how I'm feeling. My ass is sore, and I've got a massive leg cramp coming on."

He let out a quiet little sigh.

I cracked my eyes and snuck a sideways glance. "Dude. You seriously expect me to believe that this is how you manage to time travel?"

I spotted Burton's eyelids flicker for the briefest of moments. "Me? No, not usually. I prefer to lie flat on my back, looking up at the ceiling. The supine position always helps me get a new perspective. Lets me see things from a different angle."

He shifted his torso, uncrossing his legs and then stretching them out straight. "I've found that it also helps to bring along an artifact, some item that captures a moment from the era. That's why I picked up this Discman, and why I started collecting vintage clothing. That helps me focus in on the destination, and it's how *I* sift my way through the space-time spectrum, but it's only one technique. You need to find out what works for *you* and then keep doing that. Which is why today, we're starting off with the basics."

I echoed his sigh as I stretched my own legs out straight, massaging my thighs and waiting until the circulation returned before crossing them back up again. "And so this pretzel pose is just part of the basics, is it?"

"Well? To put it simply, here in 1993, even the best minds in all of science haven't come close to understanding the true nature of time. Those Buddhist monks over in Tibet are probably the closest, and meditation is a big factor in their mental clarity, so since they all sit like this, you're sitting like this. Don't be afraid to copy what works, at least when you're starting out."

My sigh of exasperation probably came out a little louder than I'd intended. "Okay, fine. Whatever you say."

"Good." He closed his eyes again, refocusing on the project at hand. "Now, for the next step, I just want you to relax. Try to clear your mind entirely, and don't think about anything at all. Forget about me, forget about school, forget about your family. If you can manage it, let yourself lose track of where we are. In space, in time, all of it. The only thing I want you to be aware of is yourself, your own existence. Don't be concerned with your external environment. There's nothing out there for you, not anymore."

"Cool. I'm there."

Burton cracked an eyelid, sporting a look of surprise. "Wait, what? You found your center already?"

"Not really, but let's just say that I have. It'll speed things up. Cool? So, go on, let's skip ahead to the important parts."

"Fine." Burton shifted his weight on those skinny legs of his. "Honestly, this whole process would probably work a lot better if you were by yourself. You can't really teach somebody how to meditate, and as far as time? Well, that's a funny thing to play with. The two of us can walk through the steps together, and I can try my best to explain how I make it all happen, but if you ever actually want to experience time travel, that's something you'll have to do on your own."

Concentration wasn't my strong suit, especially not back then, but I swear I was making an effort. "I'll try, Burton. I promise."

He nodded. "That's all I ask. Let's move on. Once you're relaxed and comfortable, I'm going to try injecting a few ideas into your consciousness. Simple concepts, but I've selected them to demonstrate how to take charge of your thinking. How to harness the power of your brain, and focus it in one specific direction. Okay?"

"All right."

"Okay, then. We'll start with a couple easy questions. First, how fast would you say 'fast' is?"

I tilted my head to the side, somehow resisting the urge to open my eyes and hit Burton with a blank stare. "Shit, I don't know. Like, how fast can a person run, do you mean? Or are you talking about, like, how fast can you drive a car? Because if it's that one, then I'd say a hundred miles an hour or so is pretty damned fast."

"Not bad," he said, with a smile in his voice. "You're already questioning the questions. But think bigger. Look beyond the limits of an Olympic sprinter or even the top speed of a race car. Spend some time thinking about your answer, and don't be in a rush to respond."

I pondered the problem for a few more seconds. "Hell, I don't know. You're not talking about the speed of light, are you? Because isn't that, like…"

I knew that we'd touched upon the subject once in Earth Science, but I also knew there was absolutely no hope that I'd be able to recall the exact figure.

"…really fast?"

Burton filled in the missing details for me. "A beam of light has a measured speed of 186,000 miles per second. Approximately."

"Yeah, like I said. Really fast."

I snuck another sideways glance and caught Burton staring back at me, probably trying to discern if I'd been impressed by his statistical wizardry.

"Now, moving right along. The next closest star to us is…" His voice trailed off, waiting for my answer like I might've had the information right there at my fingertips.

"Umm…isn't that the sun?"

"Correct! Although it's still pretty far off, at least from our human perspective. The sun is ninety-three million miles away, give or take, depending on where the Earth is in its yearly rotation."

I did my best to stifle a yawn.

"So, even though the sun's rays travel at—well, at the speed of light—it still takes them an average of eight minutes and twenty seconds to reach us here on Earth. And this is a little off topic, but I've always appreciated that fact. Did you know that big ball of gas is bound to run out of fuel someday? It's true! Even if it takes another five billion years or so, eventually our sun will burn itself out. But when that day comes, and the whole galaxy is finally set to go dark, we'll still have another eight minutes and twenty seconds of light left. Comforting, right? Assuming mankind makes it to that point without killing ourselves off, there'll still be another eight minutes and twenty seconds of normalcy waiting there at the tail end of our lives. One last little bit of warmth before the Earth's atmosphere ices over, and we all freeze to death."

"Heavy." A chilly draft swept through the living room, and I couldn't hold back a shudder.

"But stay with me now. I swear, all of this is going somewhere. Next question: you know that the sun is our closest star, right? But in our solar system, which of the *planets* is nearest to Earth?"

I rolled my eyes. I was doing my best to humor my stepbrother, but it was almost demeaning, rehashing all those second-grade science lessons. "Mars, duh. The Red Planet."

Young Burton walked into the room just then, and immediately took notice of my strange posture. I watched as he sat down on the carpet, mimicking us by twisting his legs into a bow. The kid got bored of the position after only a few seconds, though, and belly-crawled over to his favorite patch of carpet.

"Right," Burton continued. "So, how far away is that? Wait, I'll give you this one. Earth revolves around the sun once every 365 days, but Mars only makes that trip once every 686 days, so you'd have to calculate the variance. Because of these factors, on any given day, Mars could be somewhere between 34 million and 250 million miles away from Earth."

Those numbers were way too big for me to process. "If you say so."

"And you know what? Because the linear distance is so great, we should probably just go ahead and convert that into light speed. For simplicity. So then, to close the gap between Earth and Mars, a beam of light might take anywhere between 3.03 and 22.4 minutes. Mind you, those figures are just approximations. We're using imprecise measurements for the sake of discussion."

Somehow, I resisted the urge to roll my eyes. "Obviously."

But Burton had already gone and gotten himself worked up. By that point, he wouldn't have slowed down for anything, especially not my snark.

"Now, let's gradually broaden the scope of our thoughts. Okay? I'll let you suggest the next example. Pick another planet. Any one, it doesn't matter, as long as it's even more distant than Mars."

"Shit, I don't know." I gave his question about a half second of serious thought. "How about Pluto?"

Burton frowned, scratching at his chin. "Pluto's not a…" His voiced trailed away for an awkward moment before he shook his head and rushed on ahead with the lecture. "Fine, okay. Pluto it is." He rolled his shoulders back and tilted his neck up at the ceiling, almost as if he could've been poring over an endless host of facts and figures, all of them catalogued away somewhere within that powerful brain of his.

"Well, if you start from the most distant point between the two, Pluto has the potential to be up to five billion miles away from Earth." He brought his head down in concentration. "Again, that's just an approximation. I'd have to use a pencil and paper to convert the figure into light speed, but we're probably looking at, oh, maybe ten hours or so."

I'd had enough, and tossed my hands up in frustration. "Dude! What the hell? You promised you were finally going to explain how time travel works, but this shit is all just, like, astronomy! I don't get it—what in the hell do all the stars and the planets have to do with traveling through time?"

Despite my outburst, Burton's skinny face was just as calm and impassive as ever. He raised an open palm in my direction, a silent plea for patience.

"Bear with me, sis. Just one more. You know how the planets rotate around our sun, sure. But what about this? The sun acts as the center of our known galaxy, but it's just one of a countless number of stars. Have you ever considered the possibility that some of the others—or even *a lot* of them—might also be home to other planets?

I twisted my lips up into a scowl. Of course I hadn't.

"And when I say there's a countless number of stars, that's literally true. Astronomers suspect that our universe is in a constant state of expansion—that it's continuously growing, and it has been ever since the moment of creation. Assuming that theory is true, there could very well be an infinite number of solar systems out there in the vast reaches of space."

"Fascinating."

"So, with all that in mind, let me ask you this one last question. And it's totally okay if you don't know the answer. Not counting our own sun—what's the closest star system to Earth?"

Even though I'd wasted countless hours watching *Star Trek: The Next Generation*, I was completely lost. "Beats me," I grumbled, relaxing my posture, uncrossing my legs and leaning back against the sofa.

"It's Alpha Centauri," Burton informed me, as if he thought I cared. "At a distance of just 4.367 light years, that galaxy is our closest neighbor in this deep, dark, mysterious universe."

"Amazing," I yawned. "So, uh…what's your point?"

He scowled. "My point is that even using the most basic principles of mathematics, we were able to calculate that it would take a beam of light, moving at the fastest speed modern science is able to measure, over four years to cross the distance between stars. But just now, your own untrained mind was able to jump that same distance in a matter of seconds."

I didn't know how to respond to that.

"My point is, by so patiently indulging me in this discussion, you've just demonstrated the most important principle of time travel. Your mind is so much more powerful than most people realize. Your thoughts are capable of traveling infinite distances and of moving at infinite speeds."

I leaned my neck back and stared up at the ceiling, pondering the heavy material. As if the deep subject matter wasn't impressive enough, it was almost intimidating, the way Burton had managed to break the whole thing down into such a quick and easy lesson. His simple explanation made me feel like I actually had a shot at understanding it.

Almost.

"Wait, what?" I stammered. "So, you're telling me that time travel is all about speed? You can't really mean that *Back to the Future* movie got it right?"

Burton shrugged. "More or less? Speed itself—be it miles per hour, or light years, or whatever—is only a system of measurement. Since the dawn of time, humans have always sought ways to mark its passage. But for our purposes, it should be sufficient just to acknowledge the concept. Generally speaking, the faster a person moves, the more they'll be able to accomplish. At the point of infinite speed, that naturally opens the door to an infinite number of possibilities."

The puzzle pieces were finally starting to come together in my mind. All those disparate thoughts were joining up so neat and clean, I found myself terrified they might dash apart again, and drop me right back into a mess of confusion.

"So, let me get this straight," I finally choked out. "You're honestly going to sit there and tell me to my face that you have the ability to travel backwards and forwards through time somehow, and that you can do it safely and repeatedly, using nothing other than the power of your own mind? That's all there is to it?"

"Yup. That's all there is to it."

"No souped-up DeLorean with a nuclear-powered flux capacitor or whatever? No, uh…what do they use on the *Enterprise*? That big tube-looking thing?"

"A warp coil drive?"

"Sure. Whatever. So, like, you don't have a warp drive or anything like that? No technological wizardry from the future?"

"That's exactly what I'm saying."

Burton, see. That dude was always so slow to anger.

Me, not so much.

As I sat there stewing in silence, my older stepbrother eased his tall frame onto the carpet, stretching out alongside his younger self. He reached for one of the kid's Hot Wheels cars, this bright yellow fastback Camaro, and rolled it slowly back and forth in front of the three-year-old's eyes.

"Unbelievable." It was a weak reaction, I know, but by that point in the conversation, it was all I could manage.

He didn't bother to look up when he answered. "How is it so hard to believe? Ask any scientist, they'll tell you the human brain is the greatest machine ever invented. Its electric synapses are capable of millions of calculations per second, more than the most powerful computers in your time, or even mine! And haven't you ever heard the claim that humans only use about ten percent of the brain's full capacity? If that's true, then ask yourself, why is the other ninety percent even there? Don't tell me you haven't ever wondered what you're *truly* capable of?"

I turned that thought over in my head for a moment, considering the possibilities.

Like Burton had said, they seemed infinite.

"So…" I said again. "You only need the power of your thoughts in order to travel through time."

"Yes."

"In other words, this is all in your imagination."

He rotated his head my way, but I cut him off before he could answer.

"And if you *are* just imagining this, that means you're not even here at all! I mean, who's to say that all our encounters haven't just been fantasies? You know? Like, maybe you're just some kind of hallucination!"

My skin went cold as I thought about all the chemicals I'd pumped into my body that winter, and I couldn't help wondering whether any of them might've had the potential to cause lasting brain damage.

Burton raised a hand to toss out a careless wave. "You know what? It doesn't matter. Whether I'm really here or not—or whether anything you see with your own two eyes is real—these questions are entirely yours to answer. I know how crazy this all might seem, yet here I am. Right here, right in front of you."

He reached over to give his smaller self a pat on the back. The kid responded by snuggling into his touch.

"Here *we* are. All of us." He sighed. "Think about all the people you come into contact with, every day of your life. Are *they* all real? Would it even be possible to tell if they weren't?"

I looked down at little Burton.

The kid looked back up at me.

"But have you ever considered there might be a reason for these interactions? All of them. Some cosmic system of cause and effect, with an infinite number of outcomes, all of them tied together somehow? A web of interactions, outcomes and consequences, so vast and complex that there's just no hope of understanding it?"

I just stared back at him with a blank look of ignorance. By that point in the lecture, there was absolutely nothing I could contribute.

"But sis," he went on, bringing the lecture to a conclusion with an unmistakable air of finality. "All you have to do is take one look around. I'm right here, and I'm right *there*, too. Both Burtons are side by side in your living room, here in the spring of 1993. Now, tell me, what exactly is it about this situation that still doesn't seem real to you? This is happening…all of it. Why is it so hard for you to believe?"

MONDAY, APRIL 5, 1993

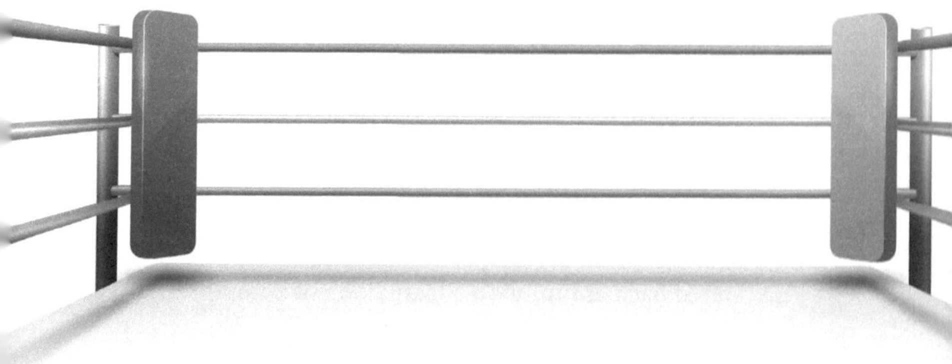

Excerpt from "Monday Night Titans" *broadcast*
Transcription by Burton Carpenter

Dr. John Burnham: And, we're back! Live, once again, from the Dallas Sportatorium, the hallowed halls which have stood witness to decades, literally decades, of professional wrestling history! It's a capacity crowd here tonight, not an empty seat in the house, and believe me, fans, every last man, woman, and child in this beautiful Texas crowd is on their feet right now. Would you listen to that, Michael Jones! They're not holding anything back at all, really letting Tommy Carpenter have it!

Michael Jones: J.B., I am literally at a loss for words. The atmosphere within this arena is unbelievable! Simply unbelievable, and by that I mean, the scene here defies all belief! For all you viewers at home, I challenge you to crack open a road atlas and mark off the distance between Dallas, Texas, and Memphis, Tennessee. The two cities must be separated by a good five hundred miles, but here tonight, we're seeing just how tight-knit the World Wide Wrestling community can be! Remember just a few short weeks ago, when the world of sports entertainment was shook, literally shook, as we witnessed Tommy Carpenter, the man they used to call "The Daydreamer," pull off a stunning upset—dare I say, the upset of a *lifetime*—ending the Tennessee Mule's career with an absolutely *crippling* submission hold. Well clearly, folks, it's not just the fans from the Volunteer State who're up in arms over that surprise outcome! Let me tell you, it's been my distinct privilege to serve as an announcer for some thirty years now. Thirty years! And I've seen a great many things from this ringside seat in that time, but I have to say, what Tommy Carpenter did to the Tennessee Mule was something special. J.B., the way I see it, that match was the biggest humiliation of a Southern man since Grant met Lee at Appomattox!

J.B.: Michael Jones! That comment was unnecessary! To our lovely audience here in Dallas, and to all our viewers tuning in across the South—a wholesome, Godly region, which I, for one, feel is the *true* heartland of America—I beg you, pay no mind to my colleague from the Big Apple. Michael, you couldn't possibly have meant that? Yes, the Daydreamer might be fresh off a single, magical moment in an otherwise hard-luck career, but I've recently heard from a number of fans who seem to think that match was nothing more than a fluke.

M.J.: The hell I didn't mean it, J.B.! Just look at the man! This is not the 'Tommy Daydream' we've been forced to watch for the past ten years. The absent-minded hippie, the golden-haired love child who was conceived in the back of a Volkswagen bus and raised in a grainy commune in the Berkshires? No, this man before us is a pure athlete, and right now, he looks like a man possessed! Can't you see the intensity? That fire in his eyes? Tommy Carpenter is ready for war! Mark my words, when this fella pulled up to the stadium tonight, he came ready for a street fight!"

J.B.: Well, Carpenter certainly does *look* like a changed man, I'll give you that! Where's his tie-dyed robe? It's nowhere to be seen! And those flowing locks of blond hair have been sheared away? Sakes alive! This man looks as if he could've rolled in straight off of a shift at the construction site. Jean shorts…work boots…an American flag draped over those massive shoulders, and a crewcut? My word! Tommy Daydream with a crewcut, I never thought I'd see the day!

M.J.: You said it, J.B! Ladies and gentlemen, just a few short months ago Tommy Carpenter was out of commission to undergo a complicated rotator cuff surgery, but it certainly looks like that procedure hasn't kept him out of the weight room! This man must've shed, what? Twenty pounds? The Daydreamer, Tommy Daydream, Tommy Carpenter…I honestly don't know *what* name he might be going by right now, but regardless, he looks fantastic. Such a magnificent physique!

J.B.: Let's pass it back down to the golden voice of Tony Schoonover.

Tony Schoonover: And now, his opponent—standing a solid six feet, six inches tall—and weighing in at four hundred and twenty seven pounds! Hailing from Rhodesia, a mysterious land deep in the heart of the Dark Continent. A veritable mountain of a man— he is— Kilimanjaro!

J.B.: Would you look at that! Kilimanjaro, chugging down the ramp, raring to get his hands on Tommy Carpenter! He's got a full head of steam…and there's the bell! Let's get it on!

M.J.: Jim Crow! That big buck's moving so fast, you'd have thought there was a platter of fried chicken waiting in the center of the ring! Or maybe a watermelon, or a welfare check, instead of a—

J.B.: —hard right hand from Carpenter! Such power behind that punch, he's knocked Kilimanjaro silly! Carpenter, taking control, cranking the mountain into motion with an Irish whip, all that bulk stretching the ropes to their limit, and right back into an outstretched arm! Ouch, that was a devastating clothesline!

M.J.: The big man is down! The big man is down! Oh, Sweet Sambo, the big man is down! For what might be the first time in his professional wrestling career, Mount Kilimanjaro is feeling the sensation of canvas against his bare back! Have you ever in your life seen anything like this before? Ladies and gentlemen, sports entertainment fans of all ages, I swear, I think I just felt the earth shake! Folks, I wouldn't risk a single blink right now. You don't want to miss a second of this match! It's turning out to be a one-sided display of pure, unbridled fury. Say what you want about Tommy Carpenter, this blue collar boy, but one thing's clear, he came here tonight with something to prove!

J.B.: Carpenter, pulling Kilimanjaro to his feet, making that lift seem almost effortless. Setting him up for…LOW BLOW! LOW BLOW! Oh, my word! Referee Earl Black glanced away for the briefest of moments, and that was all the opportunity Kilimanjaro needed to fire off a sharp jab to the groin. Oh, my! Absolutely disgusting, the way he's pleading his innocence now, when there's no doubt in anybody's mind, that punch was intentional, a textbook cheap shot. We should've expected something like this from the newest member of The Syndicate!

M.J: That gang of thugs! Leaving a black smear across the good name of World Wide Wrestling!

J.B.: But I'm absolutely certain Tommy Carpenter must've put some consideration into that organization's tactics before accepting tonight's match. Still, there's no telling what's going on in his mind right now! Hunched over, defenseless, and it looks like Kilimanjaro has gained the upper hand!

M.J.: Speak of the devil, that's The Syndicate coming in now! El Diablo, sprinting down the ramp, jumping up on the ring apron, with Earl Black rushing over to cut him off. But what's this? Look at Kilimanjaro, reaching down into his tights…J.B., what's that he's got in his hand? Is it a sap, or a piece of lead pipe?

J.B.: It's a box cutter! Oh, my God! That savage has got a box cutter! We all know The Syndicate will stop at nothing to win matches, but this is beyond belief! That maniac actually brought a *box cutter* to a professional wrestling match! Ring the bell, somebody ring the bell! Stop the fight before this ring turns into a crime scene! This is inhumane!

M.J.: Kilimanjaro, on the offensive now, striding forward with no hesitation at all! He rears back, swings, and—

J.B.: He caught it! Whoa! Tommy Carpenter, stopping that box cutter mid-slash!

M.J.: And with one hand!

J.B.: He's back upright, controlling that dangerous blade with a masterful wristlock, firmly in control now…but for some reason, he's choosing to grapple with Kilimanjaro! Going for the front lock…both men squatting low, searching for more power…

M.J.: He's stood him up! Tommy Carpenter, with an amazing display of raw strength, has somehow managed to outmuscle the Nubian giant! I don't believe what I'm seeing, folks—just look at the fear on Kilimanjaro's face! Let me tell you, I simply can't recall a time when the big man's ever been stopped in his tracks, not the way we're seeing tonight! J.B., it looks as if the unstoppable force has *finally* met his immovable object, right here in Dallas, Texas, live, on *Monday Night Titans*!

J.B.: Carpenter, cutting the lockup short with a quick boot to the midsection…wow! Wow! Just like that, pulling that boxcutter free from Kilimanjaro's grasp! Tommy Carpenter, the man they used to call the Daydreamer, looking like a completely different personality, armed with that deadly steel blade! Standing there across from his opponent, not a trace of fear in his eyes, a wild predator taunting his prey! And of course there's the referee, Earl Black, backed into the far corner, helpless to do anything more than look on…he's lost all control of this match! Michael Jones, what in the world could Carpenter be thinking? Surely, he isn't about to murder his opponent in front of four thousand, five hundred eyewitnesses, not to mention a live television audience?

M.J.: He threw it away! Oh, my word! Tommy Carpenter! He just threw down the boxcutter, abandoning any advantage over Kilimanjaro! And now it's both men duking it out in the center of the ring, bare hands their only weapons, the way World Wide Wrestling was meant to be! Ladies and gentlemen, you're viewing a street fight right now, there's no other way to describe it! We thought we were coming to watch a wrestling match, but what we've got here tonight is an old-school rumble!

J.B.: Carpenter, with a flurry of blows, shooting in beneath the big man's legs like a varsity letterman…yes! He's going for the scoop! Straining against the bulk of that African giant, legs trembling…but he's got him off the ground! Kilimanjaro, aloft, being levitated by *Tommy Carpenter,* of all people? Oh, my stars! Ladies and gentlemen, I simply cannot believe my eyes! Look at the desperation on Kilimanjaro's dark face! He's shocked, absolutely shocked, to find himself in this predicament! Every wrestling fan in attendance tonight has to be *stunned* by this development, even The Syndicate members at ringside. They're frozen in place, awed by the sheer power on display, and it's all Carpenter now, looking perfectly comfortable in the spotlight as he shoulders that great burden! And Michael Jones, is that a *smile* I see on Carpenter's face? What *could* he be up to?

M.J: Over his head! My God in heaven! Upstart Tommy Carpenter just hefted the big man up in the air, making that lift look absolutely effortless…would you look at those triceps! Panic and fear in the eyes of Kilimanjaro now, the huge beast flailing about in helpless desperation, on the receiving end of a such a flawlessly executed gorilla press! Just listen to that crowd, J.B.! It's chaos here in Dallas, absolute pandemonium! My, how the tables have turned! Every last fan in this stadium is on their feet now, screaming in appreciation for this show of raw athleticism! Wow!

J.B.: Carpenter, simply shrugging those broad shoulders of his, sending the big man back down to the mat with an air of absolute disdain! But he's not wasting a second, sliding over Kilimanjaro and wrapping a leg for the cover!

M.J.: Earl Black, count it out! One! Two! Three! And it's over! It's over!

J.B.: Tommy Carpenter, the giant-slayer, emerges— victorious!—from an epic brawl! Michael Jones, can you believe what we've just seen? By the sound of this crowd, I think everyone else must feel the same way—it's madness in here! Mark my words, this firecracker of a match, and what Tommy Carpenter's managed to pull off, is certain to make the long list of storied events which have taken place here at the legendary Dallas Sportatorium!

M.J.: Tommy Carpenter! Man, oh man! What a privilege it was to watch this wily veteran do his thing. The man has somehow, all of a sudden, embarked on a quest to salvage his career, and now he's *tearing* through the ranks of World Wide Wrestling…wait, what? J.B., what's going on? Carpenter's after that boxcutter, he's gone and picked up the blade—for the love of God, somebody cut the cameras, there are *children* watching! I can't look, J.B.! It's going to be a bloodbath!

J.B.: Wait a minute…Carpenter's pointing at The Syndicate now, all those ruffians gathered at ringside, and I'll be *damned* if they're not just as dumbfounded as we are! It looks like Tommy Carpenter is actually calling out El Diablo! The two men are exchanging words…Carpenter seems to be putting The Syndicate on notice, right here in front of all these Dallas fans! What in the world? He's waving at Earl Black now, calling for the microphone…

M.J.: Shut up, I want to hear this!

Tommy Carpenter: A boxcutter? Huh? Is that what you clowns think of me? That Tommy Carpenter's one more wet-behind-the-ears rookie? Just another twenty-something gym rat with moussed hair, some kid you can push around anytime you feel like it? Kilimanjaro, you really think you're going to reach the top of World Wide Wrestling by whipping out a blade? You think that's all it takes? Hey, you look here, boy! I'm talking to you!

Kilimanjaro: *[inaudible]*

T.C.: No, you shut up, 'cause I've got the mic, and I want to tell you something. I want to tell you something about me. Now, it's been years since I've held a boxcutter. Years! Not since I used to sweat it out on the loading dock of the Lechmere store, and that's been one hell of a long time, kid. But you better take me at my word, I still remember how to use one of these things!

K: *[inaudible]*

T.C.: Is that so? Well, fact of the matter is, blade or no blade, I just beat you, and I beat you clean. When that bell rang just now, one of us had his arm hoisted in the air, and the other was still lying on his back, counting floodlights. But listen up, Kilimanjaro. You and all your goons better hear me now, because I want you to know, this victory don't mean shit to me. Understand? That's because you don't mean shit to me, neither.

[Overwhelming applause. Approx. 10-second delay.]

M.J.: For the love of God, this is a live broadcast!

J.B.: Ladies and gentlemen, I am *so* sorry about that epithet! I hope you'll understand, that type of speech is certainly *not* condoned by the management of World Wide Wrestling, nor any of our fine corporate sponsors...

T.C.: See, Kilimanjaro. As of this moment, you're officially dead to me. You don't exist! You aren't worth one more second of my time.

K: *[inaudible]*

T.C.: Man, just look at what you've become! Mobbed up with The Syndicate, as if any one of these bitches would have your back when the shit hits the fan. And to think, I used to idolize you! Used to mimic your style, even. Years ago, back when I was lugging around all those washing machines and refrigerators, pretending—no, I'll say it—*dreaming* that it was you and me, the two of us, together in this here ring. Putting a hurting on anyone stupid enough to cross us, and then hoisting those tag team championship belts afterwards. Back then, I never missed your matches, man. Not one! You were one of the legends who kept me going, back when I was killing myself for four twenty-five an hour and thinking I was pretty damned lucky for landing even that crap job.

[Prolonged applause.]

T.C.: So I'm putting you on notice, pal. And that goes for all of you in The Syndicate, too. You guys, you can come at me anytime. But when you do, you better come with more than just a boxcutter!

[Overwhelming applause. Approx. 15-second delay.]

T.C.: Kilimanjaro! You came all the way from Africa to get your shot in World Wide Wrestling, and believe it or not, I respect everything you did to chase your dream. I do. But I damn sure know where I came from, too. And you, The Syndicate, anybody—anyone can try and stand in my way if they want to, long as they know they're going to get steamrolled. 'Cause I'm not willing to let anything stand between me and my dreams, not no longer. You know what I'm getting at, don't you?

[Applause.]

T.C.: Yeah, that's right. I've got my sights set on World Wide Wrestling's heavyweight championship…and you better believe it!

M.J.: Amazing! Doctor John Burnham, I may need a referral to an audiologist, because I couldn't *possibly* have heard that correctly! Tommy Carpenter, the young man from Lowell, Massachusetts, after besting the Dark Continent's most famous warrior in an entirely one-sided bout, went on to shame him, absolutely shame him, with a scathing lecture! What a spectacle! What a show! Let me tell you, ladies and gentlemen, I feel privileged—privileged!—to have shared this experience here with you tonight, live, on *Monday Night Titans*!

J.B.: For once in my life, Michael Jones, I'm a hundred percent in agreement with you! Tommy Carpenter—what an athlete! This young man's career might have started on the loading docks, but he's working on an entirely different level now. Diligently climbing the ladder, pulling off a pair of victories—and what, I dare say, might just be two of the most *shocking* upsets in the history of World Wide Wrestling! All you folks watching at home, I hope you were paying close attention, because what we've just witnessed should serve as proof—irrefutable proof—that the American Dream is alive and well! Remember the name, wrestling fans, and remember it well…"The American Dream," Tommy Carpenter…or maybe it's "Boxcutter Tommy" to his enemies, of which there will be no shortage! Whatever we're calling the man, one thing's for certain: you'll be hearing much, much more from him in the very near future. I guarantee it!

M.J.: Don't go anywhere, folks. We've got so much more action still to come here in Dallas, Texas! We'll be right back!

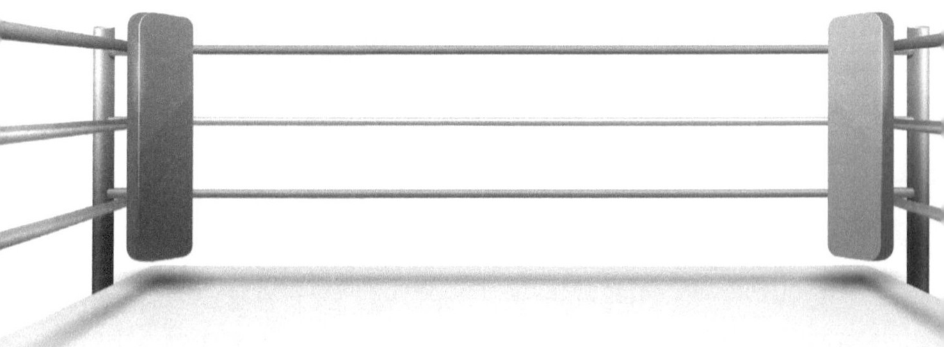

"I'M JUST STILL NOT SURE I BELIEVE IT. THAT I *CAN* BELIEVE IT. AT LEAST, not all of it."

That afternoon was a cold one. One of those days where it seemed like spring might never come, with the constant chilly drafts somehow seeping their way in past all that pink fiberglass insulation in the attic, and even the double-paned windows downstairs. That afternoon, Burton was off somewhere with Aunt Emmy, so it was just the two of us again.

Burton and me.

Kicked back in the living room, like always. He had the remote, so of course there was a rap video playing on the big screen. Me, I was doing my best not to let the music bother me, with my pre-Algebra textbook open in my lap, making a weak effort to catch up on some overdue assignments.

Burton sat there staring at the television for a couple long minutes. His eyes flickered along with the video as it cut back and forth between shots, mouthing the words to some Public Enemy song. Not that I followed those guys, mind you—but after hanging around with my stepbrother for so long, even *I* could recognize Flavor Flav, that goofy guy who always wore a top hat and sunglasses with a giant clock around his neck.

Burton seemed to be focused on the music, and it wasn't until MTV cut to a commercial for Fruitopia that he bothered to answer me.

"Well, it is what it is, I guess. And really, does it even *matter* whether you believe me or not? For this to work, I mean?" He uncrossed his legs, stretched them out straight, then tucked them back up into the exact same position. "After all, there's nothing wrong with a little skepticism, with not accepting every last thing you hear on pure faith alone."

I scrunched my face up into a scowl. "So, like, you're not going to get all offended if I ask a few more questions? You know, before I jump headfirst into all…this?"

He pondered my request. "Yeah, I guess that'd be okay. You should always ask questions, when you're trying to get to the root of a problem. I mean, that's the basis for the whole scientific method."

I saw my window of opportunity crack open, so I pressed on ahead. "Cool. So if you really *are* from the future and everything, then shouldn't you, like, be able to prove it?"

"Careful now…"

"Well, you've got to be able to tell me *something* about the world after 1993. Anything."

Burton scratched at his stubbly chin. "Do you really think it'd be wise?"

I crossed my arms up over my chest, slouching back against the cushions. "Thought so. After all that hype, and all that build-up. Turns out, you're nothing but a liar."

Sure, it was a cruel taunt, but I needed to shake him up a little. He glanced my way for the briefest of seconds, and I saw that the jab had struck home.

"Just because a person *chooses* not to do something," he began, his voice calm and collected, "you should never infer that they can't. It's called discipline. Self-control. A trait *you* obviously know nothing about." Burton twisted up that freckled nose of his and turned back towards the television set.

By that point, I had absolutely no clue what to say in response. I just stuck out my tongue instead.

He sighed, reaching for the remote control and squeezing the mute button, signaling that whatever he was going to say next would be important. I knew how much it pained that dude to silence *Yo! MTV Raps*.

"Thank you, once again, for proving my point. Self-restraint is the primary characteristic which distinguishes grown-ups from kids. It's the very essence of civilized society. Children act impulsively—they do what they want, when they want, without stopping to consider the consequences of their actions. Adults, on the other hand, are expected to make more responsible decisions." He tilted his head back, adding "And most of the time, we actually do."

I gave his words a split second's worth of consideration. "So, what? Are you saying there's, like, some kind of code of ethics with time travel?"

He shrugged.

I'd already learned how to follow my stepbrother's words. The guy hadn't bothered answering my question, but more importantly, he hadn't actually said no.

"Okay, so how about this? Just a hypothetical case. Let's say, for example, that I'd booked an airline ticket, right? Going to Paris, or maybe London. Wherever. But somehow, because you came from the future, you already knew the flight would encounter, I don't know, engine trouble or something. A mechanical problem that would cause the plane to crash into the Atlantic Ocean and kill everyone on board. Would you still keep quiet? Could you actually just do nothing, knowing full well that if I took that flight, I wouldn't survive?"

Burton dismissed the idea so quickly, it was impossible for me to tell whether he'd even considered it. "That's a ridiculous example," he snapped. "You don't even have a passport! There's no way the airline would let you board."

I'd had enough of his attitude, and chucked a throw pillow towards his head. The impact was far too soft to hurt, but I got a small measure of satisfaction from knocking those skinny headphones askew. "You know what I'm trying to say, dickweed! What, is there some kind of law against revealing the future? Would you, like, get arrested by the Time Police? And how would they even know?"

He scratched his chin again, in that irritating tic of his. "Hard to say, really. That kind of behavior isn't *technically* illegal, I guess. Or at least, it isn't illegal yet."

"Not yet, as in, it's not currently illegal?"

"Correct."

"Like, right now in 1993, or in the future?"

"Both. Although, that would make for a fascinating legal question, wouldn't it? How could a court of law ever establish jurisdiction over crimes caused by time travel? Say for example, a person went back in time and committed a robbery. Assuming they got caught, in which year might they stand trial? In the time they first came from or in the era when they committed the crime?"

I was lost, but I tried not to show it.

"After all," he went on, "this hypothetical criminal could have very well come from a completely different century! Would a future judge consider it 'cruel and unusual punishment' to put a defendant's fate in the hands of an antiquated legal system? It's an interesting dilemma, for sure."

I figured my best course of action was to just stay silent and keep nodding along. With any luck, I'd be able to jump back into the conversation at some point.

"Although, you know, it *does* seem like the government always lags behind when it comes to technological advancement. And it's the same way for ethics. Mankind has a long and recorded history of racing forward and doing bold new things without ever bothering to stop and ask whether or not we *should* be doing them. But to actually give you a definite answer, no, I don't believe there are any established laws regarding time travel. Not yet."

I saw my opportunity and went for it. "So…there's no laws against revealing the future?"

"Well, no. Not technically. But the consequences…"

"Cool! So, spill it already; tell me something about the future. Anything. I'm not picky."

Burton went silent. His hesitation was a sure sign that I'd scored a point with a mostly logical argument.

"Do you honestly want me to?" he eventually answered. "I mean, I don't want to take away any of the surprise."

I snorted.

"Okay, then," he finally sighed. "It's your funeral. But, how about this: what would you say to a compromise?"

"I'm listening."

"I'd feel a lot better about this whole thing if I just shared a couple 'predictions' about life in the future which may—or may not—come to pass. That way, you won't know for certain which of them is true…although, I promise, at least one of these scenarios will be."

The offer sounded sincere. It wasn't quite what I'd asked for, but still, it was better than nothing. Far more than I'd ever been able to get out of him before, so it counted as progress.

"Do you promise?"

"Promise." Burton raised his right hand like he was swearing a solemn vow. "Hand to God, sis."

"Okay, then. It's a deal."

"Okay." His eyes roamed across the room, eventually coming to rest on the pile of junk mail stacked up on Dad's brown leather Barcalounger. "First: in the future—not very far off from now, actually—nearly every single person in America will own a cellular telephone."

"A car phone? Or do you mean, like, one of those big Wall Street jobs, where the handset cord hangs down and plugs into a briefcase?"

"The latter. But see, these phones will be much more advanced, and so small you can carry them around like a pocket calculator! Cellular technology is going to grow by leaps and bounds, and it will revolutionize the way humans communicate."

I raised a hand to my mouth, doing my best to stifle a yawn. "Okay, so I guess everyone who went all in on a Skytel pager is going to be out a few hundred bucks. What else you got?"

He held up a thin hand. "But wait, sis. Check this out. Those mobile phones will become so advanced that eventually, you'll be carrying more computing power in the palm of your hand than in an entire 486 desktop processor! In fact, in the next decade or so, everyday Americans will have access to more technology than NASA used to pull off the moon landings."

I rolled my shoulders, stretching my back to its full extension as I imagined the possibilities. "Man. If that's the true one, then I bet all those big Internet companies—Compuserve, Prodigy, America Online, and them—they must be worth *billions* in your time! Okay, yeah, I guess I can see how that might be pretty important. So what's the next one? Tell me you guys don't have flying cars already?"

"Not yet, but I imagine someone's got to be working on it. Although soon, a few big companies will begin developing the technology to power the first generation of self-driving cars."

"No way!" I shook my head in disbelief. "How could something like that even be *possible*?"

"Advances in computing technology is all. Without getting too technical, these full-sized vehicles will be operated by remote control, pre-programmed to drive along digitally mapped routes at fixed speeds. They'll even be equipped with cameras and sensors to make sure they don't hit anything."

The information dump was just too much for me to handle. For the first time in weeks—maybe even months—that big dark cloud hanging over my heart felt like it was actually starting to clear. My shoulders felt lighter, almost, as this strange new sense of optimism crept through my body. For the very first time since Burton started coming around, I actually began to believe that in the future, anything really would be possible.

Now, if only I could make it there to see it.

By that point in our relationship, I simply couldn't dismiss either of Burton's 'predictions' outright. They were as close to proof as I was likely to get, and besides, if the future really *was* going to play out the way he described, our world would be an amazing place to live.

I stretched my legs out straight, flexing my toes and wriggling them around in the warm raglan socks Samantha had given me for Christmas. That lady might never be my real mother, but even I had to admit, she had decent taste in clothes.

"Wow. I mean, just...wow! If that's true, it sounds awesome! But enough of this technological crap—give me something cool. Like, what do you guys watch on television? Don't tell me Steve Urkel's still around in your time, acting all nerdy and wearing those same suspenders when he's, like, sixty years old?"

For the briefest of seconds, I thought I spotted a faint hint of a smile flash across Burton's face. "Not quite. But I think you'll like this one." He nodded towards the projection screen, which was still showing a garbage rap video. "You still haven't gained an appreciation for hip-hop, huh?"

"No, but let me guess. Soon, everyone will realize that it's nothing but crap? Rap music will disappear from the radio entirely, fading away just as quickly as it came?"

He snorted. "Just the opposite. All those rappers are modern-day poets! They're the Shakespeares, the Shelleys, and the Keateses of your generation. It still kind of blows my mind that you can't appreciate their art."

I shook my head, mystified by Burton's odd taste in music.

"In my era," he went on, "people have come to recognize the massive impact that hip-hop has had on our culture, on our society. Even our politics. It's a style of music that's entirely American, and so the pioneers of the genre, MCs like Melle Mel or Grandmaster Flash—"

"Who?"

Burton shook his head. "Sorry, I keep forgetting they're not teaching this stuff in schools yet. You *have* heard of Tupac Shakur, haven't you? Or Christopher Wallace, better known as the Notorious B.I.G.?"

Both of those names sounded vaguely familiar. "I'm pretty sure you've made me sit through their videos at least once."

"And you're welcome for that. See, when those guys spit lyrics, they aren't just making music. They're speaking out against social injustice, and just wait. Right now you might think that rap music is a fad, but pretty soon you'll be hearing it everywhere."

The claim sounded so wild, I suspected Burton must've just made that one up. I raised an eyebrow in his direction. "What in the hell could anybody possibly take away from garbage like gangster rap?"

"Listen, Sis. Don't be so quick to reject these ideas—or at least, don't blow them off just because you don't understand them. Modern rap music, as much as you personally might not care for it, will go on to become the defining sound of your generation."

I shrugged, anxious to change the topic. "Whatever you say, man. But if rap music really *does* become that popular, then it sounds like the future still has a lot of issues to work through."

"Yeah, you're one to talk about issues." Burton shivered, almost like he'd caught a sudden chill. "But for real, it's *not* all sunshine and roses out there. The world will probably always be working through some kind of problems. Big ones, things you couldn't even begin to conceptualize."

"Okay…"

Burton took a deep breath. "You remember the World Trade Center bombing, right? You might have seen it on the nightly news, back in February."

I thought hard, trying to remember the details. I'd never really paid much attention to the news, and besides, those few weeks of my life were shrouded in a dense fog of memory. "Vaguely. Some camel jockey drove a truck bomb down into the basement, right?"

Burton frowned at the slur. "The terrorist was from Pakistan, and I'm not sure camels are native to that region, but in any case, yeah, he *was* driving a rental truck loaded with high explosives. Parked it in the underground garage, directly beneath the North Tower. The guy was trying to blast the building off its foundation and topple it into the South Tower to bring that building down, too."

I shuddered.

Burton sniffed and tilted his head to one side. "And the dude might've been able to do it, if only he'd parked a few meters closer to one of the load-bearing pillars. There were over thirteen hundred pounds of urea-nitrate explosive packed into that cargo truck, did you know that? A mess of booster charges, too, all of it lined with poisonous chemicals. Sodium cyanide."

I let out a low whistle.

"Yup. Dozens of people were hospitalized for smoke

inhalation that day, but only six of them died. Six. Given the scale and the sophistication of the attack, that's nothing short of a miracle. It's unbelievable."

I didn't know what to say.

Burton paused, leaving me with another long moment of silence before he piped up again. "But here's the thing, sis. This won't be the last time a terrorist attack occurs at the World Trade Center. In fact, this same group of people is going to target the complex a second time."

I felt my body tense up. "You're shitting me! Pakistan's going to declare war on America? Really? Didn't those idiots see what we just did to Iraq? Operation Desert Storm lasted, what, five days? Six? Hell, if any country ever tried to cross the USA, we'd bomb those morons back to the Stone Age!"

He shook his head. "Not the government of Pakistan, but members of the same transnational terrorist organization. See, one thing you need to know is, despite all our technological advances, mankind will still maintain the unique ability to inflict violence on our own species. So yeah, anyway. When the FBI and the cops finally catch up with the 1993 bomber—when he's arrested and brought back to New York to stand trial—at his sentencing hearing, he'll tell the court that this attack is only the beginning."

"What!"

"And, sure enough, the day's going to come when a group of these same terrorists manages to pull off a much bigger attack. A more coordinated one, where they hijack a couple commercial airliners at the same time."

A chill ran down my bare arms. "Wow…so, what happened? Or, I mean, what's going to happen? Or like, what *might* happen, if it turns out this prediction is the true one?"

He paused. "Are you sure you want to know?"

"No. I'm not sure I *want* to know. But I think I have to."

"Okay. So the thing about this particular hijacking is, well, it's different. Instead of simply stealing the planes and holding the passengers for ransom, these terrorists aren't interested in money. They're militant followers of the Islamic faith. True believers, convinced they'll be rewarded with eternal paradise after death."

"Whoa."

"And so what they'll do is, they'll plan this attack for months. Even sending a few of their team to the US ahead of time to take lessons at a flight school. And the first couple planes, right after these terrorists seize control of the flight deck, they'll get turned around and flown into both of the World Trade Center towers. On a bright, clear, Tuesday morning, there'll be a pair of big fiery explosions way up high on the sides of these skyscrapers, only about twenty minutes apart. Those two big jet airliners will be fully loaded for cross-country flights, so all that fuel will explode on impact, causing massive fires."

"Shit! So, they're going to burn down the World Trade Center?"

"No, not exactly. See, jet fuel can't melt steel beams. All that gas will burn up long before the building's metal support trusses reach their melting point, but such sweltering heat *will* cause the beams to lose their structural integrity. Before long, those skyscrapers will fall in on themselves in a total, catastrophic collapse."

I shuddered at the horrible images that were playing out in my mind.

"All the passengers and crew will be killed, obviously. A couple thousand other New Yorkers will perish from falling debris and smoke inhalation and whatnot. But that's not all: another hijacked plane will head for Washington, targeting the Pentagon. And just before the government shuts down our airspace, one last plane will crash down in rural Pennsylvania. From that day forward, the bad guys behind all this will use Nine Ele—"

Burton swallowed hard, then took a deep breath to compose himself before going on.

"They'll use this attack as a rallying cry. A recruiting tool, almost. The United States will go on to declare war on this group and all their supporters, anywhere they might be around the world. The conflict will grow exponentially, enduring for decades and re-shaping the global balance of power."

My body shuddered once more, and I pulled that cable knit sweater tight around my shoulders. Burton's last prediction was simply too terrifying for me to dwell on it, which is how I knew it *had* to be the one he'd made up.

We turned our attention back towards the television, me doing my best to block out those mindless rap videos—

along with everything he'd told me—and him mouthing the lyrics, trying to forget that he'd said any of it.

And I guess that's when I realized that Burton was probably right.

Whatever the future had in store for me—for any of us—we were probably all just better off if we didn't know what was coming.

MONDAY, APRIL 12, 1993

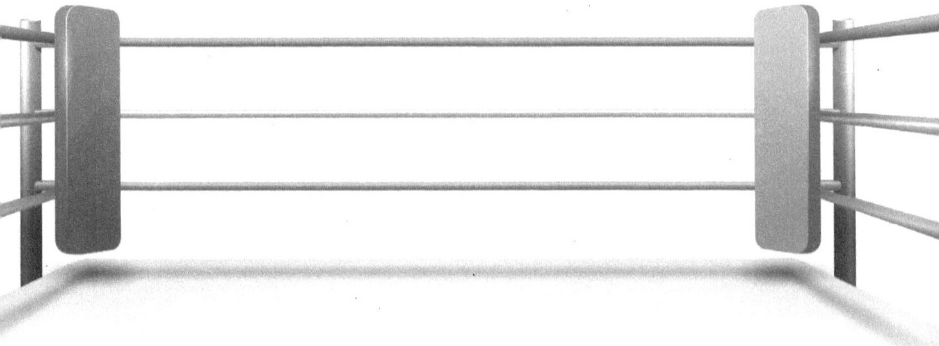

Excerpt from "Monday Night Titans" *broadcast*
Transcription by Burton Carpenter

Dr. John Burnham: Welcome back to "America's Showplace," the fabulous Philadelphia Spectrum, here in the heart and soul of the Keystone State! Ladies and gentlemen, judging by the sound of this capacity crowd, all 18,000 wrestling fans plus a few hundred more who seem to have snuck past security, the City of Brotherly Love has abandoned all of its fraternal spirit tonight! Now, I'm here with The Syndicate's self-designated spokesman, *Mister* Hector Lamas, better known as El Diablo, to get his thoughts on the challenge put forth by The American Dream, Tommy Carpenter, that was broadcast live, right here, on *Monday Night Titans*! El Diablo, could we trouble you—

El Diablo: Gimme 'dat microphone!

J.B.: Uh…it's all yours.

E.D.: Shut up! And 'dat goes for all you ee'jits, too, 'joo heard? Shut up! Shut up! 'Coz El Diablo gots something he wan' say! Now, El Diablo come here tonight—

[Speech interrupted by crowd noise. Approx. 10-second delay.]

J.B.: Wow! What a response!

E.D.: Shut up! Whassa matter, 'joo rednecks cain't un'nerstan' English? Ay, I shoulda never swam crost 'dat Rio Grande! But the on'ly reason I did come *norte*, and the on'ly reason I steel here wid' no green card, is to prove El Diablo th' best damn wrestler in the whole damn world! 'Joo heard? And so when I fin'ly do head back home, it's gon' be with' 'dat heavyweight champe'enship belt wrapped roun' my waist. That's why I link up wit' The Syndicate, see. 'Dem boys promise they gon' get me there, one way or 'nother. And lemme tell 'joo somethin', mayn! Ain't no one, 'specially not no *gringo* like Tommy Carpenter, gon' stand in my way!

[Speech interrupted once more. Crowd chants "Tommy" repeatedly.]

J.B.: Well, since you brought him up, let's talk about Tommy Carpenter, The American Dream! El Diablo, would you not agree, this man has been absolutely on fire as of late? Following his most recent, and most controversial match, where he squared off against your fellow Syndicate teammate—

E.D.: Kil'manjaro? Naw, man! Uh-uh. He ain' wid' us no more.

J.B.: What? El Diablo, did I hear you correctly? Kilimanjaro, a legend among legends in the storied annals of World Wide Wrestling—the man who shocked the world just a few months ago by turning his back on his fans and joining The Syndicate—is now, all of a sudden, no longer welcome in your crew?

E.D.: We kicked 'dat fool out. He embarrass' us, straight up, mayn.

J.B.: And what about Tommy Carpenter? Your thoughts? I would venture a guess that even you, El Diablo, would have to be impressed by Carpenter's recent turnaround! First, he ended the Tennessee Mule's career, an impressive feat in its own right. But besting the dark mountain, Kilimanjaro? And after the big man so blatantly cheated? No, that performance was superhuman, there's simply no other way to describe it!

E.D.: Mayn, I din't come here to talk 'bout da past. Wha's done 'ees done. Nah, I came here to tell you what's gon' happen next. Carpenter, you out there, *gringo*?

J.B.: Oh, I'm sure he's watching tonight, El Diablo! Along with all of us here in Philadelphia, plus the millions of fans tuned in at home!

E.D.: Tha's good, Jefe John. Tha's real good, 'coz I gots somethin' to say. Carpenter, 'joo think 'joo got what it takes to wrap that champe'enship belt 'round your waist? Well, be careful what 'joo wish for, homie! 'Coz me and The Syndicate, we been talkin' it over, see? And we decided, you gon' get that shot.

[Crowd erupts. Approx. 15-second delay.]

J.B.: What? El Diablo! Do you really mean—

E.D.: 'Joo shut yer mouth! I'm still talkin'! Carpenter, mayn. 'Joo want a chance to rip that belt away from us, you gon' have to earn it. See, way it works 'round Worl' Wide Wrestling is, 'joo want a shot, 'joo get in line, wait your turn. Now, Jefe John. 'Joo and e'erybody else, we all know the next man up s'pose to be Johnny Forbes. Right?

J.B.: Of course! Boston's millionaire playboy, the Baron of Beacon Hill! Fans, for the benefit of anyone who might not know this, both Forbes and Carpenter are sons of the Bay State, although their upbringings couldn't have *been* any more different! Carpenter's a man who's paved his own road, working with no more than raw muscle and sheer determination. Forbes, on the other hand, has only had to stroll along a well-established path to success, greasing his wheels with an endless swath of hundred-dollar bills!

E.D.: Forbes! He a good kid, 'joo know? And 'coz he been so patient, he gon' get his shot, too. 'Coz me and the boys decided, right? We gots to be fair 'bout this. Forbes think he wan'na title shot, but now Carpenter say he do, too? So, what we gon' do, Jefe John, is we gon' let these two *gringos* fight it out.

[Massive applause.]

E.D.: Like I said, tha's fair. Next month, live, e'erbody gon' see. Winner gon' get a blank check to challenge the heavyweight champ, an'ytime, an'yplace!

[Crowd noise. Dialogue inaudible for approx. 10 seconds. El Diablo exits the stage.]

J.B.: El Diablo, wait! I still need to ask you about—holy moley! Ladies and gentlemen, for all of you watching at home, I sure hope you didn't pick the wrong time to run to the bathroom just now! Wow! I can't believe it—El Diablo just threw down the gauntlet for Tommy Carpenter! What a huge opportunity for those two men, Carpenter and Forbes…though, if the prize for winning the Blank Check match is a date with The Syndicate, I'm not so sure I'd *want*

to come out on the winning end! Don't go anywhere, folks…
we'll be back in just a moment from historic Philadelphia,
where the fireworks are only getting started here on *Monday
Night Titans*!

IT WAS RAINING.

That might not have been the main reason I'd been struck by a relapse of truancy, sneaking off from school again during our lunch break, but it definitely helped. I can't remember what triggered me—maybe it was the thought of having to choke down those God-awful tater tots, I don't know. I definitely wasn't sick—didn't even bother trying to fake it. In fact, I was feeling better than I had in ages. I mean, I'd dropped into the Li'l Peach store on the way home to grab a Snapple and hadn't bothered trying to shoplift any Bartles & Jaymes wine coolers. Like, it hadn't even occurred to me to boost them.

I slipped into the house just as quietly as I could manage. Tiptoeing past the kitchen where Aunt Emmy was simultaneously microwaving her lunch, watching telenovelas on Univision, and jabbering away on the cordless phone. She was speaking rapid-fire Spanish, so I assumed she was talking to my Uncle Hector. Running up our long distance bill, like always.

And when I made it upstairs, of course Burton was already there in my room, waiting for me. It was almost as if he'd known I was going to cut class, like he'd somehow managed to find a copy of my attendance record or something. Both of my stepbrothers were snuggled up next to each other in my beanbag chair, shuffling their way through a tall stack of VHS tapes.

Our Dad's earliest matches.

I slid down onto the floor beside them, not bothering to say hello. Leaning my head back against a pillow, I did my best to ignore the match playing on my small screen. I'd seen that one at least a couple dozen times—the very first from ringside, at the Worcester Palladium.

Yeah, that'd been a good night.

Dad had been listed squarely in the middle of the card—a temporary push, so he could do the job and help put over a fresh young babyface, Chris "The Claw" Lawson. But it was almost awkward now, having to watch my Dad get himself tossed around the ring, when I knew full well what he was capable of. I did my best to ignore the expert way he sold each of Lawson's blows, trying to focus in on the crowd instead.

The sweeping camera never quite found me, even though the production team kept the focus on the lower levels to avoid showing all those empty seats. Back in the day, my Dad's matches—even the hometown ones—were a good time for the fans to visit the restrooms or hit up the beer stands.

Both men were locked in a rest hold in the center of the ring, standing each other upright in a tight clinch. The close, prolonged grip was a way to make the fans believe they were stuck in an intense struggle, when in reality they were just catching their breath and talking through the next sequence of moves.

I used the same strategy, taking advantage of the lull in the action to grill Burton.

"You know, what I still can't process is *how* you actually managed to come back here. Like, you claim that you can travel through time, and that you can do it using only the power of your own thoughts. And apparently, you can go back and forth without too much trouble."

He stood up, stretching his arms high overhead before getting down into a prone position on the floor. His younger version followed suit, lying parallel next to him on the carpet. Burton reached into the pocket of his stonewashed Bugle Boy jeans, coming back up with a bright orange Matchbox car. He rolled the IROC-Z back and forth in front of his younger self, and I watched as the kid's bright blue eyes followed the vehicle with a fixed concentration, a rare smile growing across his freckled face. The two of them went on that way for a full minute, the repetitive behavior never seeming to grow old.

Just the opposite, really.

And when Burton started to pause for a second at the end of each run, his smaller twin actually began giggling with anticipation of the next round.

Eventually, Burton gave up and passed himself the car, rolling onto his back to signal that the game was over. "That's right."

He was looking up towards the ceiling now, almost as if he was addressing it instead of me.

"We all know the human brain is the greatest machine ever invented. Why would I bother using an inferior piece of equipment?"

I gave his statement a moment of consideration, even stretching out flat myself and staring up at the ceiling to mimic him. "All you need is your brain, huh? I know I've said this before, but it just sounds too much like you're making everything up. Like this is all in your head, and in *my* head somehow."

Burton still couldn't be bothered to make eye contact. "That's putting it awful simply, don't you think?" He exhaled with a loud, deep sigh. "But yeah, I guess you might not be too far off the mark."

"So, you admit it! You're not even *here*?" I pounded a fist against the carpet in frustration as my heart pumped faster, that old familiar rage welling up in the back of my throat. It was all I could do to spit out the next sentence without choking on my thick sarcasm. "What a relief, huh? Turns out, all this has just been my imagination."

Burton shrugged, lifting his shoulders with a casual air of indifference. "Who knows? Maybe we're both just imagining this, the two of us. Yeah, I guess that *could* be possible. But what's *real*, anyway? What does *reality* even mean?"

"Ugh! What the fuck are you even talking about right now?"

"Have you ever imagined the possibility that maybe all of us, along with every last, minute detail of our daily lives, could just be a series of tiny and inconsequential figments in the vast realm of some God's infinite imagination?"

I bit my lip.

"And that maybe, if He should ever turn His thoughts to more weighty matters than our piddling little lives, this entire world of ours—and every last thing we perceive as *real*—could just, all of a sudden, up and cease to exist? I mean, if you're claiming that *I* might not really be here, shouldn't we at least examine the possibility that we're *all* nothing more than make-believe?"

I stayed silent, unsure of what I could possibly say in reply.

Burton reached over and mussed his younger self's hair, then sat upright and waved a thin arm towards the TV. "Okay, then. Let me show you another way of looking at it."

"Okay…"

"Both you and I watch wrestling, right? We never miss a Monday night broadcast. And then there's all the pay-per-view events and the recap shows on the weekends. I know for a fact that I've seen all Dad's fights now. Even the dark matches, the ones he never got around to transferring off of these VHS tapes. And as much as you might try to deny it, I'm certain you have too."

It was true, so I nodded. "All of them."

"But the thing is," he went on, "the two of us, we're not exactly a couple of marks. You know? We understand the business of World Wide Wrestling and how the company *really* works, so let me ask you: do you consider professional wrestling to be real, or is it all fake? Just a bunch of make believe?"

A chill ran up my spine at the unexpected turn in the conversation. His question was the only one I'd never been allowed to ask at home, the electrified third rail of any family discussion. It'd always been forbidden to dig too deep into my Dad's work, but suddenly, Burton had come right out and said the unthinkable.

Just like that.

I found myself at a complete loss for words, struggling to block out the doubts he'd raised.

Faced with my silence, Burton had no choice but to continue. "I mean, your entire life, every other kid at school has told you that professional wrestling isn't real. Am I right? That all the blows, the holds—they're all fake. That the sport is designed so the moves look like they hurt, while not actually inflicting any damage."

As always, Burton was right. I'd heard it all before.

"And what about the fact that these matches are predetermined? Huh? That the winners are chosen in advance? Now, I know good and well that you still read the industry dirt sheets—how can you possibly reconcile the fact that all these wrestlers hang out together during their downtime? The faces *and* the heels, they all go out drinking together, no matter who's supposed to have heat with who!"

Again, with the logic. But by that point in the conversation, staying silent seemed like my only real option.

"All right, then. So, to my point: if wrestling really *is* fake, and if you and I and everybody else already *knows* that, then why in the world do we spend so much time watching it?"

I still couldn't think of anything to say, so I just sat there stewing as Burton's words hung awkwardly in the air. Dozens of unrelated thoughts swirled around in my mind, and I found myself raising a hand towards the ceiling, unconsciously imitating my stepbrother's habit of reaching out and brushing up against random objects. I did my best to imagine that my arm was longer, long enough to touch the ceiling, and how the plaster might feel against my fingertips. My right arm wavered back and forth as my shoulder tired, with my hand wobbling from side to side, almost like it was working to sift through Burton's ponderous thoughts.

"Exactly," he finally concluded, once he'd sensed that I'd abandoned the discussion. "You watch it because you enjoy it, simple as that. You're drawn to the story, even though you know it's scripted—although deep down inside, even *you* probably still believe some of the kayfabe. Or at least, you *want* to believe. So, in that sense, you and I are absolutely no different from any of the other marks out there who're tuning in each and every week."

He craned his neck at the television, dismissing it with a loose wave.

"It's all fake, sure. But you're still watching it, so how fake could it be? And let's take this discussion a step further, okay? So, let's just say that your suspicions are correct and that *I'm* not real, either. Yeah, I'm completely made up." Burton let his arm hang for a long moment before he rested it across his younger self's shoulders. "And yet, here I am."

I stared at the two of them, unable to look away. My stepbrother, the kid who normally recoiled from another person's touch, just lay there on the carpet, rolling his toy car along on its imaginary dragstrip, looking more relaxed than I'd ever seen him.

"No, here *we* are. All of us. With you, in your own home, in the spring of 1993. So, tell me something: what exactly about this afternoon still doesn't feel real to you? Sure, this friendship of ours might be a little…unusual, but it's been this way for weeks now. Months, even. So, why is it still so hard for you to accept?"

When I refused to respond, Burton went quiet himself. He left his question hanging there for a full minute, probably hoping I'd turn my head his way.

But I just couldn't bring myself to make eye contact.

Finally, he let loose with a loud sigh of frustration. "I don't get it! If you're willing to consider the possibility that professional wrestling could be real—or at least, to believe in it enough to follow the sport—then why's it so hard for you to do the same with me? Why can't you at least *imagine* that I'm real and that what I've been telling you is the truth?"

EVERY TIME I THINK BACK ON THAT NEXT MONDAY, IT'S ALWAYS A little blurry, though I do remember one moment clearly. It was Patriots' Day—this local holiday where the state of Massachusetts shuts down for some reason or other, even as the rest of the country went on about its business as usual. I was sitting there in my Dad's recliner, legs thrown up sideways over the armrest, still wearing my flannel pajamas in the middle of the morning. My Earth Science and Pre-Algebra textbooks both lay open on my lap, neither one of them looking particularly interesting. I was glancing back and forth between them, wondering which of them I should dive into first, when my half-hearted attempt at studying was interrupted by a gentle tug on my sleeve.

Burton stood there beside me, dressed in his favorite pair of boxer briefs. I noticed his expression immediately, that normally impassive face showing an obvious look of concern. Holding a green apple in his left hand, the kid raised it towards the big projection television to draw my attention.

There on the screen, where the Boston Marathon had been broadcasting live just a few seconds ago, was a fiery scene of destruction. The sound was muted, but I swear, those images were so powerful that they told the story all on their own.

The dateline below read "Waco, Texas," so I knew the network was broadcasting live. They had to have been, if they'd interrupted the race. I couldn't quite tell what was happening, but it looked like some kind of tank was driving back and forth near a walled-off compound, with the low-slung buildings engulfed in a swirl of flames.

I looked back at Burton and that obvious look of distress on his face. It was almost creepy, as if the kid was trying to tell me something.

Trying to warn me about something.

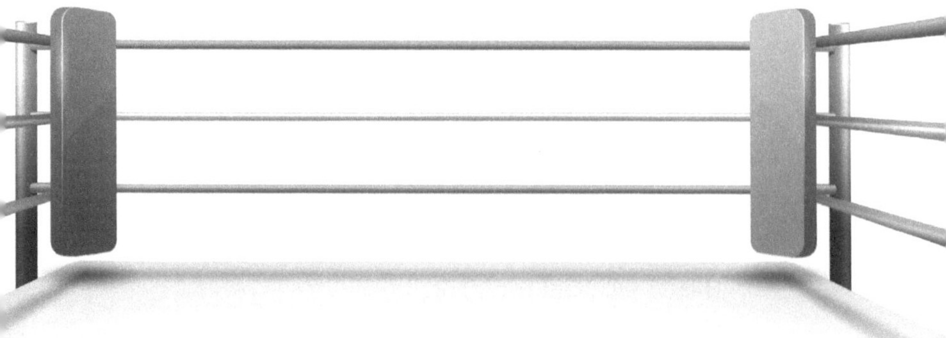

IT WAS ONE OF THOSE RARE NIGHTS WHEN BURTON HADN'T SHOWED up. That was strange in its own right, but the fact that he'd left me to watch *Monday Night Titans* on my own?

Well, that was just plain odd.

Aunt Emmy had taken Burton with her when she'd gone out, so it was just me at home, staring at the walls and doing my damnedest to plow through a big pile of homework.

While the television warmed up, my mind drifted along through the events of the past few months. The audio kicked on, and it sounded like Michael Jones and "Doctor" John Burnham were still in their pre-fight coverage, so I dashed into the kitchen to grab a can of Crystal Pepsi.

Of course I knew that World Wide Wrestling was a fantasy world.

Nothing more than an escape. But hey, at least it was a consistent one.

The moves, the holds, all of them so familiar to me. Hell, even those cheesy plot lines never failed to suck me in, the tired old works that the Creative team seemed to keep recycling every few years. In truth, professional wrestling was the broadcast version of a hot bowl of Kraft macaroni and cheese. Hardly a perfect meal, and with zero nutritional value, but you could always count on it to fill you up and leave you satisfied. So, even though I knew good and well that the acting, the kayfabe, and everything else was just for show, Burton had been right.

There I was, still tuning in.

And it wasn't just me, either. A couple million other fans were watching, too.

A sudden burst of inspiration hit me, and I reached for the cordless phone. When I dialed my Dad's Skypager and punched in our home number, it only took a minute before the handset began beeping. When I picked up, the commotion of the dressing room was evident in the background.

"Hey, Bear!" my Dad shouted above the din. "Is something wrong?"

I smiled. The sound of my father's voice was nearly as comforting as his actual presence, and a warm feeling began to spread over my body. "Hi, Daddy! No, I'm fine. Everything's fine. I just wanted to call and wish you good luck." I swallowed. "No, wait. That's not entirely true. I mean, yes, good luck and all, but there *is* something I've been meaning to ask you, and…well, it can't wait any longer."

"Well then, don't hold back. You know you can always ask me anything, Bear. Fire away."

I swallowed again, choking back my fear and bracing myself for the difficult conversation ahead. "Thanks Daddy, but this one is kind of hard to ask. What I really need to know is…is wrestling real? Or is it all, like, you know. Fake?"

A long, empty pause came over the line. The silence made it impossible for me to guess at what my Dad could've been thinking.

I mean, I'd expected a yell, or at least some kind of rebuke. Hell, if he'd been there in person, there was a good chance my Daddy might've just slapped me straight across the jaw, or maybe sunk me into one of his killer headlocks. But as it turned out, the icy chill that followed was just as painful.

Worse, maybe.

When my Dad finally did answer, his voice had dropped down to a low, serious tone. His words echoed across the staticky line, making the man sound more disappointed than angry. "Why are you asking me this, Bear? And why now, of all times? Don't tell me those punks at JFK have been bothering you again? Fucking Lowell, I swear! That town will never change. I should've sprung for private school a long time ago."

I stood up and began pacing about the room, allowing my gaze to wander, hoping that the movement might somehow help me hold back the tears that were building up behind my eyelids. "No, Daddy. It's not that. Lately, I've just been…thinking. About stuff, you know? About everything. Like, about how it was before Mom died, and then about how Samantha's become a real part of our family this year. And how through all of that, you've stayed so dedicated to your work. So committed. I mean, you've been wrestling my entire life, you know? That's the way it's always been, so I guess I've just never really questioned it."

Over on the bookshelf, one photograph in particular caught my eye. I walked across the room for a closer look, lifting it gently out from between a half-dozen other picture frames. It was an old shot, a grainy color four-by-six of my Dad. The man was grinning with pride as he held me, this tiny little swaddle of a baby, neatly up inside of his massive bicep. My Dad looked young, in his twenties, leaning casually back against the ring ropes. The handwritten cursive scrawl across the bottom of the photo read "Hampton Beach Casino Ballroom, 1980."

A shiver raced up my spine as I read the words. I swear, for a fraction of a second there, it felt almost as if I'd been transported back in time to a moment I was too young to remember.

I swallowed. "It's just that—well—everybody always says that wrestling's fake. The other kids don't tease me about it much—or, at least, not nearly as much as they used to. But I want you to know, even through all that harassment, through all the bullying, I've never doubted you. Not once. As hard as it's been sometimes, I've never questioned your work, but now, I guess—I don't know. I guess I just need to hear *you* say it."

My Dad didn't answer right away, so I rushed on before he could duck the question. I didn't have time to think about what I was asking, or to consider the consequences.

The words were rushing out of my mouth faster than I could stop them.

"And I promise, Daddy. This is the only time I'll ask you. Ever! Cross my heart, swear to God, all that. And no matter what you say, I'm going to believe it, just so long as you promise to tell me the truth."

I took a deep breath, giving my plea a few seconds to sink in.

"So what do you say, Daddy?" I finally asked. "Do you promise?"

After a long, uncomfortable pause, he finally spoke up. "I know I haven't been a perfect father to you, Bear. I know that. And I know how hard my job, my work, has been on you. And on Burton. And on your Mom, God rest her soul. I've paid the cost to be the boss, believe that."

I swallowed, waiting for whatever might come next.

"But Jessie Bear? I've never lied to you, not once. And with God as my witness, I swear, I never will."

A sudden rush of excitement surged through my body. My hands began trembling, and I had to tuck the cordless phone up into my neck for fear I might drop it. "So, you promise to tell the truth?"

"Yes, Bear. I promise."

"Thanks, Daddy." I took a deep breath, steeling my nerves to repeat the question. "So, is professional wrestling real? Or is it fake?"

There was absolutely no hesitation this time. "Yes."

"Daddy!" I nearly screamed at his vague answer.

My father took his time before responding, but when he finally did, I noticed that he'd changed his tone once again. He was speaking intentionally, pacing off the words that he'd chosen with care. In a different setting, Tommy Carpenter could've been speaking to "Doctor" John Burnham instead of me, cutting one of his famous promo monologues. "Is wrestling real? That's what you want to know, is it? Well, I guess it all depends on your perspective."

But I wasn't in the mood for any double-talk, and I sure wasn't about to let my Daddy go and hype me up like some everyday mark. "So, what's *your* perspective?"

"What's my perspective? What's my opinion? In my mind, kid—the way I see it—professional wrestling is real, one hundred percent. Or, at least, it's as real as it has to be. God knows, sometimes wrestling's even more real than I'd like it to be."

I leaned my shoulder against the bookshelf, still holding that photograph.

"Listen, Bear. Sports entertainment is what I do for a living. It's my *job*. So believe me, when I'm out here on the road, I go to *work*. Wrestling is what gets me out of bed at four AM every morning, hitting the weights seven days a week 'cause winners don't take days off. Wrestling is why I'm still out there doing my roadwork, clocking five miles a day, rain or shine, for the past…how long? Fifteen damned years, now? And you know how I hate running, but yet I still do it. 'Cause it's my damned job, see?"

I saw.

"Professional wrestling is real enough to have been a way up for me. An escape route that got us out of a slummy part of Lowell that was so damned real, I'll never be able to forget it. Yeah, sure—for some of the talent, World Wide Wrestling might just be a means to an end. A steady paycheck, a fun way to make money so long as you stay healthy. But for me? No, Bear. This wrestling shit is more than just a career. It's my *calling*. Wrestling is how I met your stepmother and your mother before her. It's how both you and your brother came into existence, and it's my *life* now. That real enough for you?"

I nodded, even though he couldn't see me. Everything my Daddy had ever told me about World Wide Wrestling, all those over-the-top stories about life on the road, they all came rushing back. The images charged up towards the front of my mind like a two-hundred-and-fifty-pound heavyweight rumbling down the ring ramp. "I know that, Daddy. I do."

"But it is a job, and one that pays well. Damn well. But what about the money, huh? Yeah, let's talk about the salary I pull in from World Wide Wrestling, because you better believe *that's* real. Real enough to keep the lights on and put food in your mouth. You were probably too young to remember, but where we're at right now? How our family's living today? Well, it's a damn far cry from where we used to be."

He lowered his voice ever so slightly, switching cadence to project a sense of intimacy.

"How do you like that roof over your head, huh, Bear? Or what about your room, that space that's all your own? That big old house we call home, it's a hell of a lot more comfortable than living in the backseat of a Toyota Tercel coupe, and I'm telling you 'cause I know! But you never stop to ask if *that's* real, do you? That fully restored four-bedroom colonial, with the central heating and air? Or what about the clothes on your back, the shoes on your feet? Your friends don't tease you about *those* anymore, do they? Because professional wrestling's real enough to provide all the name brands you kids wear, even though Guess jeans and Vuarnet t-shirts don't come cheap."

I slid down in the Barcalounger as a feeling of contentment came over me. His answer was good enough already, but I didn't dare speak up. Whenever my Daddy got himself on a roll, it'd be foolish to interrupt. Instead, I just kicked up my feet and settled in to enjoy the performance, an audience of one.

"You remember Milwaukee?" he asked. "Wrestle Fest '89, when I did the job to put over 'Superstar' Sonny Bruder? You remember that one?"

"I remember." My voice came out as a whisper as my mind replayed that horrible match in a series of slow-motion frames.

"Let me tell you something, Bear. There ain't nobody in all of professional wrestling who'd ever taken the Ring of Fire off the top rope before—no one. And, well, shit. I guess I'm the reason no one's attempted it since. The second 'Star botched the grip, got his arms wrapped up tight 'round my neck instead of down on my shoulders, I knew it was going to be bad. I swear, flying through the air, I thought I must've been a second or two away from dying. Man threw me clear over the ring ropes into that TV table. Split the damn thing in half, and that one wasn't no balsa wood breakaway. Fractured my clavicle in three places, bones snapped so loud they could hear 'em all the way up in the nosebleeds. You want to talk about what's real, do you? Well, let me tell you something, the pain I felt that night was real. One hundred percent genuine."

My shoulders shook from an involuntary shudder. I must've seen that tape a dozen times, hard as it was to watch. And each and every time, I'd be hard pressed to fall asleep afterwards. But apart from that horrible injury, it truly was one of my Dad's greatest matches. Taking that bomb had cemented his reputation as the best jobber in World Wide Wrestling, bar none.

He dropped the showman's voice, sounding like a normal father now. "So, what I'm saying is, yes. The way I see it, for all intents and purposes, yes, professional wrestling is real. It's as real as it has to be, and that's good enough for me. Now, the corporate side of the house? Well, those suits, they may, just *may*, have the authority to script out a few things in advance. But what you'll see on the screen when you tune in to watch tonight? That's all me, all Tommy Carpenter. So, if anybody ever tries to tell you that professional wrestling isn't real? That my job—my *livelihood*—is all fake, and that your fraud of a father has been feeding his two kids a steady diet of peanut butter and bullshit sandwiches? Well, just between you and me, Bear, I'd be happy to hold the ropes open for those clowns. Let any of those suckers spend just sixty seconds in the ring with me, we'll see if they still think wrestling ain't real."

My dad fell quiet, leaving me to listen to the roar of the crowd in the background.

And when he finally spoke up again, his voice was sure and steady.

"But just to save you the trouble of asking, I'll go ahead and tell you. Yes."

I exhaled.

"Yes. I already know who's going to win tonight's matches. Most of them, anyway. Obviously, that includes me versus Johnny Forbes. So, if you really need to be in on the secret, then yes, Bear, I'll tell you. I don't care if it violates my non-disclosure agreement, that I could lose my job, and pretty much everything I've worked for my entire life. That's how much I love you. For you, Bear—and only you—I'd break kayfabe."

I didn't know what to say.

Hell, I couldn't talk at all.

So in the end, I just stayed quiet. I did my best to choke back those salty tears, hoping that my Daddy wouldn't be able to hear me sobbing.

Eventually, that last moment of silence finally passed. "So, what do you say, Bear? The way I figure, there's got to be a million people tuned in to *Monday Night Titans* right now. More, probably. And yet, only a couple dozen of us actually know what's about to go down. So, what about it? Do you want to be in on the secret, too?"

It was right about then that I lost my composure entirely. A fat tear spilled down my cheek, the first of many to come. "No," I finally sniffled. "No, I don't. Your word is good enough for me, Daddy. It always has been, and it always will be. I love you…and I believe you, too."

MONDAY, MAY 3, 1993

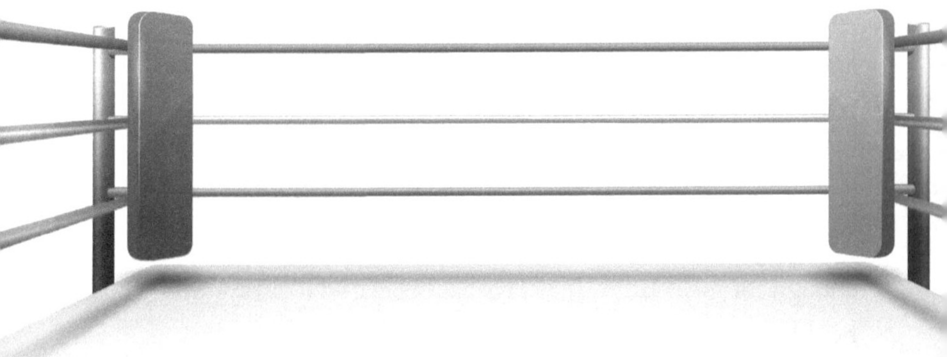

Excerpt from "Monday Night Titans" *broadcast*
Transcription by Burton Carpenter

Dr. John Burnham: And now, wrestling fans, it's the moment you've all been waiting for! Welcome back to *Monday Night Titans* and our main event! It's a packed house here tonight at the Los Angeles Memorial Sports Arena, where more than a few of Hollywood's brightest stars are in attendance, eager to experience the excitement of World Wide Wrestling! And Michael Jones, I'm told that the seating capacity here is close to sixteen thousand, but it's standing room only right now! Would you listen to that crowd roar? It's pandemonium!"

Michael Jones: You're absolutely right, J.B.! If I had to describe this scene in just one word, it would have to be 'total chaos!' No, strike that, let's go with 'complete insanity!' There may very well be sixteen thousand seats in this building, but there's not a single damn one of them being used right now! Every last man, woman, and child is up on their feet,

"

cheering for the challenger, this man who overcame the demons of defeat to climb the championship ladder! And J.B., I've got to say, by the way this man has been working, it looks like Tommy Carpenter, 'The American Dream,' isn't going to stop until he reaches the top! Just look at that expression on his face, folks…there's nothing there but focus, determination, and raw intensity!

J.B.: No doubt about it, Michael Jones! It's plain for anyone to see, when this man arrived in the City of Angels, he came here to do work! Tommy Carpenter has always been known as a paragon of fitness, but tonight, he's positively shredded! Just look at the man, folks…he must have been *living* in the gym to achieve such a physique! You can forget all about his past record—all those losses are simply irrelevant, because Carpenter's gone and hit the reset button! Man, oh man, we're in for a treat here tonight!

M.J.: You speak the truth, J.B. Even *I* can't disagree with you! The man we used to call 'The Daydreamer' has proven he's not afraid to get his hands dirty. Not afraid to roll up his sleeves and get to work, and now, we're just seconds away from watching him do it! Listen to the sound of these fans—they're more than ready to see this man go to town! Carpenter, stoking the crowd from the center of the ring, carrying a massive boombox stereo and waving that giant American flag, which was personally given to him by a highly decorated United States Marine, a wounded veteran of Operation Desert Storm! God bless our men and women in uniform, ladies and gentlemen! Please spare a thought and a prayer for our service members posted around the world tonight. And J.B., when I reflect on all the sacrifices those brave young people are making to defend our freedoms, I can't help but be reminded of the hard road that Tommy Carpenter has also walked. This man's a hustler, plain and simple, putting in the grind and doing what it takes to succeed!

J.B.: The crowd is going wild! Folks, I can't help but feel a shred of sympathy for Tony Schoonover, a man who's not accustomed to being upstaged, now having to wait patiently for his turn on the microphone! This match should've already begun, but Schoonover, the man with the golden voice, hasn't even had the chance to introduce Carpenter's opponent! Yes, I'd say it's pretty obvious whose side these fans are on!

Tony Schoonover: Thank you very much, ladies and gentlemen, for that warmest of welcomes! And now, his opponent…a direct descendant of the original Mayflower colonists! He was born with a silver spoon in his mouth… and as a child, he looked down on the common people of Boston from his mansion on Beacon Hill! Wrestling fans, please put your hands together for a *true* child of privilege! I give you, The Fortunate Son, Johnny Forbes the Third!

M.J.: Man, oh man! I haven't heard this many boos since last Halloween!

J.B.: Would you take a look at that showboat! Johnny Forbes is throwing hundred dollar bills out into the crowd! Those *cannot* be real!

M.J.: They look pretty real to me!

J.B.: Real enough to have caused a stampede down along the railing, in any case! Johnny Forbes, ever the peacock, making his way down the ramp in a slow, confident strut, but we all know money can't buy everything! Yes, Forbes might be decked out in the most expensive silk robes, and yes, he may sport a crisp golden tan year-round! All that generational wealth might furnish him a small army of personal trainers, plus thousands of dollars of vitamin supplements, but tonight, in front of this furious California audience, one thing is perfectly clear: the love, the adoration, or even the simple respect of World Wide Wrestling fans, is simply not for sale! Yes, both of these men might be natives of the Bay State, but tonight, it's plain to see, the two were born and raised *worlds* apart!

M.J.: And it's Carpenter who strikes first, not even waiting for the bell! Diving beneath the ropes, out onto the apron and slamming into his opponent! Forbes goes down hard, dropping that hand-tooled leather satchel down on the cold concrete!

J.B.: Careful with that case, men! There's a seven-figure payday inside! Fans, don't forget, the winner of this special "Blank Check" match will earn the right to crack open that briefcase and sign the contract within, a legally-binding document which guarantees a match against the World Wide Wrestling heavyweight champion with the title belt on the line, anytime, anywhere!

M.J.: Carpenter, whipping that case back over his shoulder and tossing it up into the ring, unconcerned by the possibility of marring such fine Corinthian leather with any scuffs, dings, or scratches. Clearly, The Boxcutter's got blood on his mind!

J.B.: Oh, my word! Michael Jones, did you see that? Tommy Carpenter just lifted Johnny Forbes with a powerful clean and jerk, hoisting the millionaire playboy high over his head like the man was nothing more than a lifeless set of free weights! And he…wow! My, oh my! Carpenter *launched* Forbes over the ropes, and now, he's charging into the ring himself. He's moving like a man on a mission, hot on Forbes' heels, looking absolutely ruthless!

M.J.: That's no man, J.B., that's a wild animal! A crazed beast, full of passion and fury! Forbes, struggling, scrambling back to his feet. He's going for the briefcase, and he's got it now, flailing it wildly, and—oh! Cheap shot! Cheap shot! Carpenter, bludgeoned right on the temple, and the blood is flowing freely now! Forbes ought to be ejected for that one… where the hell is the referee?

J.B.: Well it looks like Earl Black, off there in the far corner, seems to have been distracted by the antics of Jeeves the Butler! Once again, Johnny Forbes' dedicated manservant has dug deep into his bag of tricks, searching for any way to tip this match in favor of his employer! And with Earl Black occupied for the moment, Johnny Forbes is taking full advantage of this opportunity to go to town on the challenger, brutally assaulting Tommy Carpenter with that luxurious calfskin satchel! The American Dream is down on one knee, unable to defend himself, absorbing blow after powerful blow, and Michael Jones, you have to wonder, just how much punishment can one man take?

M.J.: Forbes, taking a breather now, reaches into the briefcase…what is he doing? He's not after the contract, is he? Oh, it'd be just like that pompous pretty boy to tear it into pieces, just to spite Carpenter and this capacity crowd… but no! He's got something else in his hand! Doctor John, can you see what it is?

J.B.: It's some kind of foreign object…maybe a…a pipe! Oh, my God, it's a lead pipe! Somebody stop the match!"

M.J.: Ha, ha! Aw, relax, J.B.! It's just a pocket comb! Johnny Forbes, strutting about the ring in a victory lap that's more than a little premature, coolly preening in front of this Los Angeles crowd, who're simply *incensed* by this show of vanity! Folks, in all my twenty-plus years of covering world-class sports entertainment events, I've simply never seen anything like this! A highly trained professional athlete, a full-grown man, has taken a pause from such a high-stakes match, to do…what? To comb his hair? For everyone tuning in at home, I hope you're taking in this showmanship, because Forbes' behavior simply defies all logic! If I wasn't watching it live, seeing it with my own two eyes, I wouldn't be able to believe it!

J.B.: Carpenter, working his way back up to his feet, stumbling about in a stupefied daze. This man might have gotten knocked down, but he's definitely not out…not by a long shot! Look out! Johnny Forbes has that briefcase high over his head, looking to bring it down with one last finishing shot…

M.J.: He ducked it! Tommy Carpenter somehow dodges the blow, and those powerful fists of fury are really moving now…switching gears, locking Forbes up in a tight grip…it looks like…yes! He's going for the standing half-nelson!

J.B.: Oh, how the tables have turned! Look at Forbes' face, there's panic in his eyes! The pretty boy is shook, unaccustomed to being on the receiving end of a beatdown, and that custom leather briefcase with its million-dollar promise is just laying there on the mat, absolutely forgotten!

Forbes can't be thinking of anything else besides his own survival, and I've got to be honest, his prospects aren't looking particularly good! If what we've seen out of Tommy Carpenter lately is any indication, I think Forbes would be lucky to last one more minute against this old hand! One thing's for sure—Carpenter's not just a brawler any more— the man has been transformed! Evolved, even! The wily old veteran has spent *years* of his life as a scholar of the sweet science, and he's putting on a clinic here tonight with Johnny Forbes as his hapless pupil!

M.J.: What's Carpenter doing with his free hand? Working it up across Forbes' face, going for an illegal eye rake, perhaps? Trying to blind the man and deliver an unmistakable message to The Syndicate?

J.B.: No way—that's not Carpenter's style! It looks like he's fighting to land some kind of a grip…could it be? Yes! Oh, my God! Tommy Carpenter's going for the Cobra Clutch… and he's locked it in!

M.J.: Johnny Forbes, in desperate straits now, struggling just to stay awake with that vicious hold clamped down over his carotid artery, steadily slowing the flow of oxygen-carrying blood to his brain!

J.B.: Tommy Carpenter, the American Dream, appears to have this match well in hand, and look! Now *he's* the one playing to the crowd, grinning from ear to ear! And let me tell you something, these people are absolutely *loving* it! Sixteen thousand strong, still on their feet, but Michael Jones, I have to say, I'm actually a little bit worried now! These fans might not be satisfied with a precision submission hold, no matter how masterfully Carpenter might've applied it! No, sir—these fans want blood!

M.J.: What's he setting up next, I wonder? Carpenter, with that glint in his eyes, eases into a squat, lowering the Fortunate Son gently down to the mat for a nice, peaceful slumber… and it's good night, sleep tight, Johnny Forbes! Lights out for you, and lights out for your heavyweight championship bid! Oh…oh! Holy cow!

J.B.: A suplex! Wow! He could've broken Forbes' neck, lifting the man like that, but oh, what a move! Carpenter, hustling like greased lightning, scrambles for the cover! And these fans are ecstatic! Count it out, Earl Black!

M.J.: One! Two! Three!

J.B.: IT'S OVER!

M.J.: Dr. John Burnham! I swear, that performance was simply unbelievable! Tommy Carpenter, still on the move, wisely slides beneath the bottom rope to make a quick exit before The Syndicate has any chance to react to this staggering victory! Don't forget that briefcase, Tommy—it's got your one-way ticket to greatness inside!

J.B.: Ladies and gentlemen, that's going to do it for us here in Los Angeles! That last match was nothing short of epic… no, it was so much more than that! It was amazing! It was *historic*! I have no idea what's gotten into Tommy Carpenter these past few months, but mark my words, you're going to want to be watching whenever he decides to cash that blank check! So, on behalf of all of us here at World Wide Wrestling, coming to you *live* from the City of Angels, thanks for watching, America! Good night!

THURSDAY, MAY 6, 1993

THE NEXT TIME I SAW THAT KID, I NEARLY FROZE IN MY TRACKS. Thankfully, I'd spotted him first. See, John Nguyen had this way of trudging up and down the hallways, lurching about like a silverback gorilla. So, it only felt natural for me to hang back on the other side of the corridor and observe the creature in his native habitat.

John was posted up in front of his locker, staring into that cramped and musty space with his usual blank stare of confusion. I swear, it almost seemed like it could've been the first time all year he'd bothered to look inside. The kid just stood there, motionless, only breaking his statuesque pose long enough to run his chubby fingers through that rat's nest of thick black hair. John's narrow eyes were tilted up and to the side as he picked at the thin gray wisps of peach fuzz scattered all over his wide, round face, almost like he was trying to recall some random thought. John was one of a handful of ninth-graders who had a legitimate need to shave once a week or so, but of course, he never did. That patchy half-beard of his caused me to stop for a second and reflect on what Burton had told me about John's home life. If the adult Nguyens really had been drifting in and out of the kid's life for years on end, it made sense that there wouldn't have been anyone at home with the time or the interest to teach the kid how to drag an electric razor across his face.

The late bell rang, shattering my concentration. As the hallways cleared, I summoned my courage and stepped forward to close the gap. "Hey, John," I began, in a soft tone of voice, one that I hoped would come across as non-threatening. "How's it going?"

Of course, I'd still caught him off guard. John Nguyen's shoulders tightened as he glanced back, sizing up my presence before shuffling a half step to the side and hitching up his oversized jeans. I wondered for a second why the kid wasn't wearing a belt, before doing my best to push the question from my mind. Who knows why? Maybe the accessory hadn't occurred to him when he'd gotten dressed that morning, or else it was also entirely possible that he just didn't own one. In any case, the kid looked so nervous talking to me, I thought he might take off running at any second.

While John stood there, searching for words, I used the uncomfortable silence as an opportunity to examine the dude up close. His jeans were a well-worn pair of Cross Colours, black and yellow. The brand had gone out of style just a couple weeks after they'd hit the stores last year, and the baggy fit was a clue that John must've found them on a Salvation Army rack. His sneakers, they weren't much better.

Newish, with the white leather uppers still fairly bright, but definitely not name-brand. Knock-off Reeboks, they looked like, the ones without labels that always seemed to be on markdown at TJ Maxx. What really caught my eye, though, was the kid's grubby old T-shirt. The faded black fabric was stretched thin over rolls of belly fat, pulling the bright red WWW logo out into a comical oval shape.

Finally, just to avoid wasting half my morning waiting for John Nguyen to string a pair of words together, I did my best to push the conversation along. "Cool shirt, man. Were you watching on Monday night?"

Something seemed to click inside that kid's brain, and those normally delayed thoughts began shooting past his lips at high speed. "Yeah, of course! I've seen every episode of *Monday Night Titans* since, well…since forever! Of course, your dad's my favorite, Jessie. Always has been, even back when he lost all the time."

From the corner of my eye, I caught a glimpse of Mr. Busadawicz at the end of the hall. That old geezer was marching purposefully towards the wood shop and tying his knee-length apron tight behind his back with both hands. When he spotted me, that old guy froze in his tracks and looked down through those Coke-bottle glasses to check the time on his Casio digital watch. That done, he looked back up and threw an evil stare my way. Of course, I knew I was running late for his class, but at that particular moment I had bigger things to worry about than a stupid table saw or a God-damned drill press.

I felt my face grow hot as I shot him a low middle finger in reply. Busadawicz shook his wrinkled neck and stomped off, clearly disappointed that I wasn't giving his precious woodworking projects the attention they deserved. Although, I honestly wasn't sure how a guy his age could see me at all. Those safety goggles must've been super-powered or something. I was already on thin ice for cutting out of shop class so many times before, but I doubted that Old Man Busadawicz would take the time to write out a detention slip for such a small act of insubordination.

Still, it was best not to drag my feet too long. No sense in pushing the envelope, you know? I turned back to John Nguyen and asked, "So, I'm guessing you must have seen my Dad's match?"

"Hell, yes!" His eyes lit up with an energy I hadn't expected. "I was really tired on Tuesday morning, but it was totally worth it. I stayed up late to watch the main event, the whole entire thing. I drank, like, two or three cans of Mountain Dew during the show, but, wow! You must be so excited, huh? Now that your dad has a real, honest-to-God shot at the title? Has he shown you the contract yet? It must be, like, a hundred pages long! And I'm not trying to question Tommy Carpenter's strength or insult his ability or anything, but, like, I bet he's got to have a couple bodyguards on call right now, huh? I mean, he's carrying around a shot at the title, so he's going to need 24/7 security. Who knows what The Syndicate might be planning?"

His passionate words threw me for a loop, to the point where I didn't actually know how to respond. John Nguyen sounded like he'd actually bought into that crazy storyline, and I couldn't tell if he was pulling my leg.

"Uh…yeah? I guess, right? I mean, we haven't had the chance to talk much, he's been so busy and all. But I imagine he's got to have his guard up?"

John grinned, rubbing his fat hands together with glee. "He'd better! I mean, I love your dad, and of course I want to see Tommy Carpenter win the belt. He deserves it, more than anyone! But you've seen what The Syndicate is capable of. You can't turn your back on those guys for a second! You remember last September, at Fall Brawl, when El Diablo rappelled down from that skylight and grabbed the ring bell, and used it to—"

I backed off a few steps, trying to make my way to safety before John Nguyen could wind himself up by rehashing that terrible script. "Yeah, that match was something else, wasn't it? But listen, bud. I'd better get moving. Okay? I'm late for shop as it is, and, well, Busadawicz can be a real prick sometimes. I'm not trying to spend another afternoon sweeping up wood shavings in detention, you know?"

He nodded, setting layers of baby fat jiggling into motion around his neck. The kid was grinning like a fool as he fished down in his back pocket, eventually coming up with a crushed Hostess package. CupCakes, I think, though I couldn't be sure. The plastic wrapping was all squashed and twisted, the label mangled beyond recognition. John's chubby fingers fumbled with the packet, tearing it open in a mess of chocolate frosting. "Okay, then," he said, as he sucked the sticky brown cake from his fingertips. "Guess I'll see you later."

John Nguyen just stood there, with his usual dumb smile looking just a tiny bit wider than usual. As I walked away, I couldn't help wondering where that guy was actually supposed to be at that particular moment. I mean, who knows? Maybe our teachers had just written him off entirely, the same way they'd done with me. And I'd ducked around the corner and out of his line of sight before the realization hit me: John Nguyen actually believed that professional wrestling was real! I shook my head, trying to comprehend the idea. Like, most people might've found it easier to keep buying into Santa Claus, or maybe the Easter Bunny, than it would've been to swallow some of WWW's cheesy works.

That happy thought carried me safely past Busadawicz's angry glare, past all the nasty whispers from my classmates. As I grabbed the last open stool, doing my best to ignore yet another mind-numbing safety brief about how many fingers the school's table saw had claimed, I found myself wondering if maybe I should've broken kayfabe. Lifted the curtain a little, and enlightened the kid on how wrestling *really* worked. But just a few minutes later, when our class broke up into work groups, I'd come to the conclusion that I'd done the right thing.

After all—if John Nguyen was happy enough to remain a mark, then what right did *I* have to spoil his fun?

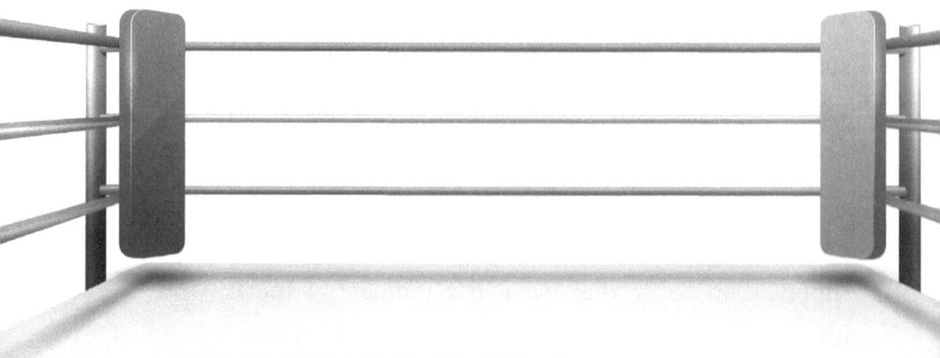

THAT NIGHT, IT WAS JUST ME AND BURTON.

Again.

Aunt Emmy had hauled my present-day stepbrother off with her to bingo, and there'd been nothing worth watching on television, so the two of us were just sitting outside on that crisp spring evening. Talking about music, video games, and wrestling.

Of course, wrestling.

Neither of us were saying anything particularly important, so there were plenty of breaks in the conversation. We'd fall into these long lapses of silence every so often, and I'd end up staring down off the hill. Into the lights of downtown Lowell below, or else off into the clear night sky. At some point, Burton had gotten up and gone into the garage to dial down the security floodlights, affording a clear view of the universe with its stars that seemed to go on forever.

Burton spoke up first. His eyes were still focused off somewhere in the night, but I knew by the way he was talking that his mind was looking out even further. Towards the most distant reaches of our constantly-expanding universe. "They all seem so far away, don't they?" he finally asked. "The stars."

I nodded. "Yep."

"Out of everything I could imagine, those countless stars are what I always come back to when I need to put things into perspective. They're just so…perfect. Like, when you think about those massive balls of gas and fire and about how far away they really are, our own problems just seem so tiny in comparison."

I smiled, extending an arm and holding it straight out. The contentment I was feeling—the happiness, even—was a new sensation back then. And as odd as this sounds, I actually found myself a little embarrassed by it. "Yeah, they really do." I held up my palm, blocking out an entire constellation, then slid it sideways to cover one of Burton's eyes and re-create the effect. "From this distance, those stars seem so small; this is all it takes to make them disappear from sight. But you and I both know how big they really are—and how close."

He nodded his approval, returning my grin. "Now you're starting to think."

I sighed in spite of myself. "Look, bud. There's something I've been meaning to tell you. I mean, I've accepted that this whole relationship could be possible, okay? That you're, you know. Real. Or at least, like, real enough."

Burton opened his mouth. The guy looked as if he was about to let loose with another physics lecture, so I held up my hand to cut him off. "You sure do *seem* as if you're here in 1993, anyway. So, unless I've been completely high for the past several months, your presence must be a real, like, *thing*. Right? I mean, everything about…*this*, no matter if I can't fully understand it, sure does seem genuine."

He sat quietly for a moment, and then nodded again. "Thank you."

"And if all of your visits have been real, and if all of our conversations have been, too, I'm going to assume that means you've been telling me the truth this whole time. And yes, I remember how you said you're able to make time travel work by like, meditation, and I'm guessing your autism somehow gives you the ability to stay focused for so long. But where I'm still lost is…I mean, I can accept that it's all *possible*, right? But *how*, exactly, is it possible?"

Burton took another long pause before answering. "Anything's possible. Just as long as you believe." My confusion must've been apparent, even in the dark, because he pulled his gaze from the stars long enough to reach down and rummage through a new Jansport backpack. "I don't suppose you've ever read this one?" he asked as he came back up with a hardcover textbook. "Or even heard of it?"

I stared down at the dust jacket, which featured a picture of an anemic-looking dude in a wheelchair. *A Brief History of Time*, huh? Can't say I've seen it on the summer reading lists. But you know what, I think I actually *have* heard of the author. Stephen Hawking? The quad, right? Doesn't he have some kind of a voice problem, so he's got to talk through one of those speak-and-spell toys?"

Burton shook his head at the coarse description, but he didn't waste any breath correcting me. "That's him. The most brilliant astrophysicist since Einstein, in your era at least. Maybe even mine. Don't be fooled by his appearance—the professor suffers from a degenerative muscle disorder, but it sure hasn't affected his mind any. As for his book, well, that's been on the best-seller lists ever since it came out four years ago. And that's in spite of the fact that hardly anybody who's bought Hawking's book is capable of understanding his theories."

I reached out to accept the thick tome, flipping through the pages more as a way to appease my stepbrother rather than from any genuine curiosity. As soon as I spotted the first complex equation—way beyond anything I'd seen in Pre-Algebra—my mind began to flounder, like it was in danger of drifting off to drown in a foamy sea of mathematics. "So like, what? Is all this stuff important to time travel or something? Why do any of these formulas matter, if all you need is your mind?"

Burton lifted his chin. "Turn to Chapter Two."

I obediently thumbed my way through a few dozen pages, coming to a stop at one of the first pictures I saw. The black-and-white technical diagram resembled a line chart, but a three-dimensional one. It looked almost as if a pair of ice cream cones had been stuck together, back-to-back, with the cylinders pointing outwards in opposite directions from the two narrow ends. "Okay, yeah. So what?"

"So what is, remember a while back when you and I were discussing the nature of time? Talking about how everybody understands how to use time as a unit of measurement, yet nobody can really explain what it actually *is*?"

"Yeah, I remember."

"Well, take another look at that diagram right there. That's Hawking's best guess of what time actually 'looks' like. This particular picture illustrates the concept that the only absolute, definite point in time—the only *truly* unchanging moment—is the one we're currently experiencing. Right here, right now."

I wrinkled my nose. "What, like the Val Halen song?"

Burton closed his eyes and took a deep, patient breath. "Not really. But—you know what? Yeah. Maybe those guys aren't all that far off. See, every *other* moment in time—no matter whether it's yet to occur or if it's already passed—you should consider it more of a possibility than an absolute, fixed event. As we continually move forward into the future, progressing along a timeline that we perceive to be mostly straight and level, the possibilities of what could be—and also what could have been—both sides quickly expand out towards infinity. The end result is a nearly limitless range of events, all of which have at least a chance of occurring, or of having occurred."

Burton must've caught the blank look on my face, but he continued the lesson without any prompting. "So, let's say for example that right now, at this very minute, you, I don't know. Haul off and punch me in the nose. Or something."

He reached up and pulled down the hood of that ratty red sweatshirt, tucking his headphones safely away at the back of his neck. "If it'd help you visualize the concept, go ahead and take a swing. It's okay, I don't mind."

"Come off it, dude. You know damn well I'm not going to hit you. I'd probably break your face in half."

He shrugged. "I doubt it, but that's not important. My point is, in that one particular moment the two of us shared just now, you at least had the opportunity to hurt me…if not the actual ability."

I sneered. "Screw you."

He sighed. "Spoken like a true Carpenter. Anyway, that brief moment of opportunity has now passed. Both of us are sitting here unharmed, which was just one of a countless number of possible outcomes. But think about what might've happened, let's say, if you actually *had* gone ahead and punched me. And just for the sake of argument, let's imagine that you broke my nose, too. That would've required a quick trip to the hospital to have it set, unless I wanted to end up looking like I'd gone a couple rounds with Mike Tyson."

"Okay…"

"And as long as we're speaking in hypotheticals, let's also admit the possibility that you—with that oh-so-impressive strength of yours—could've also broken a few of the delicate bones in your hand."

"Whatever."

"Which would mean that you *also* would've had to go to the emergency room. Or, who knows? Maybe you didn't break any bones. Maybe your hand was just sore, and all you had to do was ice it for a while. It doesn't matter, as long as you see how easily, how quickly, all those possibilities can blossom out from a single moment in time."

I scratched my head. His examples were running along a number of different threads, and it was a challenge to keep them straight. "I guess so…"

Burton kept his train of thought chugging right along. "Well, so now let's assume that maybe you *did* have to go to the hospital after all. How would you get there? That one question opens up a whole new range of hypotheticals. Are you going to call an ambulance? Would you walk, or ride your ten speed? If Mom and Dad are home that week, maybe they could drive you. Or if this all happens while they're away, I guess you could go and steal Aunt Emmy's truck again."

I was starting to catch on to the concept, but didn't dare say anything. Whenever he got himself worked up, Burton never needed much encouragement. The heavy topic was more than enough to spur him on.

"And while you're on the way to the hospital—or maybe while *I* am—what would happen if either one of us got lost along the way? Or, I don't know, we could get into a car accident or something. Or it could happen that you or I make it to the hospital safely, only to find there's some kind of problem with Dad's health insurance plan. Which opens up another line of possibilities, like getting stuck with a ton of medical bills. And that might cause financial trouble for the family! And then, what if—"

I dropped the book in my lap, raising both hands to beg for mercy. "Okay! Okay! Enough already! I get it, we could literally go on like that forever. But, why? What's the point?"

Burton lifted a shoulder, almost indifferent to my stress. "Well, that kind of *is* the point. According to Hawking, the possibilities that can develop from this one particular moment, or from any other moment in time, are literally infinite. And according to that diagram, his theory also applies to the past. There's also a countless number of events which *could* have happened."

The casual discussion made the concept sound simple enough, which was probably why I felt so frustrated at not understanding it. "I'm sorry, bro," I finally sighed, dropping my hands in defeat. "I guess I just don't get it."

He nodded patiently, and I got the impression that it wasn't the first time that Burton had had to explain the concept.

"Listen, sis. Have you ever had anybody tell you not to worry about the future? To slow down, and just live in the moment? Well, they're probably just trying to say you should relax and enjoy life as it happens, but the message is more accurate than they realize. Even if you can't grasp any of Hawking's other theories, it's enough to know that all of the possibilities we just discussed—those endless, spiraling threads blowing outward from this one single moment—all of them are equally real. Just as real as this one moment we're in, right here, right now."

I leaned back against the rocking chair, casting my gaze up towards the stars once more. That dark night sky seemed even bigger than it had just a few minutes ago.

Infinitely bigger.

Burton must've sensed that he'd finally gotten his point across. "You see it now, don't you? A countless number of alternate realities—one story, with any number of endings, any number of beginnings. All of them somehow linked, held fast by this murky concept we call 'time'."

My head spun as I struggled to comprehend it. I mean, Burton's explanation of theoretical physics might have seemed plausible if we'd been sitting inside some university lecture hall, his calculations drawn out on one of those big old blackboards. But to try to take all this stuff in, there on the front porch of my house? No, that was a step too far.

"It can't be, dude," I finally whispered.

Burton just shrugged, impervious to my skepticism. "It's tough to understand. I get that. But you know, even the airplane used to seem like a crazy dream until the Wright Brothers finally went and built one. Or the space shuttle, or the telephone, or any kind of new technology. It's the exact same concept. Look back a hundred years or so, would you? How many people do you think seriously imagined that someday humans would no longer have to rely on horses for transportation?"

I just sat there, silent, making a careful study of the night sky.

"Is the impossible *really* impossible? Or could some ideas just be too big, too bold, for people to comprehend? To be honest, it really doesn't matter. Because once you've heard a new idea, you'll never be able to unhear it. Even if you never act on your thoughts, those concepts have a way of rooting themselves down in the depths of your imagination, the same way all those alternative timelines anchor themselves to the present."

He went silent for a long time, then circled back to close out the lesson. "You're living your life with blinders on. You know that? By accepting everything you see as the truth, plain and simple, you're only seeing half the picture. Less than half! Never troubling yourself to ask *why* things are the way they are, not bothering to question *why* things happen the way they do. You're missing out on so much!"

I watched as he shifted around in the deck chair and opened his eyes wide. "Believe me if you want to, Jessie. Or don't. I don't care, because either way, it won't change a thing. It's your actions that matter—what you do. Because all of those infinite, possible realities are linked, the decisions you make in this one moment will absolutely impact the others! Tug on a single string, and all the rest will tremble right along with it."

I didn't know what to say.

But for some reason I couldn't explain, I was scared.

"Think of all the unanswered questions around how President Kennedy was shot. And, of course, you remember the space shuttle *Challenger* explosion? You can't seriously believe that those incidents—those horrible, unexplainable tragedies—just *happened* somehow?"

A chill ran down my spine.

"Nope," he answered himself. "Something did happen, somewhere. But there's no way of knowing what or when. Inexplicable tragedies like these, chances are, they're an opposite reaction to something else. A contradictory event to some other occurrence somewhere in the universe, at some other moment in space and time, which triggered a vibration that echoed out until it finally erupted in our timeline. If everything in the universe is interconnected the way Hawking thinks it is, held together by time's thin strands, then that's just how it'd work. And do you know what the worst part is?"

I shook my head. I didn't.

"There's not a single damn thing either you or I can do about it."

MONDAY, MAY 17, 1993

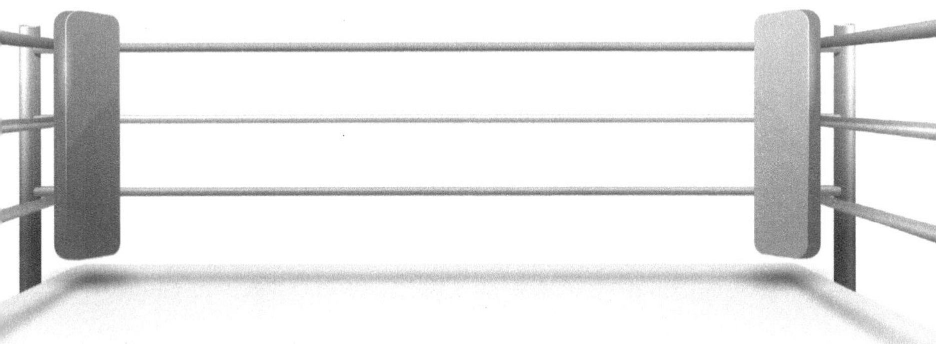

Excerpt from "Monday Night Titans" broadcast
Transcription by Burton Carpenter

Dr. John Burnham: And now, ladies and gentlemen, it's the moment you've all been waiting for! We're back live at the crown jewel of the Peach State, the fabulous Omni Coliseum, here in beautiful Atlanta! And I'm joined tonight by the man whose name is on everyone's lips, giving his first interview since he wrested a Blank Check away from The Fortunate Son, Johnny Forbes, in that unforgettable bout! Here with me now is the American Dream himself, 'Boxcutter' Tommy Carpenter!

[Applause.]

Tommy Carpenter: Thanks very much, J.B. First, let me say, it's a privilege to be here tonight. Here with you, and with all these beautiful people. How y'all doing tonight, Atlanta?

[Massive applause. Approx. 10-second delay.]

J.B.: Now, Tommy, let me ask you something. Two weeks have passed since your match with Johnny Forbes, the one-sided fight which stunned, absolutely stunned, the World Wide Wrestling community! Nobody, and I mean nobody, could've seen that beatdown coming, but here we are, fourteen days later, and it seems like the whole world is still talking about that fight! Still analyzing each and every blow! So, first, I have to ask you, is there any message you want to pass along to The Syndicate? Those despicable men who've done their best to stop you at every turn?

T.C.: The Syndicate? Man, those clowns are just whack. All I've got to say to those losers is, if you want to get at Tommy Carpenter, you know where to find me. You want to act tough on TV, run your mouths? Man, y'all go ahead. Run your mouths. You want me to listen, though, you better come on down here, step into the ring, and say that crap to my face!

[Applause.]

J.B.: Now, Tommy, I'll say this to your face. It's no secret that you've experienced a number of…well, let's say, *setbacks* during your WWW career…

T.C.: You're talking about all the matches I've lost? That what you're getting at, Doctor John?

J.B.: That's—that's not quite what I meant to say—

T.C.: It's okay. It's cool. My record's no secret. Sure, I might've spent more time on my back than a professional mattress tester, but you know what? All those beatdowns, they helped make me into the man I am today. See, the difference between me and those Syndicate goons is, I ain't afraid of losing no more. I've paid my dues—every penny! Unlike Johnny Forbes, ain't nobody never handed me jack. Everything I got, I had to earn it through steady hustlin', twenty-four hours a day, seven days a week! And let me tell you something else, J.B. When you're climbing the ladder of success, working your way to the top, you're bound to stumble every so often. It's inevitable! But if a man's scared to take a tumble from the lowest rungs, how the hell's he ever going to make it to the top?

[Applause.]

J.B.: Well, there's certainly no denying the success you've achieved! But on that note, to what, if anything, do you attribute your spectacular results? Tommy, every wrestling fan wants to know—no, we *need* to know—what *is* your secret?

T.C:. My secret? J.B., are you even listening? This recipe ain't no secret. It's one part hustle, one part loyalty, and one part respect. The only skills I ever learned in this life was how to work hard and how to believe in myself, but man, that's enough! So, for all you kids out there, listen up. There's anything you want to do in your lives? Anything you want to be when you grow up? Well, so long as you can believe it, you can make it happen. All your dreams are possible— all of them! Anybody ever tries to tell you different? Tries to stand in your way, tries to run you down and say you ain't good enough? Well, you've got my permission to knock those fools on their asses, right then and there! Tell 'em the American Dream, Tommy Carpenter, told you to!

[Massive applause.]

J.B.: Powerful words from the man himself! And, Tommy, one last question, if you have just a moment—the one everybody's been dying to ask! Now, you're the legal owner of that priceless Blank Check—

T.C.: Got it right here, J.B. I've been carrying this nice, new briefcase around, day and night.

J.B.: But when exactly are you going to cash it?

T.C.: How about right now, Dr. John? That soon enough for you?

[Massive applause. Approx. 20-second delay.]

J.B.: Wait, what? Tommy, Tommy Carpenter! Did I just hear you correctly? You're going to cash the Blank Check right now? Right here, live, on *Monday Night Titans*?

T.C.: That's right, J.B. What do you think about this? I'll sign over the Blank Check, right here, right now…but I want my shot during Summer Smash-Up.

[Massive applause.]

T.C.: And hey, I'm going to make this a little more interesting! I don't even care who I go up against! I'll let The Syndicate pick somebody, anybody they want, as my opponent. What do you say to that, folks? Would anybody like to see that match?

[Interview interrupted by crowd response. Approx. 30-second delay. Carpenter signs the check, hands it over to Dr. John Burnham, and exits up the ring ramp.]

J.B.: Ladies and gentlemen! You heard it here first, on *Monday Night Titans*! Boxcutter Tommy Carpenter—the living, breathing embodiment of the American Dream— has just thrown down the gauntlet! But oh, my word, what could the members of The Syndicate possibly have to say in response to that? Be sure to tune in next Monday night to find out…and don't forget, tickets for the 1993 Summer Smash-Up pay-per-view event are officially on sale now! That's going to do it for all of us here at the Omni Coliseum, down in beautiful Atlanta, Georgia. Goodnight! And remember, as the man himself just said, don't ever stop believing! Wow!

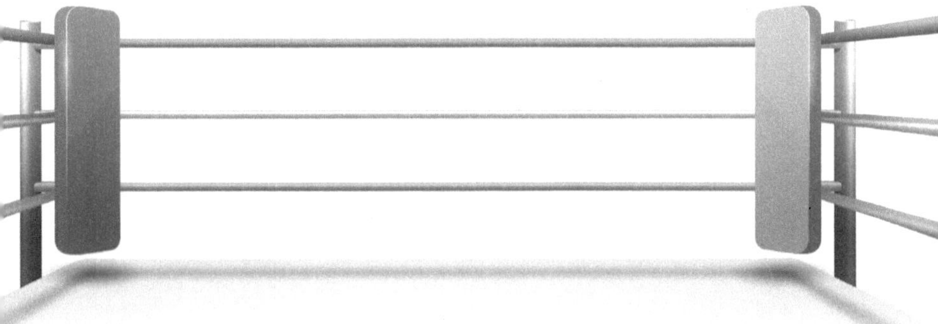

LOOKING BACK ON EVERYTHING, IT'S KIND OF FUNNY TO ME NOW, HOW well John Nguyen and I got along. After those first few awkward encounters, I mean. Once I'd figured out the one thing we both had in common, the connection came easier each time.

Like, we weren't exactly friends or anything.

Not even close.

But I *was* able to tolerate the kid's presence a whole lot better than before. And for his part, John Nguyen had even started acknowledging me every so often. He never turned into the creeper I'd feared, not stalking me or tailing me around campus or anything. I'd usually just get a quick head nod instead, or maybe a mumbled "hey" whenever we'd pass in the halls. If John was in a good mood, the two of us might chat for a couple seconds about something from World Wide Wrestling—a recent match, or a promo comment which caught his ear. And just like Burton had promised, all I had to do was be nice.

To be honest, it wasn't an overly taxing assignment.

Sometimes, just not being a dick was all it took to pull a smile out of the kid. Our relationship was a manageable one, and with only a couple weeks left in the semester, it was starting to look like the both of us might actually make it to graduation.

Then came that one morning. A Friday, I think it was. I'd arrived at JFK a couple minutes earlier than normal, which is to say, I'd made my way inside before the late bell rang. My Dad had scored a rare couple of days off, and I was still riding a warm, happy glow from his visit. Even though Samantha and Burton had tagged along when we'd gone out to eat at Papa Gino's, their company hadn't bothered me nearly as much as it would've just a few months before. In fact, the whole outing was kind of…nice. That feeling of happiness—that rare, odd sensation when I'd dared to believe that things might actually turn out all right— that was probably the reason why I lengthened my stride after spotting John Nguyen.

"Hey, John," I called, hustling across the corridor to pull up alongside him. "Where 'ya headed, bro?"

"Hey," he said with an awkward, high-pitched wheeze. "Homeroom. Obviously."

I swear, no matter how solid and stocky the kid might've looked on the outside, the very act of speaking always seemed like such an exertion, as if stringing together a full sentence might put him at risk of an asthma attack or something.

"Huh. Okay. Well, how's your day going so far, man?"

John slowed his pace. I guess having to think up a response had sapped some of his momentum. "Good, I guess. Maybe." He came to a halt, lifting his head towards the ceiling while he scratched at his ear. "It just started, you know? So, like, it's kind of hard to tell."

I nodded, and we shuffled off down the hall in silence, all the other kids giving us a wide berth. I spotted more than a couple curious looks from the usual smartasses, but by that late point in the semester, I was determined to ignore them all. I mean, what could any of those clowns have had to tease us about?

John Nguyen might've been a spaz, sure, but at least the kid knew it.

As for me, anybody who watched World Wide Wrestling wouldn't have called my Dad a loser anymore, so that was out, too. And seeing as how I was apparently on some kind of top-secret mission from the future, I guess I was just beyond caring about other people's opinions.

I was busy, you know? I had things to do. And if anybody didn't like that, it was like my Daddy had said—they could just step to the side, and get the fuck out of my way.

The first bell rang as we stopped in front of his locker. The crowd around us began to thin as kids reluctantly filed off into their classrooms. They moved slowly—dragging, almost—same as the final days of the school year were doing. And just then, a sudden burst of inspiration hit me. I reached out to lay a hand across his shoulder and said, "Hey John, listen. I was talking with my Dad this week, when he was home for a couple days, and your name came up, if you can believe that. Didn't you tell me before how you don't get the pay-per-view events at your house?"

"Yeah," he sighed. "It really sucks; they're just too expensive." That nervous smile of his glinted out of sight just as quickly as it'd appeared. "But it's all right. They always show the most important highlights on the next *Monday Night Titans*, anyways. And sometimes…" He shot a glance back over his shoulder, just in case one of our classmates might've been listening in. "…you can ask around. If anybody ordered the match, they probably recorded it on the VCR, so sometimes you can borrow somebody's tape for a few days."

I nodded. "Yeah, well. Listen. You know how *Summer Smash-Up* is coming up, right? It's next Saturday night. And you obviously know my Dad just cashed the Blank Check, and even though we still don't know who he's going to fight, this thing is going to be huge! But because he's been with WWW for so long, we always get the pay-per-view shows for free."

John sniffled. "Lucky." He rubbed a fat hand across the base of his runny nose. I shifted my eyes away, wishing that I had a handkerchief or a tissue or something to offer him.

The kid wasn't catching my drift, so it looked like I was going to have to come right out and say what was on my mind. "Well, how about this?" I sighed. "Do you—I don't know—maybe want to come over and watch it with us?"

I pressed on ahead, nervous that the kid might get the wrong impression. After all, I sure as hell wasn't asking John Nguyen out on a *date* or anything.

"There'll be some other people there…but just a few, you know? Me, my Aunt Emmy, my little brother Burton, and my…" Somehow, I managed to stop myself before I slipped up and said the name twice. "…my, um, new tutor."

John Nguyen didn't say anything.

He didn't have to.

The kid just stood there, grinning, as a few more kids hustled by. They cut us a wide berth as they raced to class.

Ten seconds went by.

Then twenty.

And just when the break in our conversation was beginning to feel way more awkward than usual, the second late bell rang and shattered the moment. I took the sound as an excuse to break contact, throwing one last wave back over my shoulder as I jogged away.

"Show starts at eight, all right? Don't be late!"

*Excerpt from "Monday Night Titans" broadcast
Transcription by Burton Carpenter*

Dr. John Burnham: Welcome back, wrestling fans, to The Gateway to the West! We're here in the beautiful, historic state of Missouri, coming to you, *live*, from the fabulous Saint Louis Arena, where so many legends of World Wide Wrestling have left their mark in the beloved "Checkerdome"! And even though tonight's matches have been excellent, with such a remarkable degree of talent and athleticism on display, I get the feeling that people are more concerned with this year's *Summer Smash-Up* event! That'll only be broadcast via pay-per-view, so if you still haven't ordered your subscription, I don't know what you're waiting for! And of course, there's one match in particular everyone wants to see: The American Dream, "Boxcutter" Tommy Carpenter, facing off against an unknown opponent, with the WWW heavyweight title on the line! And that's why tonight, we've arranged a special interview with the voice of The Syndicate…

El Diablo: "Voice of th' Syndicate"? Oh, no, Papa John! El Diablo is so much more'n 'dat! Soul of the Syndicate, 'dat's more like it! And 'speakin of souls…

J.B.: Take it away, El Diablo—it's your two minutes! But before we begin, allow me to pass along my sympathy regarding that *awful* slip and fall you suffered in the locker room at the top of tonight's show. Although, from the camera angle I saw, it didn't look all that serious…

E.D.: 'Dat floor was wet, Papa John! Man, 'joo know what? I oughta sue this dumpy little stadium. I coulda' been kil't! But hey, no matter. Wha's done is done, right? But in any case, as my personal doctor Manuel jus' tol' me, I'm in no kind'a shape to be wrestlin'. Sooo…as much as I wan'na go upside of Tommy Carpenter's crewcut head, as much as I wan'na lay the smack down on that *gringo*, it looks like I'm just not gon' be able to make it.

J.B.: Unbelievable! El Diablo, what does this mean? Of course we're *all* familiar with the questionable circumstances which transpired last year, that series of calamitous events which allowed The Syndicate members to obtain the heavyweight title in the first place…

E.D.: Questionable? Damn right, they was questionable! Man, Papa John, I'm *still* tryin' to figure out how tha' steel chair got inna' the ring!

J.B.: But tonight, the question we all have is…what's going to happen at *Summer Smash-Up*? Does The Syndicate have anyone available who can step in on short notice? Kilimanjaro? Johnny Forbes? Carpenter's already beaten both men, and done so handily! Does this injury mean you're planning to drop the championship belt and just *give* it to Tommy Carpenter?

E.D.: No, no! Mayn, we ain't droppin' this hardware, not when we had to work so hard to earn it! 'Joo dig? But hey, a deal's a deal. Carpenter gon' get his shot…even if th' match ain't gon' last long. I tell 'joo what I'm a-do, hey? Since I got my arm tied up in this here sling, I asked one of my oldest, most down-ass *vatos* to step in an' take my place. He gon' fight for me, you dig? Here, Papa John. Why don't 'joo jus' go ahead and hold this belt for a min'it?

J.B.: Holy Moses, that's heavy!

E.D.: Don't go gettin' attached! We gon' want that back, jus' as soon as the ambulance comes to haul Tommy Carpenter away. 'Joo heard?

J.B.: Ladies and gentlemen, this man is *truly* putting his money where his mouth is, laying the title belt on the line! But El Diablo, you still haven't answered the question! Who could fill your shoes? Who could possibly step in to fight a heavyweight championship match on such short notice?

E.D.: You really wan' know, J.B.? Mayn, be careful what you wish for…

J.B.: You're up to something, El Diablo—I can sense it! There's no one foolish enough to step into the ring with Tommy Carpenter right now—not a man alive!

E.D.: A man alive? No, prol'ly not. But wha' 'bout a dead man?

[Massive applause.]

J.B.: No! You can't mean!

[Applause continues, grows louder.]

E.D.: Tha's right, Big John! Comin' out of retirement fo' this one match, and this one match on'ly. 'Cause when The Syndicate calls, even a dead man gon' pick up the phone!

[Massive applause. Approx. 20-second delay.]

J.B.: The Gravedigger! The Man From Beyond The Tombstone, back in action after all this time? I don't believe it! If what you say is true, El Diablo, then Tommy Carpenter is in for the fight of his life!

E.D.: 'Joo mean the las' fight of his life, huh? But hey! Carpenter, mayn! If 'joo at home watching this, 'joo ain't got to be scared, hey? 'Cause when I talk' to the 'Digger, I ask him to make it a quick one, so there ain't much sufferin'!

J.B.: Holy Cow, ladies and gentlemen! You heard it here first! El Diablo, throwing a curveball in Tommy Carpenter's direction, and oh, what a pitch it was! Could The Gravedigger—The Man Without A Soul—really be coming out of retirement? If this is indeed true—and believe me, I'm sure the World Wide Wrestling corporate offices are already working to confirm the details—then it's entirely possible that Tommy Carpenter might have bitten off more than even *he* can chew! Folks, I honestly don't know what to think right now, but one thing's for sure, if you still haven't booked your pay-per-view subscription for *Summer Smash-Up*, you need to pick up the phone and call right now! I'm not sure how we're going to top that announcement, ladies and gentlemen, but we're sure going to try! Stay tuned for even *more* wrestling action, *live,* from Saint Louis!

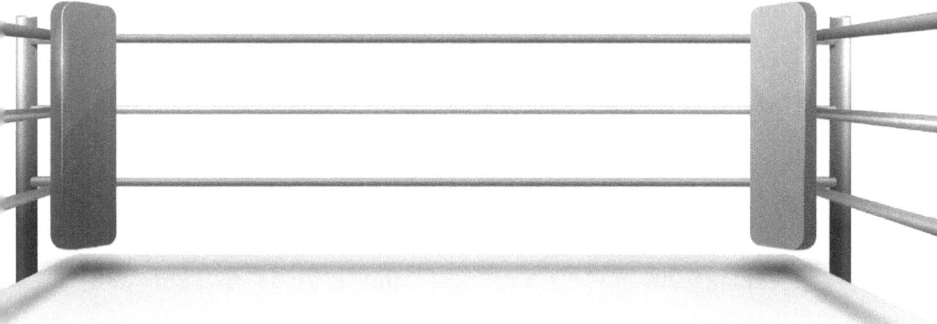

WHEN EIGHT O'CLOCK FINALLY ROLLED AROUND, IT WAS BEGINNING to look like the *Summer Smash-Up* party might be going down without John Nguyen. The curtain jerkers had come and gone, and even the 16-man Lumberjack Brawl had been settled by the time that kid finally showed his face. It was definitely an above-average program, but there was just one match we'd tuned in to see. The announcers might as well have been filling dead air, for as much attention as we were giving them.

When we heard that soft, almost hesitant knock on the door at around nine-thirty, my Uncle Hector raised a thick eyebrow. It was only then that I realized I hadn't given him a heads-up we'd be having company—more than just Burton, I mean. My uncle leaned forward on the couch, staring down the hallway with a protective glower across his brown face. I swear, it was almost as if the dude thought I might've been trying to smuggle in my secret teenage lover or something. I guess it was a little rude for me to have caught him off guard, but honestly, my uncle kind of deserved it. No matter how many times I'd pestered him, the man staunchly refused to drop even a hint about Dad's match. Said he didn't want to ruin it for me.

And you know what?

As much as I might have whined and complained, I loved him for doing that.

John Nguyen didn't bother offering any kind of explanation for his tardiness, and I knew the kid well enough not to ask. When I opened the front door, he was standing there on the porch, shoulders slouched forward and looking just as stupid and confused as always. I couldn't tell for sure what he was going to do next: come inside or take off running. John was wearing that same old WWW T-shirt, and it looked like it hadn't seen a washing machine in a while. The collar was freshly torn, a grungy look which matched the dark purple bruise on the side of his neck. Somehow, I managed to check the urge to grill him about what had happened.

"Hey, kid," I grunted. "Better late than never, I guess. Come on in."

I took a step backwards and motioned with my arm, hoping the visual prompt might help propel him into motion. "You missed a couple matches, but nothing huge. And hey, my Aunt Emmy and Uncle Hector ordered some Little Caesar's. You cool with pepperoni?"

"Thanks," he said, cracking a smile as he stepped inside. John Nguyen kicked off those white, no-name sneakers of his, exposing a matching pair of holes in the toes of his worn-out tube socks. "Sorry I'm late and all. What happened was, my Dad…" The kid's voice trailed off as he glanced past me and back to the end of the hall where my Uncle Hector was standing. "Holy shit!"

Uncle Hector froze in place. He'd been on his way to the kitchen during a break in the action, holding an empty twelve-ounce can of Bud Lite in each hand.

John Nguyen took a hesitant half-step forward. Hand quivering, he held a chubby finger at the level. "It's him!" he shouted. "El Diablo!" He tilted his head sideways, staring at me with a look of genuine fear on his face. "And he's here, in your house!"

My Uncle Hector turned sharply and strode toward us. Those snakeskin cowboy boots of his clomped against the hardwood floors, the tall heels echoing with each and every step. He came to a stop, stacking the beer cans in his left hand and extending his right. "Hiya, kid. Call me Hector, won't you?"

John Nguyen went silent.

I swear, I could almost hear the low hum of his lip as it began to quiver.

"So, you're a friend of Jessie's, huh? Do you go to John F. Kennedy, too?"

John Nguyen swallowed. "No way I'm shaking your hand." He bit his lip, struggling to hold back the tears. "You're a low down snake! A real son of a bitch, and I know *exactly* why you're here."

It was a bold response. And it was definitely *not* how most people tended to speak to my Uncle Hector.

Honestly, I had no idea what might happen next.

I watched the two of them closely, unable to look away. Uncle Hector set both of those beer cans down on the telephone table, carefully, slowly. Then he mounted his hands on his hips, flexing those massive forearms out to make them bulge even more than they normally did.

"Excuse me?"

John Nguyen's wide neck swiveled from side to side as he shifted that dumbfounded gaze from Uncle Hector to me, and back again. I watched as the kid's familiar look of confusion shifted into an expression of anger, as the gears in his autistic brain struggled to process the unexpected encounter.

"Come off it, El Diablo," he wheezed, once he'd found his voice. "You're busted, so you might as well come clean. We caught you in Tommy Carpenter's house, tonight of all nights, just as he's about the wrestle The Gravedigger with The Syndicate's title belt on the line?" He took another half-step forward, bravely positioning himself in between me and my uncle. "And what happened to that sling you were wearing? Huh? I've got news for you, bub. Everybody knows you're faking that injury!"

Uncle Hector scowled. "Oh, is that right?" he hissed, his voice low and mean.

"That's right! Because you're a coward! You're too scared to fight Tommy Carpenter, not without the rest of The Syndicate backing you up."

That moment—that long, awkward silence—was absolutely extraordinary to witness. I swear, in all my life, that was the only time I'd ever seen my Uncle Hector at a loss for words. His jaw hung open—stuck there, it looked like. The confrontation had caught him by surprise, and the fact that it was a kid like John Nguyen who'd had the balls to stand up to him?

Well, that was unbelievable.

John Nguyen must've been emboldened by the lack of a response, because he kept right on pressing his luck. "How'd you get in here, anyway? And what were you planning to do? Kidnap Jessie, maybe hold her for ransom, while the rest of your crew ambushed her father on live TV?"

Eventually, my Uncle Hector recovered his composure. Somewhat.

He glanced past John Nguyen, fixing me with a wordless, questioning stare. But I'll say this for my godfather—even under pressure, the man was a true professional. As soon as he saw me mouth the word "kayfabe," he instantly snapped into character.

"Lis'sen, kid," he growled, switching on that corny stage accent of his. He reached up to smooth his thick handlebar mustache, then puffed out his chest and bent over at the waist, crowding uncomfortably close to John Nguyen. "'Joo a smart boy, 'joo figured it out. 'Joo know how me and The Daydreamer got heat, right? Prol'ly been watching all his matches. Am I right, *cabron*?

John swallowed again, but somehow managed a nod. His Adam's apple bobbed shakily along, making the full circuit down his neck and then right back up again. Jittery as he was, though, I had to give the kid credit. No matter how scared—how terrified—he might've been, that thirteen-year-old autistic kid stood his ground.

Fucking John Nguyen, of all people! Facing down the leader of The Syndicate, and doing it all by himself.

Uncle Hector crowded in closer, placing his dark brown eyes level with John's, only an inch or two away from the kid's face. "Well lis'sen up, *vato*," he hissed. "'Coz I want 'joo to know the truth. 'Joo listening, hey?"

John kept silent, but somehow found the courage to nod once more. Just a single dip of his chin, down and up again.

"Well, kid. I wan' 'joo to know, tha' shit ain't real. None of it. Nada. 'Joo un'nerstan'?"

I gasped.

"It's all bullshit. An act. Fake. 'Joo *comprende*?"

I bit my lip, shocked that my Uncle Hector would even consider revealing the secrets of World Wide Wrestling to an outsider. His words made it sound as if he was about to let John Nguyen in on everything. To quickly—almost cruelly—shatter the illusion, once and for all.

A cold bead of sweat trickled down my forehead as my brain kicked into overdrive, struggling to think of a way to signal my uncle and clue him in to the fact that John Nguyen wasn't an ordinary mark. In that tense situation, I guess I should've shoved my way in between the two of them and whispered the word "autistic" into Uncle Hector's ear.

But for some reason, my feet just wouldn't move.

My hightop sneakers could've had a pair of lead weights inside of them, the way they stayed glued to the floor. In the end I could only stand there, frozen and fearing the worst.

"It's not real?"

John's words came out as a whisper, barely audible, as the rumbling of the television threatened to drown him out entirely. One of the two Burtons must've cranked up the surround sound speakers, and the noise of that Madison Square Garden crowd was enough to shake our house to the foundation. There were 20,000 fans packed into that stadium, and even though none of them could've possibly known about the drama going down inside our house, to John Nguyen, it must've felt like every single one of those voices was screaming directly at him. There was no way to tell what that kid might've been more scared of— that World Wide Wrestling was real, and he was about to get his ass kicked by El Diablo—or that professional wrestling was nothing more than a sham, and every last bully at JFK had been right.

No matter which of those two answers my Uncle Hector was about to give him, though, one thing was clear.

John Nguyen was about to get himself an education.

I watched, terrified, as the man rocked back on his heels, sucked in a deep breath, then broke eye contact long enough to shoot me a discreet wink.

"None of it, mayn. Not one dam' bit."

He clapped a heavy hand down on my classmate's shoulder. Hard.

John Nguyen jumped with surprise. Shocked to find himself still breathing, probably.

I looked on, enthralled, as Uncle Hector clamped the grip down even tighter. Squeezing into John's flesh with a set of hairy, swollen knuckles.

He leaned in closer. "'Joo see, mayn? That beef me and the Boxcutter got goin'? That heat, well, it jus' ain't real. Is' all for show, dig? Carpenter, me and him, a little while ago we…how 'joo say? We kin' of come to 'an arrangement.' Like, him and me, we got this agreement where I let him in on what The Syndicate's plotting. Yeah, they always lyin', cheatin', tryin' to keep the babyfaces…"

I winced at the slip.

"I mean…th' good guys, right? The Syndicate always tryin' to keep 'em down, but you and me both know, tha's only 'cause they cain't win fair. And tha's why me and The Dream decided, we oughta start workin' as a team. In secret, tho'. 'Joo dig?"

"Uh…I think so…"

"Well, I'm Carpenter's man on the inside. Passin' him secret information 'bout wha's gon' happen next. How 'joo think the Dream was able to snatch that boxcutter away from Kilimanjaro, huh? Mayn knew tha' sneak attack was coming, tha's how."

John's round eyes went wide as he processed the new information. However improbable the story sounded—even by WWW's creative standards—the kid had to admit it was possible. "You mean…you're actually trying to *help* Tommy Carpenter win?"

Uncle Hector nodded.

"So you're like, what? A spy?"

Uncle Hector shrugged. "If tha's wha' 'joo wanna call it, then yeah? Sure. On the real, tho', I'm a good guy. Okay? Only I jus' can't tell anybody yet, so neither can 'joo."

He wrapped both hands around John's fat neck, pulling the kid forward until the tips of their noses pressed together.

"So, what'choo say, kid? Huh? Can we trus' 'joo? 'Joo, me, and the American Dream?"

John pondered the offer for a long, tense moment. I swear, I don't think I exhaled for at least thirty whole seconds, not until I saw the kid pump his head up and down with a new sense of energy. "Of course! It all makes sense now!" John Nguyen couldn't quite hold back his huge smile, but he did his best to put on a serious face as he answered. "Your secret's safe with me, El Diablo. Man! The Syndicate is never going to know what hit them!"

Uncle Hector held his gaze. It was a long, meaningful stare, and when he finally broke off, he wrapped both arms around John Nguyen's torso in a massive bear hug. "I'm tellin' 'joo, kid, everything's gon' be fine. 'Joo jus' listen to El Diablo, now. Okay? We gon' take care of e'erthing. Say, mayn…'joo wanna beer?"

"He's underage!" I screamed as the two of them traipsed into the kitchen, walking arm in arm now.

"'S no problem! Emmy babe! Get my frien' here a Zima, hey?"

As his words hit my ears, this strange, warm sensation began seeping over my body. I savored the glow for a few short moments, then made my way back into the living room to rejoin that weird group of people who made up our family.

Uncle Hector was doing his best to stay in character, showcasing his macho side by shotgunning two beers at a time. The routine had John Nguyen doubled over with laughter.

Aunt Emmy sat next to him on the couch. She was dressed in her finest track suit, talking over the broadcast into the cordless handset and running up our long-distance phone bill, like always.

Both of the Burtons were there, too.

My little brother was sitting up in his older self's lap, snuggled comfortably in his own skinny arms. The kid had fixed his stare on the big projection screen, looking way more attentive, way more focused, than I'd ever seen him.

And as for Burton? Well, that dude just sat there with a small smile across his lips. He looked calm and happy.

Peaceful, almost.

And then, even before I knew what was happening, I was smiling, too. The expression came on slowly, gradually, pulling my cheeks out wide, changing my expression and shifting my entire attitude for the first time in a long time.

In a very long time.

And it was right about then—at that one moment in time—that I realized both Burton and my Uncle Hector had been right.

Somehow, someway, everything really *was* going to turn out all right.

For all of us.

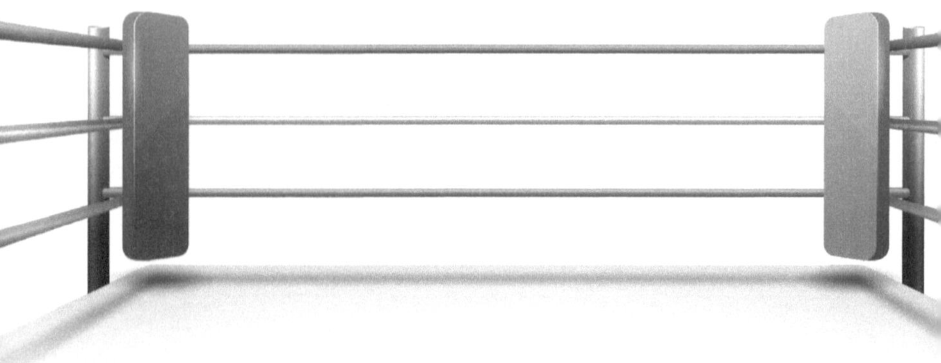

Excerpt from "Summer Smash-Up" pay-per-view broadcast
Transcription by Burton Carpenter

Dr. John Burnham: Welcome back, wrestling fans! And now, it's the moment we've all been waiting for, tonight's main event! Coming down the ramp first, our challenger, the young man whose career is positively on fire right now…known as "The American Dream" to his friends…or "Boxcutter Tommy" to his enemies…

Michael Jones: And when it comes to enemies, he's certainly got his share!

J.B.: …Tommy Carpenter! But as we all know, with that surprise hand that El Diablo dealt last week, the WWW heavyweight championship might not be all that's on the line tonight! This match could well become a battle for his very soul! Can you believe it? Out of all the possible opponents, out of all the legends of World

Wide Wrestling, The American Dream got stuck facing off against The Gravedigger! The Man From Beyond The Tombstone, coming out of retirement for one last match…Michael Jones, could you *ever* have predicted this?

M.J.: I'm sorry, but I'll have to interject! Dr. John Burnham, you're wrong on at least two counts!

J.B.: Well, by all means—enlighten me.

M.J.: First off—yes, even though there may be a handful of "Tommy-Come-Latelys" here in the audience tonight, all of us *true* wrestling fans have been waiting years for this match. Maybe even our entire lives. We just didn't know it!

J.B.: Well, I'm not going to argue that point. And by the sound of this New York City crowd, I don't think anyone else is either!

M.J.: Second—it's not just one man's soul on the line tonight, it's all of ours! Tommy Carpenter, this seasoned veteran, has somehow transformed himself into the fresh face of a new breed of World Wide Wrestling superstars! A potential champion! A man who's put in the work and clawed his way up the ladder, winning over a countless number of hearts and minds in the process!

J.B.: Michael Jones! *Now* we're a hundred percent in agreement, and I think that's *got* to be a first! Fans, you might want to mark this day on your calendars!

M.J.: I tell you what, J.B. As a professional commentator, I probably shouldn't be cheering for one athlete over another, but as a human being, I simply don't give a damn! In all my years of broadcasting, I've never seen anything like this man—this beast—Tommy Carpenter! My money's on "The Boxcutter" tonight, all or nothing. If there's any man alive who can top the mystical, undead strength of The Gravedigger, it's going to be the pride and joy of Lowell, Massachusetts!

J.B.: Just listen to that crowd! It sounds as if the entire Empire State is in full agreement with you! Every last man, woman, and child here in Madison Square Garden is on their feet now, cheering for Tommy Carpenter as he jogs down to the ring. The kid looks loose. He looks limber. He looks confident—

M.J: He looks like a champion, is what I think you mean to say! And that physique…it's unbelievable! Such a level of fitness is never God-given, ladies and gentlemen, it has to be earned! Hours upon countless hours spent in the gym, never a day off…

J.B.: What? What the hell?

M.J.: Oh my God! It's an ambush! A surprise attack from The Gravedigger…now, where did *he* come from?

J.B.: From the depths of hell, that's where! The Gravedigger, all six feet, eight inches of stinking, rotting flesh, emerges from his Underworld lair, crawling out from beneath the ring apron to get the drop on his opponent! What a lowlife! An absolute lowlife! I ask you, Michael Jones, are there no depths to which this depraved soul would not stoop, no dirty tricks he would not pull, in order to win this match and reclaim the WWW heavyweight championship!

M.J.: There's the bell—this fight is on!

J.B.: Carpenter, finding himself in an all-too familiar position now, on the receiving end of such a brutal beating!

M.J.: It's the Gravedigger, kicking, stomping, landing blow after blow, using those steel-toed motorcycle boots to his full advantage! Shot after shot, while Carpenter can only lay there, helpless, down on the cold concrete! This isn't a fight, J.B.—it's a beatdown! For all of our pay-per-view customers watching at home, if you've got any young children around, any tiny tots who might've stayed up past their bedtime to witness this historic bout, you may want to reconsider! On behalf of the World Wide Wrestling corporation, I want to apologize for this senseless, unsportmanlike display of carnage! And now, referee Earl Black is risking his personal safety, maybe even his own soul, to dive between these two men!

J.B.: Oh, my word! Can you believe this? On an ordinary night, that attack might've rated a disqualification, maybe even a suspension! But like every other matchup we've seen here on *Summer Smash-Up*, this brawl is extraordinary! It's beyond belief! Somewhere over the course of the last three hours, WWW has taken the rule book and thrown it out the window! They've discarded all procedure, all decorum, with nary a second thought! The Gravedigger now, hitting Earl Black with an intimidating staredown, the smoldering, fiery intensity of the undead just burning away in his eyes…and no surprise at all, the ref chooses to back away to safety.

M.J.: The Gravedigger, actually showing a lick of common sense, climbing up into the ring! Leaving poor Tommy Carpenter there on the floor, abandoned and forgotten, and it looks like he's having some words with Earl Black now!

J.B.: Seems to be an awfully one-sided conversation.

M.J.: It looks like he's *ordering* Earl Black to start the count! The Gravedigger isn't going for a pin…no, he'd be perfectly happy with a simple disqualification! If Tommy Carpenter can't get himself up and into the ring within twenty seconds, this match will be over just as quickly as it began! And if that happens—if The Gravedigger should emerge victorious—The Syndicate will retain the heavyweight championship belt, and tomorrow morning, it'll be a rude wake-up call for The American Dream!

J.B.: I don't believe what I'm seeing, Michael! This is a crock! A disgrace! An absolute travesty of sporting justice! Just look at Carpenter…the man's damn near crippled! There's absolutely no way he'll be able to climb across the ring ropes, not in his condition. I mean, Jesus! I'm not even sure he's still alive! He could have fractured ribs, a concussion, anything! But let me tell you, if Tommy Carpenter *does* somehow manage to make it out of this match alive, I hope he's got a good lawyer on retainer, because that ambush was absolutely criminal! Carpenter ought to sue The Syndicate for all they're worth!

M.J.: Is it just me, J.B., or is Earl Black counting just a bit faster than usual?

J.B.: Don't judge the man, Michael Jones. He's doing his best, I'm sure, and I'll tell you what—if those evil eyes of Satan were boring into *you*—if it was *your* nose filling up with the thick smell of sulphur and brimstone—I bet you'd be doing whatever it takes to survive, too!

M.J.: And…wait! What is that? Yes! Movement from Tommy Carpenter! He's awake, or at least, he's stirring! I'm not sure the man's fully conscious, but he's still fighting! Struggling, dragging his body along the floor now, powered by nothing more than sheer will! It's absolutely amazing what we're seeing here tonight, folks! What a contender!

J.B.: Hats off to Carpenter! All respect to this man and his fighting spirit! He's literally *crawling* towards the ring now… it's amazing! I tell you what, if I was that young man, I'd be headed off in the exact opposite direction, putting any distance I could between myself and The Gravedigger, but no! Tommy Carpenter, refusing to give up, is still looking for a fight! No doubt about it, this man is a true champion!

M.J.: And The Gravedigger, finally taking notice of the action behind him, slides back out beneath the ropes to tangle with Carpenter once more. The giant stands his opponent up with ease, launching him in under the ropes! The Spawn of Satan is ready for another round, set to unleash another barrage of pain, and J.B., I'm not sure how much more punishment Carpenter can endure! I don't know how much longer *I* can continue watching this level of brutality!

J.B.: I've never seen anything like it! This isn't a professional wrestling match any longer—this is savagery! Carpenter, the challenger, looks out on his feet, leaning up against the turnbuckle with nowhere to run, nowhere to hide, and no other choice but to absorb blow after blow from The Gravedigger's cold, dead hands! And what about this crowd?

Stunned into silence, these fans are, all 20,000 of them! They can only stand and watch as the cracking sounds of slap after vicious slap echo throughout the arena!

M.J.: And it's The Gravedigger still, pulling Carpenter out of the corner and setting the man up for even more punishment. Doctor John, I'm not sure how the American Dream could still be standing upright, but off he goes with an Irish Whip, into the ropes and ricocheting back out at full speed. The Gravedigger, with that arm ready…

J.B.: He ducked it!

M.J.: Holy shit! Carpenter ducked the clothesline!

J.B.: Language! Michael Jones, you *know* you can't talk like that on the air! Amazing, the presence of mind of Tommy Carpenter.

M.J.: …bounding off the far ropes, launching into the air with a flying kick! My, oh my! It looks like he's stunned The Gravedigger!

J.B.: But can he follow up on this opportunity?

M.J.: You read my mind, J.B. The Boxcutter, not wasting a second, showing no hesitation in locking up with the soulless giant! The hustler is back in his element now, flexing that rock-hard physique, layers upon layers of muscle! Embraced in that tie-up, he's summoning all his strength, calling on all the forces of goodness and light as he grapples against the demon of darkness, with absolutely no holds barred!

J.B.: Both men look sorely weakened, yet neither one is giving an inch! They're locked in that perilous death grip, struggling for any leverage, any advantage at all! It's brain versus brawn, and Michael Jones, with absolutely no disrespect meant towards The Gravedigger, I've got to think that the tactical advantage might actually tip towards Carpenter in this situation! He's got the speed. He's got the power. And what about all those new submission holds he's mastered?

M.J.: No doubt about it, Tommy Carpenter's giving it his all, really bringing it to the beast, in the fight of his career! Slipping loose from the tie-up, with a wild haymaker and— oh, my God!

J.B.: DDT! It's a DDT!

M.J.: The big man is down! The big man is down! Great God in Heaven, the big man is down!

J.B.: ...nothing short of a miracle! The up-and-comer, Tommy Carpenter, has done the impossible! He's put The Gravedigger on the mat using one of the most devastating moves known to World Wide Wrestling, and that perfectly timed kick to the ankle was all the distraction he needed to pull it off!

M.J.: The Dream's moving like greased lightning, back on his feet again, fully in charge of this match now! It's a complete reversal of fortune, a full one hundred and eighty degree turnaround. The Gravedigger appears dazed—if such a creature could be capable of feeling any kind of emotion, he's got to be shocked, simply shocked, to find himself on the defensive!

J.B.: On his back in a most unfamiliar position, staring up at the overhead lights and writhing about like Doctor Frankenstein's heinous creation! Let me tell you something, Michael Jones: there's no way to know for certain whether that man…that thing…can process the sensation of pain, but if he truly can, then he's got to be swimming in a world of hurt! Carpenter, letting fly with a series of massive elbow drops, raining down blow after blow, back on his feet just a split second after striking the mat!

M.J.: But where's he going now, J.B.? Across the ring…is Tommy Carpenter turning off the heat? Or does he simply need a breather? Don't tell me this fine physical specimen is running out of steam, when we're just now crossing the five-minute mark—

J.B.: No! Look at that! Clambering up the turnbuckle like a spidermonkey on steroids! Folks, I'm not imagining this, am I?

M.J.: If I wasn't seeing this with my own two eyes, I wouldn't believe it!

J.B.: Six foot three! Two hundred and forty-five pounds! All that muscle, poised and balanced, walking the ropes for the very first time in his World Wide Wrestling career, and yet…and yet, looking so cool, so calm, it's almost as if the man was *born* up there! Tommy Carpenter's just taking it all in now, admiring the view!

M.J.: Strutting his stuff like a bird on a wire! A hawk, a fierce and deadly predator, ready to strike at his wounded prey! And would you listen to this crowd? It's pandemonium here in New York City tonight! Powering up with a low, low squat…

J.B.: What a leap!

M.J.: Oh, no! That crack, it hurt me just to hear it! And it looks like The Dream may be hurt, ladies and gentlemen…yes, Tommy Carpenter is most definitely hurt! The powerhouse from Lowell went down hard, flying full throttle and powering his arm into The Gravedigger's skull, and by the sound of that impact, there's got to be one bone shattered, at least! Oh, my! What a blow, just as this promising contender was about to achieve such a momentous victory!

J.B.: Carpenter may be writhing in agony, but at least he's still awake! The Gravedigger, on the other hand, has been knocked out cold! His mind—if he has one—is off in some black nether world, communing with the demon spirits!

M.J.: Carpenter, lying there alongside The Gravedigger—and I do mean right next to him—writhing in pain, screaming loud enough to wake the dead, no pun intended! And just take a look at Earl Black…the ref simply doesn't know what to do! Should he stop the match? Both men are obviously incapacitated. And if they're unable to carry on… wait! What is this, now?

J.B.: Tommy Carpenter, the American Dream! Ignoring the pain, fighting through what looks to be a separated shoulder, somehow, someway, finding the strength to roll himself over and flop on top of the big man, securing the cover! Could this really be happening? Count it out, ref!

[Broadcast inaudible due to crowd noise. Earl Black pounds the mat three times, then signals for the bell.]

J.B.: It's over! It's over! He actually did it! Tommy Carpenter, accomplishing what no other athlete has ever managed, besting The Gravedigger by pinfall—and in doing so, capturing World Wide Wrestling's most prestigious prize—the heavyweight championship belt!

M.J.: Somebody call an ambulance! My God! Carpenter, writhing on the mat in obvious pain, but man, oh man—what heart! Folks, this warrior will almost certainly need some time off to tend to that awful injury, but by God, like everything else in this man's life, he's earned it! Lying there, clutching that belt, unable to raise it more than a few inches in the air, the pain on his face clear to see—but still, ladies and gentlemen, there can be no doubt about it—this man is a true champion!

J.B.: Deadly as a Boxcutter…he *is* The American Dream! Your *new* WWW heavyweight champion, Tommy Carpenter!

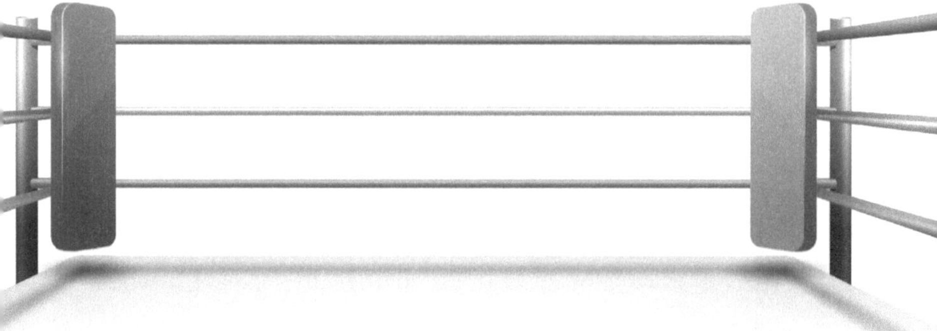

THIS MIGHT NOT COME AS ANY KIND OF SURPRISE, BUT THAT WHOLE next week was kind of a blur. It was just as well the semester was over, because I don't know how I would've reacted to everyone at school who'd seen that match.

Daddy didn't make it home from New York City until Wednesday night, and by that time, my report card had already arrived in the mail. Mostly C's, backended by a couple of sad and lonely D's. Somehow I'd even managed to scrape out a B- in American History, which could only have been a result of Burton's influence. But the grades themselves weren't all that important—what really mattered was that I'd managed to graduate from the ninth grade.

My time at John F. Kennedy Junior High School was over and done with, never to be repeated again.

After that match, though, life for my family was… different. First of all, my Daddy had become an honest-to-goodness celebrity overnight, a mid-list jobber no more. Everybody in Lowell who'd pretended not to know the man back when he was losing? Well, now that he held the title, all those same people seemed to want a piece of his time. Even the Boston Globe, which normally didn't cover professional wresting; they sent one of their sports reporters up Interstate 495 to interview my Dad, right there in our living room. The article made the front page of that weekend's sports section, one of those "North Shore Kid Makes Good" kind of stories. The paper played him up like he was some kind of overnight success story, almost as if the man hadn't spent his whole adult life working towards that goal.

But us neighborhood kids?

We knew better.

I swear, first thing Monday morning, there was a long line of grade schoolers posted up on the sidewalk out front, blocking our driveway in the hope of catching a glimpse of The American Dream.

And the question they all seemed to be asking was, "What's next for Tommy Carpenter?" Turns out, Daddy'd only snapped a collarbone during that leap. Not a career-ending injury, but of course, World Wide Wrestling did their best to sell it like it could be. They claimed the doctors needed to do a full reconstruction, a process which might keep The Boxcutter out of action for six months or more. What they didn't say—at least, not publicly—was that even though he'd be taking a break from wrestling, my Dad would still be plenty busy.

See, Tommy Carpenter wasn't content to be a paper champion, holding on the the heavyweight title when he wasn't capable of defending it. So, just a few days later, when

WWW was broadcasting *Monday Night Titans* live from the Philadelphia Spectrum, he climbed back into the ring with that championship belt in one arm, and a sling wrapped across the other. And even though he only appeared before that crowd for about five minutes—or maybe it was ten—those Pennsylvania fans were on their feet the whole time.

Every one of them.

And when the applause finally broke, my Daddy just dropped the belt. Left it laying there on the canvas, so every other WWW superstar could have a fair shot at earning it.

You know—if they really wanted it, and were willing to put in the work.

And once it quieted down long enough for Daddy to pick up a microphone, he just told the crowd that it wasn't a big deal for him to walk away from the championship like that, since it wouldn't be long before he'd be back to reclaim it.

And at the very end of his speech, he dropped a hint about how during rehab, he'd also be busy traveling out to Hollywood to film his first action movie. Yeah, I'm sure his agent absolutely loved that last bit.

And what everybody was thinking—but not actually saying out loud—was that it looked like Tommy Carpenter's professional wrestling career might be over, right as he'd reached the top of the mountain. Of course, no one except me and Burton could've had any way of knowing that *Summer Smash-Up '93* was just the beginning for the American Dream.

And after the dust settled, my Dad had a rare opportunity to spend a couple consecutive weeks at home. Hell, even Samantha managed to take some time off in between the road shows.

Which meant that Burton just didn't have the chance to drop by anymore.

And as weird as this might sound, the two of us never really even said goodbye. The last time I saw Burton—I mean, the second-to-last time—was that Saturday night, while everyone was still going crazy over Dad's victory. From the corner of my eye, I watched as the guy just kind of showed himself to the door, drifting casually out of my life, pretty much the same way he'd come in. In fact, the very last thing my stepbrother ever said to me was "See Ya." He mouthed the words silently as he slipped off down the hallway, unnoticed in the chaos.

So, that was that.

No heartfelt goodbye, no final words of future wisdom. Nothing.

But since Dad and Samantha were both home, I didn't really feel the void from Burton's absence. Or at least, not much. Not like you might've expected.

And what's more, I found myself tolerating my family a lot better. Even Samantha, once I actually noticed all the ways she cared for Burton. Like, this beautiful, blonde, WWW starlet never hesitated to get down on the carpet to play Hot Wheels cars with her son. That kid got her undivided attention whenever they were together, before everything else going on in her busy life.

And even though I can't say that me and Samantha became friends—at least, not right away—I guess you could say that I was beginning to get used to her. Yeah, whatever our weird little family was supposed to be, that lady was definitely a part of it.

So, I guess that's why I actually muted the television that one afternoon when she and my Daddy walked into the living room with concerned looks on their faces. It was obvious that they'd come to talk business.

"Honey," my Dad began, in that deep, serious tone of his—the one he normally saved for the most important promo shoots. "We need to talk about Burton."

I clicked off the television altogether.

"I know you two have been spending a lot of time together over the past few months. Has he ever spoken to you? Or have you ever heard him try?"

I looked him dead in the eye. Meeting his gaze head-on but revealing nothing.

And just then, my Dad—the great Tommy Carpenter—began to break down.

Right there in front of me.

His voice choked up as he went on, describing a condition that I already understood all too well. "I mean… the kid *looks* healthy enough, at least on the outside. You know? But he's three years old, and damn near four. Most of the kids his age, they're already…well, what I'm saying is… with how quiet Burton is, and then all those tantrums that come out of nowhere? Well, it's just not *normal*."

So, that's how, even before the month was out, Burton got enrolled in the Bright Horizons half-day preschool at Phillips Academy, this uppity private school down in Andover. And because my Daddy had absolutely hit the roof over my last report card, I got shipped out right alongside him. I'd heard the tuition at that place was outrageous, a year of high school costing just as much as college, but I guess by that point we could afford it. The only real obstacle left was my grades, which is why my Daddy sat me down for a long, intimidating lecture, donning an awesome heel persona and staying in character for a full thirty minutes.

Call me a mark if you want to, but ever since that day, I've never earned less than a "B+."

In any subject.

In fact, between getting settled into the new school and all those day trips down to the Boston Children's Hospital, the summer seemed to fly by. Burton had dozens of appointments with a small army of psychologists, but when it was all said and done, that autism diagnosis came as no surprise.

Or at least, not to me.

Dad and Samantha managed to find a behavioral therapist right there in Lowell, and the guy came out to Phillips Academy three times a week. I suppose it would've done me some good to sit down for a couple of counseling sessions myself, but to be honest, I didn't even think to ask. See, I'd already made a clean break with the ninth grade. Said my goodbyes and left junior high school in the dust, savoring the closure that came with graduation.

And you know, I guess that explains why I didn't think much about that red hoodie.

Not at first, anyway.

It happened on the morning of Burton's first visit with the psychologist. After I'd been staring at those sterile hospital walls all morning, and I finally broke down and went for a walk. I trudged my way across the Back Bay and up to Newbury Comics where I browsed through the CD racks until the clerk caught on that I wasn't buying and threw me out.

And that's when I saw it.

Right next door, in the window of some kind of thrift store. A low-rent pop-up business, one that looked so out of place among the boutiques of Newbury Street, it was almost certain to be gone before the end of the year.

A Champion hoodie, solid red. Slightly worn around the sleeves, but in good condition. And basically unremarkable, except for that black-and-white "Anarchy" symbol safety-pinned across the chest.

Exactly like the one Burton used to wear. But without all those splotchy stains.

It was eerily similar, so much so that I walked in and dropped the last five bucks I had to my name. Wore it for the rest of the day, even though it was damn near ninety degrees outside. Despite the heat, that sweatshirt just felt so…comfortable. Like, wearing it was the best way I had to say goodbye to my stepbrother.

And speaking of goodbyes. After that *Summer Smash-Up* party, I never actually spoke to John Nguyen again, either.

Never got the chance.

This might sound bad, but with everything else going on in my life, that kid was just about the last thing on my mind. I mean, John Nguyen probably only entered my thoughts, like, once or twice more. And even then, only for a few seconds.

Burton and John Nguyen, the two of them, I don't know.

I guess they both just ended up being a couple more people that I closed the door on. Like everything else from the spring of 1993, those two kind of got left behind.

Out of sight, out of mind, right?

You know how it goes.

TUESDAY, SEPTEMBER 11, 2001

THAT ENTIRE DAY PASSED IN A BLUR, WHICH I GUESS IS understandable.

Funny thing, though—as confusing as that one day was, somehow it seemed like the past eight years had been blown away too, vanishing right along with those skyscrapers. And when I finally managed to pull myself away from the television, the second I put my hands on that old middle school yearbook, it almost felt as if I'd been transported back in time.

Sitting down on my bed, I closed my eyes and thought about Burton.

And pulled my legs up, crossing them over like a pretzel.

I imagined him sitting there next to me, and almost by instinct, I began skimming through the pages, thinking for some reason that maybe I just might find his photo in there, lined up next to my classmates. Crazy, I know. But my future stepbrother had been just as much a part of my ninth-grade experience as any of those random people had been.

More, really.

And I also remember finding time that night to call my family, but for the life of me, I can't remember what we said. Just that Dad and Samantha sounded amazed to hear I was still alive; their level of panic was so absurd. Like, immediately after all those terrorists pulled off the deadliest sneak attack in history, they were going to suddenly flank north, and invade New Hampshire? Like the Granite State was some kind of strategic territory in Osama Bin Laden's campaign of global jihad?

And then later on, it got even crazier when Uncle Hector and Aunt Emmy called to check in from somewhere out on the road. I have no clue what we might've talked about, but honestly, it didn't matter. I could never understand those two when they got excited and slipped back into Spanish.

In fact, the only conversation I recall clearly was when Dad rang for the last time and passed the cordless phone over to Burton.

And the most remarkable thing about that chat, was the fact that the kid was talking at all.

Phillips Academy had cancelled classes at lunchtime. Burton was unusually chatty, excited by the unexpected disruption to his routine. We must've spent at least ten minutes talking about how the Red Sox were pretty much out of the pennant race, and for some reason, we had a friendly argument about which level of *Goldeneye 007* was the toughest. I sat there listening, amazed at how well the kid was able to hold a conversation. His progress was simply amazing—even if it had taken him eight years of hard work to get there.

It was just like Burton had said, about how his development would take off as soon as he got connected to the right resources. And yet, I couldn't help but marvel at how, secretly, I was the only person in the world who knew just how much he was still capable of.

But from that terrible day, the one phone call that still sticks with me was the one that didn't go through.

Of course, I didn't have John Nguyen's phone number. Never did. And even though I hadn't thought about the kid in years, that night I went so far as to pull up the White Pages online and work my way through the listings for every last Nguyen around Boston. Most of those numbers were out of service, which is why later that evening, I ended up sitting back down on the floor. Feeling strangely desperate, cradling that old middle school yearbook in my lap. Holding onto it just because I was scared to put it down.

The book felt different—like it had changed, somehow. I know that must sound crazy, but, well? My entire world felt like it had been flipped upside down in a matter of hours. So, why couldn't an old yearbook be affected too?

My mind flashed back to all those late-night conversations with Burton, and I realized that the yearbook must have somehow managed to trap a piece of the past inside of it. Captured a small bit of 1993, and preserved it for all eternity. I swear, as I held that book in my hands, I could almost feel the energy pulsing through the cover. Finally, I understood why my older stepbrother had dressed the way he did, and why he'd carried that old Discman around everywhere he went.

In fact, I could almost picture the guy sitting there beside me. That old, red sweatshirt of his, with the hood pulled up. That thin, yellow headphone cord dangling down from his neck. Both of those artifacts must've helped him to hold firm to the past whenever he was there.

With the TV still muted, I closed my eyes again, then pulled my legs in and crossed them up over each other once more.

The same way Burton had taught me.

I took a deep breath. Held it. Then exhaled slowly, relaxing my mind.

Focusing on that moment, and that moment only.

But after a couple minutes of trying, there was nothing, and I slumped back against the bed in defeat. Obviously, the one thing that hadn't changed in all those years was my lack of patience for this kind of bullshit. But when I opened my eyes, I flipped back the cover and watched in amazement as the glossy pages fell open on John Nguyen's graduation photo.

The kid's round, doughy face was lined up right alongside our classmates, fitting in better than he'd ever managed to back in school. One calm second of the kid's tumultuous life had been captured forever, in a single, glossy, black and white photo. John looked much more put together than usual— he'd even managed to scrounge up a clean shirt for the occasion. Who knows, maybe all of his raggy old T-shirts had been in the wash or something. But cleaned up, John Nguyen almost looked like he could've been any other student.

In fact, the only thing that set him apart at all was that blank text box underneath his photo. There weren't any lists of clubs or activities, like the kids on either side of him had. No inside jokes, thank-you notes, or heartfelt goodbyes.

Nothing.

Just a painfully obvious block of white space. A silent testament to the loneliness and isolation that John Nguyen had endured for three straight years. I swear, even after all the horrible scenes broadcast on television that day, for me, that big, empty section underneath John's photo was the saddest sight of all.

And then, for some reason, my fingers began twitching.

Moving all on their own, flipping their way towards the back of the yearbook.

I thumbed past the superlatives, past all the photos of the clubs and the sports teams, all the way to the very end where local businesses had purchased ad space to help cover the school's printing costs. I paused to gaze at the half-page my Dad had shelled out for. The old picture looked enormous—or at least it did next to all the two-inch by two-inch squares that the other parents had bought. Even worse, it was one of my most embarrassing baby photos. The one that showed me peeking up out of the bathtub wearing nothing but a rubber duck and a smile.

"Congratulations, Baby Bear!" the message read. "We're so proud of you! Love Dad, Mom, and Burton."

Looking back on it eight years later, it seemed like such a nice gesture, but at the time I could only be pissed that he'd dared to call Samantha my mom. And what normal person congratulates their kid on graduating from ninth grade, anyway? Like, it's not really one of life's great milestones.

As for John Nguyen, of course his parents hadn't submitted any messages. They probably couldn't afford it, if they'd even realized that their kid was graduating at all. But a chill ran down my spine when I turned the page and spotted his chubby round face once more. That same exact photo stared back at me from above the fold of a yellowed newspaper clipping, tucked away inside the book's back cover.

Slowly, hands shaking, I pulled the newsprint loose and folded it open. But then I spotted my own yearbook photo in miniature underneath—along with a handful of our classmates' pictures—and I froze in shock.

I'd long since forgotten their names, but it didn't matter. The Globe's headline said it all.

"Summer School Slaughter: Six Students Shot, Killed."

The article held my full attention, even if I couldn't bring myself to read it.

I mean, at first, I thought it might've been a prank. Like, some kind of cruel joke.

But what sick person would go to all that trouble?

After a while, I recognized the newspaper clipping for what it was. Another artifact, a leftover scrap from some other timeline. One which had to have been irrevocably altered by Burton's sudden appearance.

When my hands steadied, I saw that the clipping was from July of 1993, just a few weeks after school let out.

Eventually, I found the strength to skim through the text. The details were light, I guess because the massacre had just occurred a day before, but the gist was that John Nguyen had stolen his Dad's gun and opened fire during one of the remedial classes at JFK.

My body froze in place. My mind, too, incapable of processing the words I was reading.

By traveling back to 1993, had Burton actually succeeded in altering the events of our timeline?

Could it actually be possible that he'd saved my life—and the lives of my classmates—by doing so?

And most importantly, maybe—what did that mean for John Nguyen?

Burton's mission must have changed the path of that kid's life, too. Like, drastically. So, could this new sequence of events that he'd created have anything to do with the horrible events playing out on my television screen?

These were just some of the thoughts that were rushing through my mind, coming at me fast and loud.

Just like a low-flying jetliner.

And as soon as I could move, I lunged for the desktop computer to start clicking my way through the White Pages all over again.

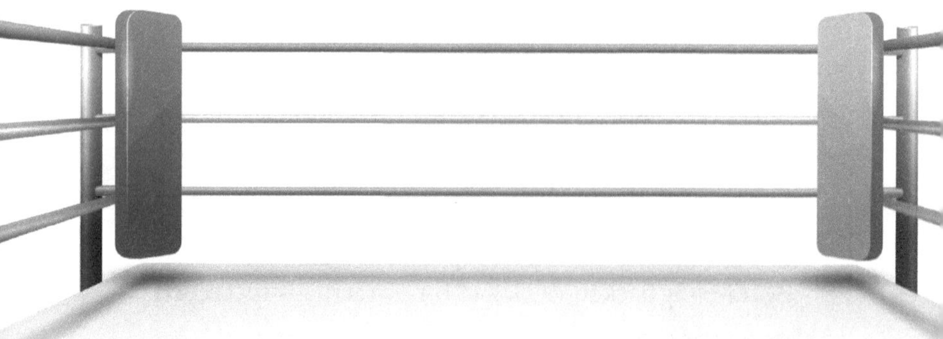

AND SO THEN, THE VERY LAST TIME I EVER SAW MY STEPBROTHER— the older one, obviously—was at John Nguyen's funeral. I hadn't bothered to let anyone know I was coming down to Lowell for the day, so it was just me and him.

No one else, save a couple hundred mourners.

It was just as well, since seeing my family would've required too much explanation. A sudden arrival might've been upsetting for Burton, too. That little guy was doing awesome in school—one of the top students in his class— but we still had to tiptoe around his established routines.

As for my Dad? Well, he was off in Colorado, or Wyoming, or somewhere out West, scouting locations for his next movie. I'll say this for those Hollywood film people, they're nothing if not opportunistic. Plumes of black smoke were still streaming up from Ground Zero, but some enthusiastic producer had already secured funding for an action movie about Navy Seals shipping off to Afghanistan to kill terrorists. They didn't actually have a story or anything yet, but some hack writer could probably hammer out a script in a couple weeks. And even though Samantha and I were on much better terms by then, so she wouldn't have hesitated to wire me money for an Amtrak ticket, I just didn't feel like answering any uncomfortable questions. I set my alarm clock instead, heading out at dawn to catch the Peter Pan bus.

The trip was slow and uneventful. The service at St. Patrick's had already wrapped up by the time we pulled in, so I set out for the cemetery down the street. The morning air felt chilly and harsh, unusually so for this early in the fall. Those thick gray clouds hung low, matching the grim expressions of everyone who'd turned out.

The size of that crowd was just unbelievable. I shook my head, amazed at how popular John Nguyen had become. I swear, if that kid had only died a month before, the funeral—if he'd even had one—would've been a quick and private affair. Maybe with his parents and a Catholic priest on hand, but that's it. Because of the way everything had gone down, though, there must've been three or four hundred people crowded around, most of them holding those small American flags that every store in town had started selling.

Everywhere you went, no matter who you talked to, it seemed like everybody had some kind of personal connection to September 11. Some kind of story to tell.

And in the town of Lowell, Massachusetts, John Nguyen was ours.

Just another hometown kid. One who'd never done anything notable in his life…at least, not until he'd booked his first-ever airplane trip on American Airlines Flight 11.

God, it was so depressing.

Like, that little paper boarding pass he must've been so excited about, it turned out to be the ultimate losing ticket in life's great Powerball draw.

The graveside service was already underway, so I eased my way up to the edge of the crowd, doing my best not to draw attention. Looking around at all the faces, I was shocked by how few people I recognized. I'm not sure why I was surprised, though—after I'd left Lowell for college, it was almost as if I'd ceased to exist in the eyes of that town. Not like I'd died, or anything. Just disappeared. And that morning was a cold, hard reminder of how quickly time moves along. Never stopping to wait for any of us.

Eventually, my eyes came to rest on one Asian lady. A teary old bird, who could only have been John Nguyen's mother. She was surrounded by a group of wrinkled old retirees, men and women who apparently had nothing better to do on a weekday morning.

Not far past them stood Nelson Madeiros and Manny Ramirez, and I'm sorry, even if they *had* made the effort to show up to the funeral, those two bullies were still losers. You know the type, I'm sure. Kids who'd been born in Lowell, raised there, and for some strange reason, seemed bound and determined to die there, too. Wasting their entire lives away in some shitty old mill town.

After a while, I'd seen enough. As the first thin mists of rain began to fill the air, I pulled up my collar and began plotting an exit.

To be honest, I still wasn't exactly sure why I'd come. There wasn't a single person in Lowell I particularly wanted to see—at least, not right then. I guess I just felt like I needed to be there, for some reason or other. Same as everybody else.

As my eyes wandered over the mourners one last time, I spotted a familiar face, and finally realized why I'd showed up.

My stepbrother Burton was standing there at the far side of the crowd, hunched over and shivering. The dude hadn't dressed for the weather at all, hadn't even bothered to throw on a windbreaker over that same old, red hoodie.

My old, red hoodie.

And the guy still had that same wispy layer of stubble across his face. Honestly, he looked as if he hadn't aged a day since I'd seen him last.

Maybe he hadn't.

And then, almost as if he could feel my gaze upon him, Burton shifted his weight and turned my way.

I guess it was just as likely that he'd been expecting me. Hanging around in the past, waiting there in the rain for me to show up and make an appearance.

Burton wore a blank look of calm composure, holding my gaze longer than he'd ever done before.

At last, when it almost felt like I was going to scream, or take off running, or do something, anything, to prompt a reaction, he lowered his chin in this single, slow nod of acknowledgement.

And then he turned away, looking back over at the empty casket.

But I just couldn't bring myself to return the gesture.

It was an even less satisfying goodbye than our other one, but I knew good and damned well, that'd be the last time I'd ever see my older, younger stepbrother.

Later on, riding that big bus back to school, the gray afternoon passed by in a blur. The world outside my window rolled along, moving by just as quickly as the past eight years had, and at some point along Interstate 95, I saw Massachusetts fade away into New Hampshire. I guess Burton had been right after all: time really *was* a flexible concept.

Stretchy—elastic, even.

And I'll admit, it was pretty damned terrifying to me, that I'd known all along what was going to happen, even if I hadn't realized it. And that even if I *did* control my own future, how powerless I was to change so many other things.

But even after everything America had been through— after all that horror we'd seen on television, and quickly become numb to—for me, at least, the scariest part about 9/11 was what had happened to John Nguyen. As much as I tried to reassure myself that I couldn't have been responsible for that kid's horrible death, I couldn't shake the nagging feeling that I—or Burton—or both—somehow were.

If Burton really *had* succeeded in changing the path of our timeline—or rather, if he'd been successful in getting *me* to change it—then that would've been the only reason my classmates and I were still alive.

Logically, I knew there was no reason I should feel responsible for John Nguyen's death.

After all—hadn't my actions bought him a few more years?

As the big silver bus chugged steadily north, I slipped on my headphones and pressed the play button, sending an Outkast CD spinning into motion. I slid my hand over that worn, old Discman Sport, thumbing the volume dial and wishing I could somehow make the bass loud enough to block out all those nagging doubts.

And just then, one last thought hit me.

I sat up straight in my seat, almost like I'd been struck by a bolt of lightning.

With everything going on, I hadn't stopped to consider what might've happened in the original timeline. The one I'd been meant to live out, if only Burton had never showed up back in 1993.

And if John Nguyen had gone and shot up John F. Kennedy Junior High like he was supposed to, so our timeline wouldn't have been pulled off its original course.

Or at least, not nearly as far.

But he hadn't, so it had.

Which is why I couldn't shake the feeling that when the attacks had taken place, our timeline had finally, powerfully, snapped back into place.

Rebounding with exponential force.

So now when John Nguyen's life finally ended, rather than taking along just a handful of bystanders, his plane had snuffed out hundreds of innocent people instead.

A warm tear ran down my cheek as I thought of that musty, old newspaper clipping.

If that article had been correct—and if I really *was* supposed to die at the same time as John Nguyen—that meant Burton's visits must've changed our timeline in a number of ways.

Maybe an infinite number.

Which also meant that *I* was also still changing the timeline, stretching our reality further and further from its original path, with each and every day I was still alive.

Was there any way to know how much time I had left? Or, like before—would I even want to know?

And worst of all— when my time finally came around, did that mean that I was destined to go out in a blaze of destruction, too, the same way John Nguyen had? If so, how many other people would I take along with me?

There was absolutely no way of knowing, I told myself. Over and over again.

I did my best to stay calm. Taking deep, controlled breaths. Reminding myself that the mathematical probability of two separate disasters of such catastrophic proportions had to be extremely low.

So low, the very idea was almost inconceivable.

Impossible, even.

But see, that right there was the worst part. After all I'd been through—after everything I'd seen—I finally realized the truth.

That nothing is impossible, so long as you believe in it.

And that was the problem. I did believe.

And I probably always will.

ACKNOWLEDGMENTS

Writing a book can be solitary work, but publishing one never is.

To the team at Fractured Mirror Publishing—Patterson Hood, Emily Kudeviz, Allison Chernutan, and Alex Vicarel— thank you for your vision, support, and dedication throughout this process. I would not have been able to tell this story without you.

Endless thanks to my wife, Tracey, and the technicians at DriveSavers Data Recovery Services, for rescuing the earliest drafts of this book after Mr. Wang borrowed my laptop. 2020 was wild.

A very special shout-out to the staff of the Arlington, Virginia Public Library's Central Branch, where *Jet Fuel Can't Melt Steel Beams* went from an idea to a manuscript. Thank you for patiently re-shelving so much reference material in 523.1 and 530.11.

And for all the inspiration: special thanks to Nathan D. Paoletta, creator of the World Wide Wrestling role playing game; to the Geek Salad Radio and Hysteria 51 podcasts;

to my old, hometown crew; and to fans of professional wrestling and conspiracy theories around the world. The truth is out there, y'all.

ABOUT THE AUTHOR

JAMES VACHOWSKI works in the field of global security and investigations. When he's not overseas, James divides his time between his home states of Massachusetts and South Carolina.

www.ingramcontent.com/pod-product-compliance
Lightning Source LLC
Chambersburg PA
CBHW032357310726
48973CB00007B/2054